DUEL OF THE MONSTERS Volume 1

Cover Art: Lungga Creatives

Peter Rawlik
Matthew Dennion
Kevin Heim
Dustin Dreyling
Tyler Shepard
Alex Dumitru
Breyden Halverson
Robert Galvin
Cody Bratsch
Christofer Nigro

Preface: Matt Hickman

Editorial staff: Dustin Dreyling, Andres Perez, Kevin Heim, Neil Reibe.

DEDICATIONS

This book is lovingly dedicated to my grandmother Gertrude "Trudie" Nigro, the wonderful woman who raised me, loved me more than anyone else ever has, and graciously dealt with my difficult side no matter how difficult it ever got. Her family, the community, and the world was truly blessed to have her for 95 years now and I love her more than anyone else. And to the memory of her sister, my aunt Concetta "Connie" Denisco, who always believed in me, and was always there for me and everyone else she knew whenever she was needed. I miss her terribly.

I also dedicate it to the Wild Hunt Press staff for working so hard to help make this dream a reality, and to the many creatives in horror fandom who made this genre a force to be reckoned with in pop culture and for saying so much that needs to be said about the human condition and society via the metaphorical lens of fantastic fiction.

Table of Contents

INTRODUCTION

So, what exactly was the inspiration for me to publish a series like this? Well, a few things.

One of them was most certainly an awesome little story penned by the late, great comic book writer Archie Goodwin for Warren Publications' *Creepy* #7. This was published before my time, circa 1965, and I first noticed it while perusing the back issue section of later Warren mags (those little glimpses of what had come before fascinated me to no end!). One of the several on display there that really caught my eye was an amazing painted cover of a werewolf duking it out with a Gothically-attired vampire reminiscent of the Dracula image made popular by a certain Hungarian actor. That cover was rendered by no less a personage than the legendary Frank Frazetta, so it is no wonder that it stood out to me so much. What also stood out was the large-fonted cover blurb announcing the title of this story within the mag: "Duel of the Monsters."

I knew I had to have that issue and read that story… someday! It took me a long, long time but I finally managed to acquire an affordable copy of that great vintage comic. Goodwin's yarn was as good as I had hoped for. It was a period story featuring a vampire and werewolf playing a deadly cat and mouse game with each other over who owned the human victim pool of a small medieval European hamlet. It ended in a brief but mutually fatal battle promised on the cover of the mag, along with a typically ghoulish twist ending (you'll have to read the story to figure out what that twist was, but I did provide a little hint in this sentence!).

The concept embodied by that story was inspiring, and this anthology series -- along with the cover of this first volume -- is a complete homage to that story and the creative coolness behind it. And so is the lead story, composed by yours truly, but do not expect the same setting or circumstances as Goodwin's classic tale. Thinking back on that highly inspirational story and the idea behind it provided the title for this anthology series, which I hope to be an enduring tribute to that memorable contribution to horror fiction by scribe Goodwin, cover artist Frazetta, and interior artist Angelo Torres.

As for the second inspiration... well, monsters fighting each other is simply a cool concept. Don't get me wrong, I enjoy stories and films featuring desperate "everyman" humans, or sometimes human monster hunters, soldiers, scientists, etc., battling for their very lives against the many and varied monstrosities that the human imagination and folklore have concocted over the centuries. Nevertheless, I am one of the many horror fans who cannot help but wonder who (or is that what?) would come out on top if two of these macabre fiends were pitted against each other rather than only human protagonists. This ties into my fascination with shared universes, of course. In such a universe where many types of monsters co-exist, it would be inevitable that they would run into each other from time to time. And when they did, I cannot imagine that such encounters would be friendly.

Furthermore, while growing up I was enthralled by vintage films like the classic Universal monster mash-up *Frankenstein Meets the Wolf Man*, the first crossover from the studio's shared Golden Age monster universe. I was even thrilled with the cobbled together 1971 Al Adamson schlock-fest *Dracula vs. Frankenstein*. I have fond childhood memories of my grandmother, who worked as a secretary for the film industry, bringing me home the pressbook and several ultra-gory stills from that flick ("Who gives you these horrible pictures?" my grandfather lamented when I proudly showed them to him -- yup, those were the days!).

Neither of these films are considered among the best of the best that earlier eras of horror cinema produced, but again the concept they embodied, however imperfectly, was perceived as amazing and creatively inspiring by this fledgling writer and horror fan. And, I'm guessing (and hoping) for some of you readers as well, am I right?

NEW! DIFFERENT! SHOCKING!
The KINGS of HORROR BATTLE to the DEATH!
All NEW! All COLOR!
TOGETHER IN ONE FILM - THEY MEET IN A FIGHT OF FRIGHT!
DRACULA VS. FRANKENSTEIN
RATED
The most shocking HORROR SHOW of the year
Starring
J. CARROL NAISH LON CHANEY ANTHONY EISLEY
REGINA CARROL ANGELO ROSSITTO
Special Guest Stars – RUSS TAMBLYN and JIM DAVIS
And Introducing ZANDOR VORKOV as "COUNT DRACULA"
Music Score by WILLIAM LAVA
Released by
INDEPENDENT-INTERNATIONAL Pictures Corp.
COLOR by DeLuxe
GP
ALL AGES ADMITTED Parental Guidance Suggested

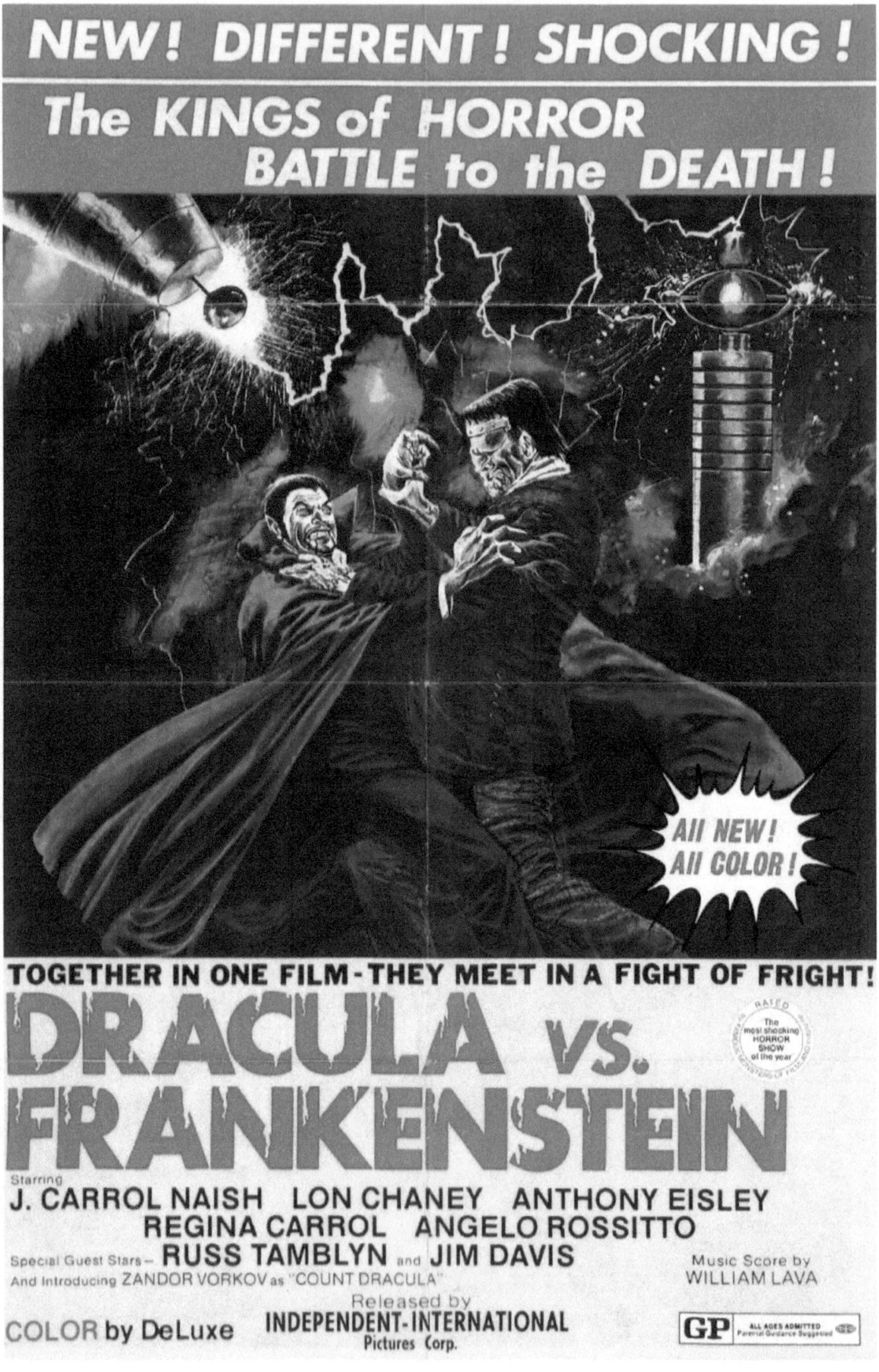

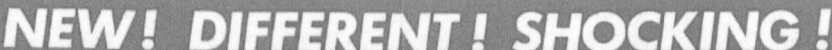

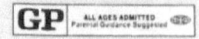

Then there were the kaiju conflicts from Toho and Daiei's classic series of films featuring Godzilla and Gamera, respectively, which I spent many hours of my youth watching. The four-way tag-team monster battle from *Godzilla vs. Megalon* that I saw when it played at the drive-in was nothing less than awesome to me (I don't care how maligned that particular G-film may be today; I loved it!).

Then there are the great monster battles that the stop motion artistry of Ray Harryhausen treated us to in his Sinbad films -- particularly the cyclops vs. dragon sequence in *The 7th Voyage of Sinbad,* the cyclopean centaur vs. the griffin in *The Golden Voyage of Sinbad,* and the troglodyte vs. saber-toothed tiger in *Sinbad and the Eye of the Tiger.* You can bet the first of the latter three flicks has a homage in this very edition, courtesy of masterful kaiju scribe Matthew Dennion.

Along with this were the fairly frequent dinosaur battles we got in films across the decades. RKO's original *King Kong* (1933) started it all by giving us the titular giant ape against a T. Rex, cave-dwelling Elasmosaurus, and a Pteranodon[1] -- and later that same year his apparent offspring Kiko squared off against a cave bear and a vicious quadrupedal dinosaur in *Son of Kong.* This basic monster combat scenario would be repeated over the many years between then and now. The succeeding decades saw subsequent versions of the iconic giant ape being pitted against Toho's celebrated kaiju king Godzilla in *King Kong vs. Godzilla* (1962), one of the most remarkable monster crossover battles in the history of cinema; giant carnosaur Gorosaurus, a sea serpent, and a robotic doppelganger in Toho's *King Kong Escapes* (1967); a giant snake in Dino De Laurentis' *King Kong* (1976); several carnosaurs simultaneously in Peter Jackson's remake of *King Kong* (2005); an island-dwelling species of monster called Skullcrushers in Legendary Pictures' *Kong: Skull Island* (2016); and a long-overdue rematch with Godzilla in Legendary's *Godzilla vs. Kong* (2021).

---

[1] Yes, I know several years earlier Willis O'Brien brought us a T. Rex vs. Triceratops battle in *The Lost World* (1925), which is arguably the first ever onscreen monster battle. However, that battle was so brief and one-sided in favor of the T. Rex that it hardly counts IMHO.

Of course, the dino-battles were far from limited to films featuring King Kong. We saw such creature combat sequences in flicks like *Unknown Island* (where we got to see a T. Rex battle a giant ground sloth!), *One Million Years B.C.*, the film version of *The Land That Time Forgot*, and *The Last Dinosaur*. With rare exceptions like the giant ground sloth, these dino-battles usually seemed to pit a T. Rex (or a similar carnosaur) against a Triceratops (or a similar member of the horned ceratopsian dino family). *The Valley of Gwangi* not only pitted the titular Allosaur against a Styracosaurus, but also had the carnosaur deal with some serious pachyderm power when he faced off against an elephant.

Then, we had the great monster battles regularly featured in the comics during the horror boom of the 1970s. Prominent among these were *The Tomb of Dracula, Werewolf By Night, The Frankenstein Monster, The Man-Thing, Ghost Rider,* the Living Mummy in the *Supernatural Thrillers* title, and Morbius the Living Vampire (soon to appear in a movie of his own from Sony) in both *Vampire Tales* and *Adventure Into Fear* from Marvel; *Swamp Thing*, "The Spawn of Frankenstein" from *The Phantom Stranger* title, and the "I, Vampire" series from the *House of Mystery* title (featuring titular vamp Andrew Bennett) from DC; and the various series characters from Warren's *Eerie* and *Vampirella*.

Each of these strips routinely pitted their titular monster protagonists against a host of monstrous adversaries – and occasionally against each other during crossovers within the shared universe of each respective publishing company.

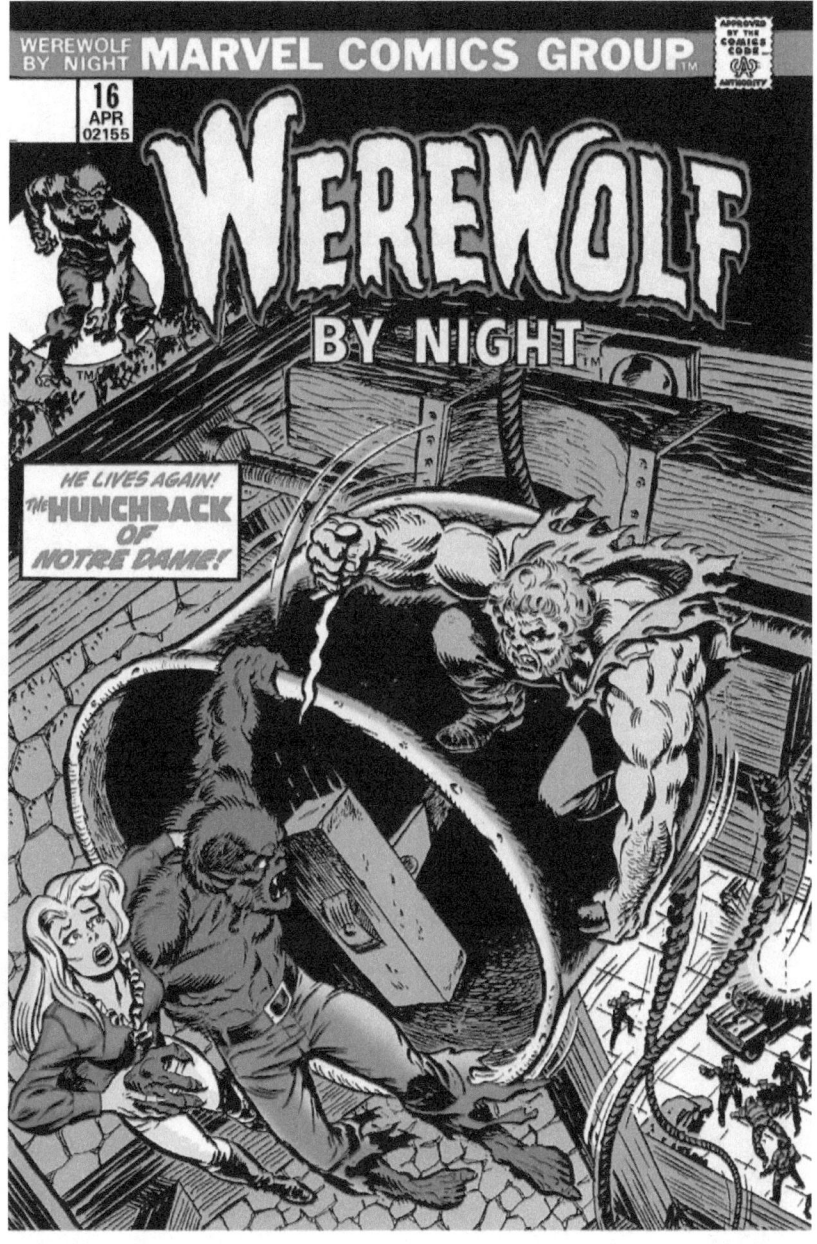

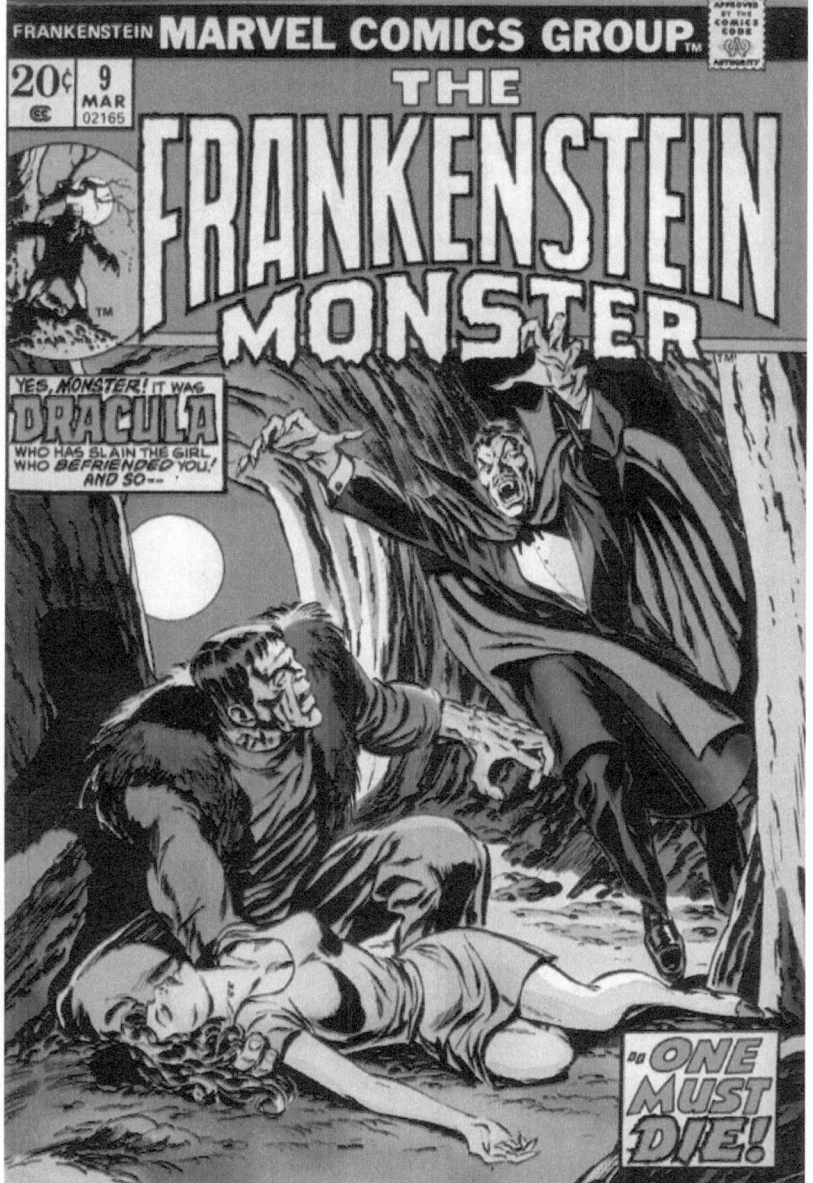

Then, I remember the uber-grotesque covers of Eerie
Publications' low-grade but prolific series of horror anthology
comic mags of the era[2], which included *Terror Tales*, *Weird*, *Tales
of Voodoo*, and *Witches' Tales*. These covers routinely depicted
monsters doing horrific things to each other during hypothetical
(and horrifically outlandish) clashes as often as they did against
humans who had the misfortune of falling into their clutches. The

---

[2] Eerie Publications should not be confused with Warren's comic
magazine title *Eerie*.

stories within rarely (if ever) featured such mash-ups, but the
emotionally stimulating imagery of these lurid covers nevertheless
made their mark on budding horror writers: if many types of
monsters were real, they would fight with each other whenever
they crossed paths!

Above is the first Eerie Publications cover that I ever saw. I came across this particular issue of *Weird* (don't ask me the issue #!) while going through a pile of back issues at Fantasy World, an awesome comic shop from yesteryear in Buffalo, New York back during my middle school years (waves to Norm, the shop's equally awesome owner/proprietor). This gore-infested cover stuck with me as much as the Frazetta cover for *Creepy* #7, in part due to the centrality of the monster vs. monster theme.

Added to this, I would be remiss to leave out the influence of the two-fighter combat oriented video games that first achieved popularity during the second arcade and home video console boom of the 1990s. These games allowed one or more players to actually take control of a virtual combatant, with the outcome of the battle always in doubt (at least if the two human players were reasonably equally experienced in the game play). Granted, earlier versions of said game franchises like Capcom's *Street Fighter* and Midway's *Mortal Kombat* featured super-martial artists taking each other on, but some of these fighters had truly monstrous attributes, such as the green-skinned, orange-haired beast-man Blanka from the former game's universe; and the four-armed human-dragon hybrids Goro, Kintaro, and Sheeva; the centaur-like Motaro; the human-raptor hybrids Reptile and Khameleon; and the bestial mutant Baraka from the latter game's universe.

These fighting video games finally gained true relevance to this topic when they branched into kaiju kombat territory with *King of the Monsters*, *War of the Monsters*, and Atari's trilogy of Godzilla video games (*Godzilla: Destroy All Monsters Melee*; *Godzilla: Save the Earth*; *Godzilla Unleashed*), where players could take the role of various Toho kaiju characters. This sub-genre of video combat also included such memorable examples as the multi-player giant monster competitive game *Rampage* (which recently spawned a movie version) and the dinosaur fighter game *Primal Rage*.

Finally, we had the more recent silver screen crossover battles such as *Freddy vs. Jason, Alien vs. Predator* (and its sequel, based on a long-running series of crossover combat courtesy of Dark Horse Comics); the Legendary Pictures' flicks that pit giant robots against kaiju in *Pacific Rim* and its sequel; and further kaiju-film mash-ups like *Godzilla: King of the Monsters* (2019) and the aforementioned *Godzilla vs. Kong* (the latter still a few months from release at this publication date). Regarding the latter two titanic rivals for kaiju supremacy, even fan films got in on the act with Zimaut Animation's excellently produced all-combat short film "Godzilla vs. King Kong" (you can watch the complete video at Zimaut's YouTube channel here: https://www.youtube.com/watch?v=IpCQEmmAyTY).

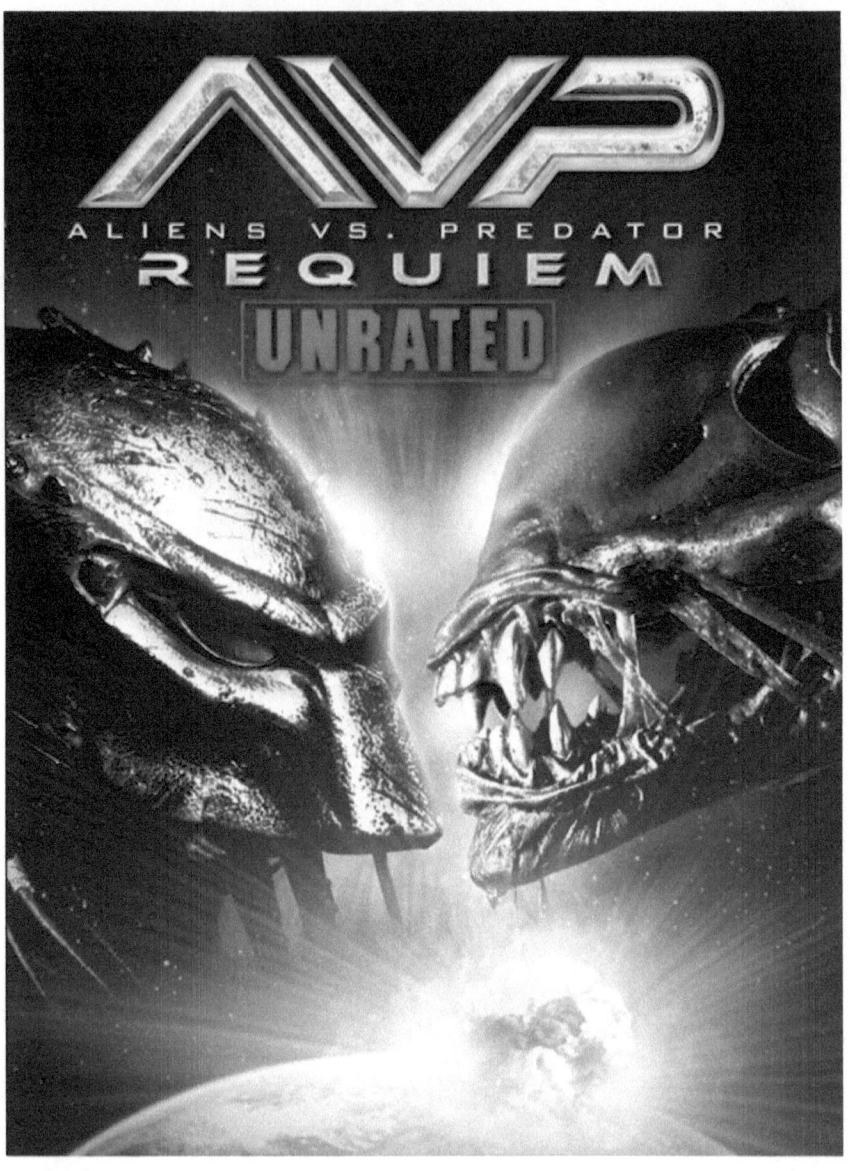

Above pic ©Zimaut Animation

And so, here we are with *Duel of the Monsters* Volume 1, where we take the concept into prose. We aren't the first publishing company to do this -- earlier this decade 18ᵗʰWall Publications beat us there with a series of terrific cryptid combat novels; and Capstone Press had its well-received (but sadly out of print) Monster Wars series of short children's books by Michael John O'Hearn -- but we nevertheless wanted to put our own inimitable stamp on the concept. We have a myriad assembly of monsters pitted against each other in this tome, brought to you by an equally myriad assemblage of authors. Here you will find monster types from across the spectrum of folklore, literature, cinema, and the annals of cryptozoology & Forteana doing their worst to each other to prove who would be supreme if they crossed swords (or fangs and claws, whatever the case may be).

The rules of the stories in this and subsequent volumes to come are simple and brutal: Within these tales, two monsters of a different type will appear. Human (usually) protagonists will have to deal with them, as occurs in all good horror stories. But these two creatures will ultimately have to deal with each other as well, as the human victim pool isn't big enough for both. These monsters will battle, and one of them -- and *only* one -- in each story will go down for the count. Which one it will be was entirely the decision of the individual authors, and the answer will keep you guessing from the beginning to the bloody end.

I hope you enjoy this nostalgic, contemporary contribution to the concept! Your comments will be more than welcome, whether on Wild Hunt Press' Facebook group or via reviews on Amazon, GoodReads, your individual blogs, and wherever books are reviewed.

Christofer Nigro
October 2019

PREFACE

Matt Hickman

One day, at the Mansion of the Macabre…

The Full Moon rose over a dusty old manor house resting on a hill. Inside the Gothic mansion was a full complement of abandoned furnishings covered in dust and grime, along with and dozens upon dozens of bookcases filled with tomes of all different sizes in many different languages. It appeared from the sheer amount of dust over everything that no one had been here in a very long time. Yet in the middle of the library, next to a set of moldy old chairs, stood a man and a woman.

The man was about 6'2" with platinum blonde hair a long black trench coat, red dress shirt, and black suit pants. He was holding a skull-headed cane and his face was covered with black and white clown make up.

The woman stood next to him, hanging off his arm. She was about 5'8" and her appearance was the very picture of duality. On her left side, she had long black hair, her make-up was perfect, and her red ring mistress jacket was spotless -- as was her long black dress pants and her red and black skirt, which ended in a shiny black kitten heel. Resting atop her head was a tiny top hat. On her right side, her head was mostly shaved, and the sparse amount of hair remaining was dyed all the colors of the rainbow; her make-up was severely smudged. This half of the ring mistress was dirty and filled with holes, while the right half of the pant leg had been replaced by fish net stockings; a dirty red tennis replaced her kitten heel.

This was Dave, The World's Greatest Vampire (he made me say that, or he'll eat my cat) and Teri/Dawn (or Dawn/Teri, depending on which one of them you asked). They are known the world over as the psycho clowns, the leaders of the Jolly Time Gang of performers… and oh no, not these assholes again.

Coming to you live from the Mansion of the Macabre, they will be your hosts for this debut edition of *Duel of the Monsters*.

"Where are we?" Dawn asked in a posh accent while rubbing her eyes and looking around the room she found herself in.

She then twisted in a spastic fashion and her voice suddenly became more manic and high-pitched. "Looks like a real shithole! These people need a maid! Preferably of the French variety! Hey, Dawny, remember that maid from when we were little, and how we..."

Dave cut Teri off by putting his hand over her mouth before she could relay that particular bit of their history.

"Ladies, while I do agree this place needs a good dusting, I believe we are here for a higher purpose," the vampire clown said as he removed his hand from the woman's lips.

She twitched again. "Higher purpose?" Dawn asked in her posh voice while tilting her head and causing her long black hair to fall to the side.

"Yes, dear. I believe we are to act as horror hosts. You know, not unlike that fellow on the Classic TV station out of Chicago. Or, that redneck fellow. Or, that woman with the huge tracts of... land."

He reached out to give the woman's breasts a squeeze to show what he really meant, causing her to let out a soft purr.

"Might as well get to it, then. Spotlight!"

Dave raised his arms and the already dark room suddenly became even darker, save for a bright circle of light (from an unknown source) illuminating his person. He cleared his throat before putting on his best game show host voice.

"Ladies and gentlemen! Boys and girls of all ages! The dreaded Mansion of the Macabre brings you, through Wild Hunt Press -- those proud purveyors of genre fiction -- *Duel of the Monsters Volume One*! Eleven exciting tales of monsters in mortal combat! Yes, it is a Grand Guignol of sport!

"In 'Rave for Blood', a vampire and a werewolf find themselves at an Oktoberfest celebration in Berlin, battling over who gets to eat some tasty co-eds. A tale as old as time; we've all been there!

"In 'Jason's Lament', we travel to glorious ancient Greece to find the legendary hero Jason caught between the one-eyed wonder called a cyclops and a scaly powerhouse known as a dragon as they battle to the death!

"Next, we have 'House of Secrets', where a new homeowner finds that he not only has ghost problems, but the place is also a haunt for some 'friends' from outer space. Needless to say, each of the uninvited guests will have to go through the other to get to the poor cretin! It's going to be so much fun to watch and see who gets slaughtered!

"Then there is the tale of 'Hades' Bride', where a duo of alpha serial killers run afoul of a member of the Griffin clan, that crop of wacky invisible mad scientists. Who will end up killing whom? Spoiler: Expect a lot of normal folks to get killed between the two! Ha!

"This next fight is just too hard to pick! It's the tale of 'Why Don't Cannibals Eat Clowns?', wherein a vampire and his crazy as a loon sidekick fight a killer clown and his own savagely crazy sidekick. It's like if me and the girls here fought each other somehow (the reality-wrenching events of '85 notwithstanding, of course).

"Then we have 'A Distraction of Monsters', where a certain infamous early 20th century alpha serial killer must face a zombie horde of his own making. And just wait 'til you see who else shows up to help make that happen!

"Next on our nefarious list we travel to the Great White North for the tale of 'Wrath of the Okanagan Lake God', where the legendary lake monster Ogopogo must fight against an invading giant eel for the title of the lake's apex predator. It will not be pretty, as the unfortunate people caught between the two aquatic beasts would readily attest if they were still intact.

"Up next, it's the lover of bridge collapses known as the Mothman vs. Mother Leeds's least favorite child, the Jersey Devil, in 'The Battle of the Pine Barrens.' Let the winged cryptids clash! Wah-hoo!"

"After that, you'll stare in shock and awe as an aging yeti warrior just wants to be left in peace... but the flying cryptid known and feared as the Owlman has other plans in 'Death Song.' You won't be hearing that one on any Top 40 station, I can guarantee you that much!

"Next up, watch as everyone's favorite hairy eater of human flesh, a wendigo, takes on a skeletoid creature that would make

Ray Harryhausen proud. Read and see what happens when the 'Gashadokuro Battles the Kee-Waku.'

"And finally, we bring you a short little romp featuring two monsters with the dumbest names! A goofus bird races a hoop snake while a stoner fool finds himself caught in the middle in a tale we call 'How High Am I?'

"So, turn down the lights, grab your favorite drink, prepare your junk food of choice, and turn the page, because here we go! To blood, guts, and battles! Ha!"

WEREWOLF VS. VAMPIRE: RAVE FOR BLOOD

Woodland area just outside of East Berlin, early evening during Oktoberfest celebration circa 2018

Eduard Russoff's sensitive ears were accosted by blaring techno trance music as he stood at the ribbon barrier that indicated the entrance into the rave. Such acute hearing – usually an asset, but occasionally not in situations like this – was common to werewolves, which they retained to a limited degree even in human form. And it was this standard hominid mode that Eduard was required to hold at this time. Otherwise, intermingling with a crowd of humans surreptitiously would be quite impossible.

Eduard's shortly kept light brown hair was matched by eyes of the same hue, and he made a point to consistently shave the section of his eyebrows that met in the middle of the forehead to conceal this clue to his true nature (and he always wondered why so many lycanthropes in past centuries had evidently failed to do this). He was attired in a black zip-up hoodie, flexible black sweatpants ("perfect for dancing," he would say, though they served another useful purpose that will soon become clear), and dark-colored shoe boots.

He smiled at the presence of his recent acquaintance Nadja Westhoff, a quiet and unassuming girl who stood beside him and their mutual friend, Simona Ionescu.

The latter was infamous for her aggressive personality and love of loudly spouting volatile "far left" politics at anyone who had no choice but to listen. This, of course, greatly contrasted with her far demurer "bestie." The fairly tall Simona was further distinguished from the petite Nadja in terms of their physical features as well.

Simona possessed shortly cut, spiked, dyed blue hair that matched her piercing azure eyes. She had a pierced septum accompanied by two cyber bites piercing her lower lips. Her attire consisted of ripped blue jeans with a white tee shirt that had the words "Proud Feminist Bitch" emblazoned on it in English.

Nadja, on the other hand, couldn't possibly look more "normal" and undistinguished in comparison. She had barely shoulder length mousy brown hair, brown eyes, and a fair complexion unmarred by make-up or piercings of any sort. Her simple but doubtlessly enticing garb consisted of a blue crop top with a rainbow on the front, neatly kept blue jeans, and a simple pair of white sneakers.

"Well, are you gonna let us the fuck in, or what?" Simona griped at the partly inebriated guy saddled with the thankless task of managing the flimsy entrance line.

The young college man held a translucent plastic cup of beer in his hand as he approached the trio. "Um, sorry, didn't see you. Things catching my attention and all that. You got the cover charge and you're in."

"About time!" Simona said as she pulled five euros from her scruffy jean pockets and slapped them in the entry attendant's palm.

Nadja was a bit embarrassed by her friend's brusque demeanor despite loving her like a sister. As would be expected, she was much more polite in handing over her entrance fee.

Eduard was silent and gracious in doing so as well. Despite his inner lupine nature, he preferred to only tear humans apart when absolutely necessary. In fact, he even preferred to hunt wild animals in the woodlands outside the city when his bestial nature all but completely took over on the nights of the full moon – or when his rage got the better of him and catalyzed an unwanted metamorphosis.

Moreover, his eyes had caught sight of Nadja weeks earlier. The diminutive girl's plain look and demure personality was highly attractive to his individual preferences, and he thought she would make a fine mate (as his pack preferred to call an exclusive paramour). However, he wasn't as confident she would prefer the opposite traits to herself in a man, as she evidently did in a best friend. Eduard thus decided to play it cool with his prize girl. Hence, he spent the last several months hinting at his interest to her and working up the nerve to share his full feelings as soon as he felt confident she had come to reciprocate them. And he decided, with some advice from Simona, that this rave may be the perfect time and place for that.

The line attendant briefly detached the multi-colored ribbon demarcating the entrance into the rave and allowed access to Eduard and his two lady friends. The threesome looked around at the sights before them, which was typical of such a festive event celebrating Oktoberfest. Young college students interspersed with a few somewhat older guests were dancing wildly to the feverish music. Many were coupled up and grinding against each other in an exuberant sexual manner that would have done the ancient Bacchian cult proud. Some were dressed in standard "club" clothing despite the exterior location of the revelry; others were made up like some of the more colorful attendees they could expect to see at one of Hamburg's Dom Fun Fairs.

"Funny I don't see any LGBTs here," Simona complained.

"Don't be so sure," Eduard replied while pointing around the dancing area. "I see girls all up on each other over there. And a few of them have rainbows on their shirts. Just like Nadja."

Simona made a scoffing sound. "Mmm-hmm. Anyone can wear an emblem. They don't gotta believe in what it means; if it's popular, they'll wear it. And newsflash, straight dude: girls dance with each other like that all the time. It doesn't really matter if they're stick shift only or not. Women in general don't tend to have the same hang-ups about that shit like you men. And I don't see any men doing the grind over there."

Eduard snorted. "Well, pardon those of us men who had the nerve to be born straight. And sorry that we straights do not get our jollies by rubbing off on other men just to make some political point. I'm sure there are some gay and bi men here, though. These raves are cool with everyone, just like the flyers said."

"Then it seems you were told all the usual shit to cover up the oppression," Simona said as she angrily stood face-to-face with Eduard. "You probably wouldn't even have come here if you thought this rave was honestly 'open to all.'"

Nadja shuddered a bit as she suddenly thought better of her decision this evening. *I knew it wasn't a good idea coming here. Especially with the two of them together. I should have stayed at home and finished the book, like I intended. But both of them insisted I should "get out more." And I had the feeling that maybe Eduard was going to…*

Eduard shook his head at Simona. "Seriously, girl? Not everything in this world is a conspiracy to oppress minorities. Grow up or shut up, will you?"

"Fuck you and the breeders that brought you into this world," Simona said as she moved an inch closer to Eduard's face.

The young man in the dark hoodie gritted his teeth and released a sound that the more-nervous-than-ever Nadja could swear resembled a snarl. He could feel his teeth tingling, which they often did just before they began elongating into fangs, a clear indication the transformation was happening whether he wanted it to or not.

Eduard clenched his fists and tried forcing himself to calm down and suppress the change. Fuck! Not here; not now!

Suddenly, he was very thankful that he could come close to mastering the training by the pack that showed him how to initiate nighttime transformations at will no matter the phase of the moon. However, if he became unusually angry, the metamorphosis would sometimes be triggered spontaneously.

And if I change under those circumstances… I can be almost as out of control as I am during the full moon transformations.

The brown-haired youth knew he needed to leave immediately, without exchanging any further words with the fiery Simona. Not only did he still consider her something akin to a friend, but she did introduce him to Nadja. His sense of honor made him feel he owed her for that much. She was not someone he wanted to vent his animalistic fury on; not for something as relatively petty as her attitude and political beliefs. However, his anger was such that he had to let the change happen and to quickly vent the fury on *something*. Every iota of his will could only hold back the change for a few minutes at most, so he had to make haste.

The quickly changing Eduard suddenly turned and ran from the two ladies. He pushed several people aside as he ran as quickly as he could towards the woodlands beyond the small area where the rave was being held.

"Hey, what the fuck, man!" one of the shoved guys hollered as he spilled a cup of beer all over his jeans.

"Watch it, asshole!" one of the young women he knocked over exclaimed after her beer landed on her chest and the honey-colored liquid seeped down between her cleavage.

Simona sniggered and shook her head. "Pffht. Just like a man. Can't hold his ground when a woman actually stands up to him."

Nadja could finally speak up at this point. "Eduard, wait!"

"Let him go, baby girl," Simona insisted, grabbing her much shorter friend's arm and pulling her towards the dancing crowds. "I heard enough of his bullshit mansplaining. Maybe he'll get a beer and cool down a bit. In the meantime, let's get a few cold ones ourselves and do some serious grindin' in the grove. The music is hot, and so are we!"

Nadja resisted being pulled after a few seconds. It was an atypical act of resistance that took Simona aback. As was what she said next.

"You know, I really don't mind these 'far left' politics you recently adopted. You always were the brave and assertive one between the two of us. I just wish you'd put a cap on them at times, at least when it comes to nicer guys like Eduard. I think he might actually like me."

Simona didn't want to lie to her friend, since Eduard had already confided that much in her, and was hoping this rave could be a place for him to get Nadja "loosened up" and share those feelings with her as well. She didn't want to sabotage a chance for her friend to find some fulfillment along those lines. However, she also wanted to keep things "real" as she saw it, and to support her BFF against any attempt by a man to try and take advantage of her.

"Nadja... baby girl... I'm sorry, okay? Not for my views, but for maybe ruining things between you and Eduard. I understand you're straight and never gonna give a decent woman a chance, so that means leaving yourself to a man. And Eduard is okay as far as they go, but I can't help worrying that the main reason he likes you, and not a straight version of me, is because you're so... you know, passive. He could walk all over you and get you to do shit you may not be ready for yet."

Nadja considered her longtime friend's striking blue eyes, slightly illuminated by the various glow sticks in the crowd shimmering off the metallic dots embedded into her lips.

"Look, I... know you mean well. And I respect your beliefs. But just... just chill sometimes with that, okay? Just because a girl is on the quiet side doesn't mean she is submissive or naïve, or easy 'prey' for some 'nasty' guy. If you're gonna hate, just leave it for the men who actually deserve it. I... don't get the impression that Eduard is in any way predatory. Okay?"

Simona could not overlook her friend's bright and large brown eyes when they were utilized to form an expression like the one she now displayed.

"Okay, okay, but how well do either of us really know him yet? I only met him last semester."

"I would like the chance to find out, is my point."

Nadja then retreated into her usual persona with stooping little shoulders and a downbeat countenance. Simona couldn't help but feel a bit badly now.

"Alright, let's hit the dance grounds to let off some steam and have a beer afterwards. Then we'll look around for Eduard and get him to join us. Then I'll leave you two a bit of time to talk alone while I mingle with a few friends I know should be here. Okay?"

"Yea. Thanks, hun." Nadja smiled, which was so rare that it was completely radiant every time it did happen. "But only for a short time. Then I'm going to go looking for him, alright?"

"Suit yourself, baby girl. In the meantime…"

As the two girls headed for the dance grove, Eduard continued rushing as far as he could into the wooded area. He was praying to the god Fenris that he could find some wild game to "vent" his rage on once it reached its apex upon completion of the metamorphosis.

Unfortunately, he was unable to run far enough before the change was complete. He barely had enough time to unzip his hoodie and drop it to the grassy ground before his increasing bulk would have ripped it to shreds. The stretchy sweatpants expanded with his greatly increasing mass (thus revealing his main reason for wearing them so often), and he swiftly doffed his shoe boots as his feet morphed into a non-human shape.

Within minutes, Eduard stood transformed into a slavering man-wolf in the middle of the woods a mere 70 meters from the outer perimeter of the rave. His height was now well over seven feet, and his girth resembled that of an Olympic-level weightlifter. His largely exposed body was covered with a coat of matted grayish fur, and his now enlarged hands had five long human-like fingers with razor-sharp talons. Though his arms and hands remained humanoid despite their enhanced musculature, his legs – particularly the lower part below the knees – were bent into a shape and size resembling a mastiff. Nevertheless, he chose to remain in a bipedal stance, though it appeared as if he could just as easily move on all fours.

Eduard's head had re-shaped into something resembling a huge timber wolf, sporting an extended canine muzzle filled with extremely sharp teeth that looked as if they could bite through virtually anything. His ears pointed upwards like that of a canine, his snout likewise resembling something of the dog family; and just above them were eyes that shown an almost iridescent yellow in the darkness.

The werewolf's gaping jaws emitted an unsettling growling noise and dripped salivary fluid as if this no-longer-human beast could think of nothing other than tasting the flesh of something living.

***

Forty minutes earlier…

Gunther Radu looked around at the festive, often inebriated and/or stoned individuals surrounding him at the rave. While (almost) all others present saw peers intent on having a good time, providing each other with fun memories and potential couplings of shared pleasure, the refugee from Romania instead saw potential prey. Gunther forced himself to sip tiny amounts of beer, pretending to actually enjoy the beverage while discreetly pouring portions of it onto the grassy ground when others weren't looking. This was to be expected, as beer was not exactly the beverage of choice for a vampire.

His dark eyes were complimented by shoulder-length black hair, and his general features were striking though his skin tone had become a bit pallid since his transformation into one of the Undead. He was tall and thin, but also somewhat athletic looking. His person was accentuated by a dark leather jacket covering a black shirt with a vintage "Metallica" emblem on it, as he hoped at least one song from this classic band would be played at the rave (*yeah, right!*). He wore dark denim pants and gray sneakers, all of which gave him a degree of stealth coloration for operating in the dark. He had a pewter signet ring on his left ring finger, which contrasted his dark features and attire by gleaming whenever the light from a nearby glow stick reflected off it.

Gunther had been transformed into a vampire several years earlier at the age of 22 and was ultimately forced to flee his homeland of Romania after his vampiric depredations brought both the local constabulary and a prominent group of professional vampire hunters down on him in a major way. He would forever be frozen at this attractive youthful age, which was undeniably to his advantage (particularly since his lifespan would be indefinite).

Upon taking refuge in Berlin, he enlisted in night courses at Humboldt University to learn as much as he could about German culture and to matriculate towards a degree in management. His eventual goal was to open and operate a nightclub that would serve multiple purposes for him. Among these were a legitimate human cover identity, a means to earn a sizable income towards the purpose of operating within the human financial world, to hire bodyguards for protecting him during the day while he slept, and to have a ready supply of potential candidates for building a harem of she-vampires.

Even before being "turned" Gunther was raised by a proud family to think big, grandiose goals. Since he was sired into the Varnaean strain of vampires – the same bloodline to which Dracula, the recognized Lord of all Vampires and the head of the Vampire Society, himself belonged – Gunther was determined to eventually work his way as far up the ladder towards a position of honor and prestige amongst the Undead as possible.

"Hey!" a loud, somewhat slurry voice suddenly called out to Gunther to interrupt his internal musings. That voice was from his fellow Humboldt student and acquaintance Bog, a drug-loving young man who had accompanied him to the rave. "Do you want a hit of this shit or not? I'm talkin' to you, bro!"

"My apologies, Bog," Gunther replied in his slightly distinct Romanian accent. "I was distracted by some of the fine ladies here tonight."

"You can fuck with all that later! Right now, I'm wondering if you want some of this before it's all gone."

Bog held up a pill of a sort that Gunther did not recognize and did not care to at any rate. As a vampire, he no longer had any interest in the college drug culture that enamored so many of his peers.

"No, thank you. I will stick to the beer as my… vice of choice for tonight."

"If you say so," Bog replied. "More for the rest of us, then."

With that said, the tall and burly young man with an unkempt mop of brown hair and bloodshot eyes dropped the pill in a cup of beer. He swirled the liquid around for several seconds to hasten the speed of the tablet dissolving. After the pill had become a fine ring of powder floating atop the golden beverage's surface, Bog swallowed it in a single gulp.

"Ahhh! Goes down perfectly with the *Spaten Oktoberfest!* Never is this sweet beer sweeter than when it's mixed with this stuff. Then it becomes, well… pure ecstasy! Haha!"

Gunther forced a smile to pretend he was amused at his mortal friend's too-obvious pun. A moment later, his darkish eyes turned to look at another of his college cohorts who had accompanied him to the rave this evening. That turned out to be none other than the lovely Anika Sitz, whose model-perfect figure and long sandy blonde hair moved about gracefully in the dance area to the resounding tune of "I Can't Stop" by Flux Pavilion. She was alternately grinding her buttocks and pubic area against that of her athletic, blonde paramour Nicolae Reicken ("Nick" to his friends). Anika's boyfriend made certain to proudly show off his relationship with her by exploring both her upper and lower anatomy with his hands as their bodies flowed harmoniously with the beat of the tune.

"Hah! I see you're eyeing Anika," Bog noted as he procured another plastic cup of beer for himself. "I won't lie, *alter* … I was doing the same. But no way are you gonna get to fuck her with Nick in the picture. He'll kick your foreign ass all over the campus if you try to move in."

Gunther did his best to control his anger, lest his burgeoning bloodlust slipped from his control and he ended up taking the drug-infected life fluid from his obnoxious "friend." No, the vampire's intentions were to take Anika this evening. He wanted her for more than just sustenance, however. He desired to have the girl as the first and most treasured of the vampiric harem. To this end he simply had to get the studious but popular and attractive Nicolae out of the way. And possibly the annoying Bog as well.

"Yes, I suppose I couldn't possibly be a match for a football player like Nick," Gunther falsely acquiesced. "That, however, would seem to leave you out of the equation as well, my friend."

Bog took a sip of beer before scoffing. "Hah! Riiigghht. I work out just as much as Nicky-boy, and I already have two talent scouts considering me for the *Deutscher Fußball-Bund* after graduation next year. Can he say the same? I will kick his ass all over the fucking pavement if he has a problem with Anika and I having a bit of fun together."

Gunther saw his "friend's" hubris as a possible opportunity. "That's quite a strong boast, Bog. I imagine you will prove it to be fully legitimate. Eventually."

Bog interrupted a sip of beer to look cross at Gunther for the implications of his remark. The drug he was taking, mixed with a few cups of beer, had obviously begun taking its toll. The 21-year-old athlete tossed his nearly empty cup onto the grass and walked up to Gunther. Bog then grabbed the front of the other man's leather jacket and roughly pulled the dark-eyed Romanian towards him.

"What the fuck you say, you dick-smoking mother fuck?"

Gunther again forced himself to control his temper. Hence, he avoided the temptation to grab Bog's wrist and snap his carpal bones like a twig (which he could easily do). Nevertheless, the covert vampire could not help but grit his teeth a bit at the temerity of his obnoxious friend's act of battery. As such, it took an even greater act of will for Gunther to suppress the protrusion of his fangs and the appearance of his fiery red eyes that would typically manifest whenever his full wrath was provoked.

"You may have read into that wrong, Bog!" Gunther said with feigned worry. "I meant 'eventually' as in *soon*. Please don't be angry. I am certain you will prove your point to me and everyone else as soon as possible."

The now drug-addled brain of Bogdan "Bog" Theodorescu seemed to waver between thrashing the (correctly) perceived insolence of his friend and giving the young man the benefit of the doubt that he may indeed have taken things the wrong way due to his substance-clouded mind After all, that wouldn't be the first time something like that happened to him during a binge. As a result, the arm he held Gunther's jacket with quivered furiously as his muddled psyche remained conflicted over which conclusion to draw.

It was about then that Anika and Nick witnessed the impending incident from several meters away on the dance grounds. The pretty blonde noticed this first, and she tapped her boyfriend on his shoulder and pointed in the direction of their two friends.

"Nick, look! I think Bog is burning out again! He looks ready to fuck Gunther up! He's such a nice guy. We can't let Bog do that shit to him."

"Yeah, you're right," Nick concurred. "Let's get over there and deal with this before Gunther gets hurt and we all get banned from future raves."

The two rushed from the dance floor in the hope of averting the looming violence. Before things could be taken further, Nick arrived on the scene and grabbed Bog's wrist while it was still grasping the lapel of Gunther's jacket.

"Bog, let him go, man! It's not worth it, okay?"

"Listen to him, Bog," Anika pleaded as she put her hand on the burly art major's shoulder. "I don't know what Gunther said to piss you off, but you're not in your right mind now."

"Yeah, man, I think you've been taking a bit too much of that stuff tonight," Nick added.

Bog then released Gunther's jacket and turned to Nick. "What the fuck did you mean by that? Are you calling me some type of fucking addict?"

Nick swallowed and pondered whether he should handle this gently or be more honest to his acquaintance.

Deciding in favor of the latter he replied, "Bog, please listen. You seriously have a problem with this shit, okay? Maybe it's time to stop."

Bog took a step closer to Nick. "And who are you to judge, Nicky-boy? Are you a drug counselor suddenly? Or, do you just think you're better than me because Anika is currently sucking your dick instead of mine?"

Anika scoffed loudly as Nick stepped towards Bog. This, of course, is exactly what his inhibition-challenged rival wanted him to do. Gunther simply stepped aside and tried not to noticeably grin with satisfaction.

"You brain-fried fucking asshole!" Nick exclaimed as he shoved the equally burly Bog.

The latter retaliated in kind and the two young men quickly had each other in a mutual headlock. Anika looked terrified, and no one else at the rave seemed to notice, nor were any of the few designated security guards anywhere in sight. She was aware they were likely off getting drunk or laid in their vehicles.

"Gunther!" the blonde girl hollered. "Do something!"

The long-haired Romanian threw up his hands and took a few steps back. "My apologies, Anika, but I'm not getting between those two brutes! I nearly got thrashed by one of them tonight as it is."

"Damn you!" Anika yelled at the (not actually) timid Gunther as she ran to break up the fight herself.

The young woman ducked between the two brawling men and did her best to push them away from each other while verbally demanding that they cease the fighting.

"Stop it! Both of you, stop it! I mean it, or I'll call the fucking police on my cell!"

Anika finally managed to push the two apart after some serious effort. Bog was in no shape to have inflicted much damage on Nick, and the latter was inebriated just enough that he was a bit too wobbly to take full advantage of his challenger's condition.

"What's the matter with you, Bog?" Anika queried. "I know you're high on all that shit you take along with the alcohol, but still!"

The only response from the guy with the unkempt hair was to almost slip and fall to the grass with no help from anyone else. Bog was nursing a bloody lip, and Gunther had to force himself not to salivate at the sight, let alone pounce on the man right then and there.

If only I could take a single quick lick of that precious blood...

Anika then turned to her boyfriend. "Nick, I think we should leave."

"Oh, fuck that!" the flaxen-haired athlete said. "I'm not going to leave because this fry-brained piece of shit had to go into full asshole mode on us. I came here to have a good time, and I'll be damned if I leave here on account of him before I do. We were having a good time out there before he started his shit!"

"You would have to carry on the macho bull and keep this conflict going, wouldn't you?" Anika spat.

"I'm not keeping anything going!" Nick insisted. "I didn't start this bullshit!"

Anika's voice was now raised, as she became increasingly irate over what she perceived as her boyfriend's pig-headed machismo. "No, but you have way too much male pride to leave here and avoid any more of this shit, right?"

"Can we not all get along?" Gunther said with bogus innocence and a bit of subtle sarcasm.

"Maybe that asshole *ausbrennen* should leave instead?" Nick insisted while pointing at the semi-coherent Bog. "Why should people who play by the rules suffer because of people like him?"

"Fuck you, dick cream!" Bog shouted at his rival.

"Fuck you up is what I'll do!" Nick yelled back.

Anika screamed in anger while throwing up her arms in frustrated surrender. "I've had enough of you shitheads for one night! I need some air! I'm going for a walk in the woods!"

"I think that is something we both need right now," Gunther opined. "I'll walk with you."

"Don't let her, Nick!" Bog yelled. "He wants to fuck her too! He told me that while you were dancing!"

Gunther clenched both his fists and gritted his teeth, struggling to keep his fangs and red eyes from becoming visible. *Bog, you stupid son of a bitch. I may have considered sparing your pathetic life before, but you are now on my list. When you least expect it. And it will be painful. So very painful... and quite* prolonged. *Moreover, you will not receive the honor of entering the ranks of the Undead.*

"You speak nonsense," Gunther told Bog. "You know I said no such thing!"

"Uh-huh," Bog retorted. "I caught you ogling her on the dance grove, and you didn't deny anything when I called you out on it! You do so want to fuck her!"

"Oh, what the hell!" Nick hollered at no one in particular. "I can't trust any of you fuckers! Not a single one!"

"Jesus, I am out of here!" Anika announced as she ran for her planned, lonesome walk in the wooded area outside the perimeter of the rave.

Gunther carefully eyed the exact route she was taking. *Since I cannot accompany her from here thanks to that dick-headed junkie, I will have to go around the other way and intercept her along the trail I am fairly certain she will be using. It will take even me several minutes, so I need to leave now and let these two fools enjoy each other's company.*

"Um, I think I'm going to leave too," Gunther said quietly. "I believe I will find my own way home. I don't think either of you will be too concerned, as I'm certain none of us are particularly desirous of each other's company anymore this evening."

With that said, the covert vampire walked off quickly in the opposite direction of the path taken by Anika. He knew he would have to trek all the way out past the perimeter of the rave on the eastern end, which led to a road that ran alongside a small wooded copse. There he would take refuge behind a tree and morph into bat form so he could swiftly fly to the trail he was near-positive Anika would be walking. Then, he could easily take her unawares.

Shape-shifting into certain nocturnal animals was one of the greatest abilities possessed by typical members of the Varnaean vampire strain that was only rarely possessed by average members of most other Undead bloodlines. Suffice to say, Gunther was as pleased as a maggot in shit to have that power among his repertoire of vampiric abilities.

After he took Anika, Gunther planned to quench his hunger with her blood and then remove her body from the area. He would hide it for the three days on average it would take for the mystical virogens in the vampiric blood he forced her to imbibe would cause her to rise again as one of the Undead. He was certain she would then think of Nick as no more than food and be delighted to have Gunther himself as her new paramour – not to mention enthusiastically accepting the honor of becoming the head of his vampiric harem.

After nearly a year of dreaming about this, Gunther could scarcely believe this plan was finally going to come to fruition! Unless something went horribly wrong, of course. But then, what was the chance of that happening during the mere several minute interval it would take the vampire to reach the road just outside the rave on foot; and the few minutes more it would require for him to fly back to the woodlands in bat form? Nothing to worry about, right?

***

Anika strode through the thick trees of the darkened woods several dozen meters outside the perimeter of the rave -- with tears streaming down her eyes. She wanted to leave this place but was reluctant to do so without Nick. The young woman had yet to decide if she was going to try to find a way home on her own, or simply walk around the woods for a while until he had cooled down. And Bog had hopefully passed out or something.

She couldn't really give a shit about Gunther, who increasingly appeared good for not very much as she came to know him better (to think she used to believe he was such a nice guy!). Needless to say, Anika was far too pissed at Nick to talk things out with him. Maybe she should simply let those two macho bastards beat the hell out of each other, even if it meant they were kicked out of the rave and banned from future parties.

"Damn him… damn him," the saddened and angered girl complained to herself as she leaned against a large birch tree and pounded her fists softly against its thick bark.

Little was she aware that the sounds she made had caught the attention of a large hirsute creature lurking in the nearby trees. After Eduard had fully morphed into his werewolf form, he had caught, and was in the process of devouring, a raccoon. That is, until his astute lupine senses had detected something much more appetizing.

The lycanthrope raised his large canine head and his pointed ears perked up. He sniffed the air and immediately caught a scent that he quickly identified as a human being… and female, judging by the sweet texture of the scent. And though Eduard would kill just about any human when he lost control of his animal side, for some reason incomprehensible to both the human and animal aspects of his psyche he had always found female flesh to be tastier than that of the male of the human species.

The werewolf, still well outside of Eduard's control, quietly peered through a tangle of concealing foliage, his yellow eyes fixed on the despondent young woman standing a scant few meters in front of him. Her emotional state was clearly registered, and the chimeric beast was aware that this served as an added distraction on her part. Thus, the lycanthrope surmised that at the speed he was capable of achieving on all fours, it would take him no more than a few seconds to dash across the small clearing and pounce on his prey. And she was far too distracted in her apparent melancholy to hear it coming.

It turned out that the simple math conducted by the werewolf was absolutely on target. Anika was aware of nothing until something huge, hairy, and feeling as if it weighed a ton smashed into her from the side. That quick glimpse was all she saw of her attacker before being knocked onto her back. It was the last thing the young woman would ever see. She had no chance to regain her faculties or get past the sudden blazing agony of a broken arm and three fractured ribs before the man-beast tore her throat out. The werewolf then moved towards her gut and ripped open her abdomen with the ease a child may tear apart the paper from a birthday gift.

The lycanthrope salivated at the sight of the exposed internal organs that he could now savor the taste of.

***

Gunther swooped over the treetops leading towards the trail he was certain Anika would be taking. His leathern wings were connected to what looked like a black-furred, unusually large specimen of the *Desmodus rotundus* species. Those not familiarized with the nomenclature would know it as a rather uncommon variation of the common vampire bat. His senses in that form were quick to navigate the direction he headed at a speed and altitude that rendered him unlikely to be spotted by anyone at the rave (and likely to be presumed an ordinary bat if he was).

Gunther finally reached the clearing where he was confident he would intercept Anika's chosen path… only to spot what seemed like a dead body lying below him. A female body, no less.

No. It cannot be. Not her. Nothing could have…

The vampire was not one to cavort about wondering rather than acting. He descended to the clearing and morphed back into humanoid form. As always, the entirety of his clothing -- including the contents of his pockets -- mystically reconstituted around him as he did so. Gunther approached the lifeless body, praying to whatever twisted deity a vampire could pray to (possibly the legendary Varnae… or perhaps Lord Dracula?) that the female corpse would not turn out to be whom he feared it would.

Upon reaching what was left of Anika's body, Gunther clearly confirmed the cadaver's identity since her lovely facial features were left mostly intact. The rest of her once beautiful body… not so much. A stream of still fresh blood dribbled from the side of her mouth, and a large gaping hole in her abdomen was surrounded by her strewn bowels and stomach. The rest of her viscera appeared to have been removed and largely eaten, though small chunks of leftovers could be seen staining the grass. The flesh on her legs and arms was stripped off, right through the tattered remains of her jeans and shirt. Her breasts were missing from her upper torso and were not seen among the other innards scattered about the horribly maimed body.

For a third time that evening Gunther had to use his will power to rein in a knee-jerk violent reaction. In this case, it was to resist shouting a stream of curses.

Anika! How could this have happened as quickly as it did? No species of animal in these woods could possibly have done something like this. Let alone over the course of just fifteen minutes.

Gunther then pulled himself together, bent over the body of his would-be beloved, and carefully sniffed over the worst of the many ghastly injuries inflicted upon her. He was hoping this would turn out to be the work of a particularly efficient human serial killer. Or, perhaps one of those mysterious out-of-place big cats periodically reported roaming about the European continent. For the second time in a single night he issued a prayer to an unholy source, this time that his suspicions of what the culprit of this slaughter was wouldn't prove true.

Unfortunately, within a moment the vampire's senses confirmed his worst fears. This was indeed the work of a werewolf, ancient enemies and sometimes conscripted servants of his kind. Gunther cringed, something he had rarely done since becoming one of the Undead.

Then, however, a different concern abruptly overcame him as his bloodlust became so acute that it was actually painful. He turned back to the maimed corpse of the girl he had once fancied.

I must get my fill of the blood while it's still fresh!

The non-culinary implications of poor Anika's death were momentarily lost upon Gunther as he attempted to feed off the proverbial scraps. He bent down and ravenously licked the stream of blood trickling from her open mouth. To his consternation, it had mostly been diluted by salivary fluid at this point. He then licked as much blood as he could from her torn throat. But she had largely bled out by this time, so it wasn't nearly enough to satisfy his gnawing hunger.

Next, the famished vampire ripped what remained of her bowels from the gaping hole in her stomach, tossed the odiferous organs aside, and lifted her pulverized body off the grassy ground as if it weighed mere ounces. He held the dangling form of a once beautiful girl over his open maw and shook it violently, hoping to force any blood remaining within the body to trickle out and into his anxiously waiting gullet.

Only a small amount did so, however, along with a few pieces of leftover viscera that were insufficient to sustain a vampire. Gunther spit out the chunks and angrily tossed the remains of Anika against a nearby tree. He now strongly considered uttering at least a few curses aloud as the hunger pangs grew close to unbearable in his belly. That is, until he heard some soft but audible (to him) footsteps walking over the grass a few meters away. A moment later a sweet, distinctly female voice caught his ears.

"Eduard!" came the voice of Nadja. "Eduard, are you out here? Can we please talk? Simona didn't mean anything by what she said. You know she can be irksome at times, but she really isn't a bad person at heart."

"Yessss…" Gunther hissed to himself in satisfied delight as he bared his sharpened fangs and ducked behind a nearby tree.

"Eduard, are you out here?" Nadja again called as she stepped out of a bundle of thickets and into the clearing lit by a bright waxing moon.

The concealed Gunther was not within her line of sight. Instead, what at first resembled a discarded female mannequin lay before

Nadja at the base of a large birch. Her eyes just barely had time to register the horror of what actually lay in front of her before a hand of tremendous strength suddenly grasped and covered her mouth from behind. It was so strong, in fact, that she could feel the left side of her jawbone crack in its grip. The hand felt entirely human, save for the skin being unsettlingly cool to the touch.

Nadja was unable to utter a scream as Gunther wasted not a fraction of a second before sinking his fangs into her jugular and drinking deep of the precious red fluid coursing through her circulatory system. The young woman's eyes opened freakishly wide as she felt everything that sustained her system flow into the mouth of another, siphoned out to sustain *him* now instead. Within several seconds she had lost a sufficient amount of blood to cause her to pass out and then expire in quick succession.

Gunther felt his great vampiric strength rapidly return to him and his hunger pangs fade as he ravenously fed. He intended to drink more than his required fill for the evening until his ultra-sensitive ears detected the sound of more footsteps approaching from about a dozen meters behind.

***

Several minutes earlier…

Eduard walked calmly but anxiously back towards the perimeter of the rave. He had regained sufficient control after his buffet of raccoon and human female that he was able to force himself to resume human form. Then he dashed back towards the bushes where he hastily hid his hoodie and shoes and redressed as fast as he could before heading back to the party. Thankfully, he had only lost his socks, and his stylish shoe boots were intended to cover most of his socks anyway, so it wouldn't be too easy to notice if he was no longer wearing them.

The pangs of remorse had now replaced those of raw hunger, and the young man found himself torn apart in a manner far more metaphorical than that of the hapless Anika (whose identity he didn't know).

I wish that girl, whoever she was, hadn't come into the woods. I really didn't want to do that. If she hadn't stepped in, I could have

caught a couple more coons and I would have been satisfied.
Goddamn her! Why did she have to step into the woods before I
had the chance to hunt some wild game? Why?

Eduard wiped the tears of sorrow he shed as he crossed the
perimeter back into the rave to rejoin Simona and his love interest
Nadja. After looking around for a few moments, he spotted Simona
passionately grinding on the dance area with another woman he
didn't know. Nadja was nowhere to be seen. He would have been
happy to leave Simona to her fun, as he had no interest in speaking
to her again this evening. But he needed to interrupt her to query
about Nadja's whereabouts, hoping she hadn't left with someone
else.

Eduard realized he had no choice but to run up to the dancing
justice warrior and interpose upon her revelry. He had to shout
over the haunting but danceable tune of Zhu's "Faded" as it blared
out the oversized speakers to the irritation of the extra-acute
hearing he possessed even while in human form.

"Simona!"

"Shit, you startled the fuck outta me!" the blue-haired young
woman screeched.

"Where is Nadja? I don't see her anywhere."

"Um, after dancing here for a bit she went into the woods to
look for your ass. Didn't you run into her there?"

"No. I didn't see her anywhere. Are you sure she didn't come
back?"

"She never came out of those woods. And she wouldn't have
gone anywhere but here if she did."

Had Eduard been covered with the grayish pelt that coated him
in wolfen form, it would now be standing on end. Some
preternatural sense he could not explain told him that he wasn't the
only unusual predator in those woods this night. He needed to
locate Nadja, and fast.

"I have to find her!" Eduard yelled before taking off back
towards the woods as quickly as he could.

"Wait!" Simona called to him. "What do you think is going on?
Wait up, I'll go with you! Aw, fuck!" She turned to the chunky but
cute young nursing major she had been dancing with. "Babe, I'm
sorry but I need to go. A friend of mine may be in trouble! And
I'm not gonna let that man go after her alone!"

Simona's companion nodded in understanding a nano-second before the blue-haired girl took off after Eduard with all the speed one would expect of an athletically fit young woman.

***

Also several minutes earlier…

Nick faced off against Bog. "It's your fucking fault she ran away. Because you had to start your shit!"

"Hey, ain't my fault you're not the only guy who wants to fuck her," Bog retorted through a glass-eyed expression.

Nick tried to keep his temper in check, but only because he knew Anika would have wanted him to. "I thought you were a friend, Bog. You caused a lot of trouble tonight, just like you've done before under the influence of that shit. You need some help. Seriously, man. Take that advice in the spirit it was intended."

Bog cocked his head, almost looking confused. Then he laughed. "Really, man? I drink to your ignorant, judgmental ass." The mop-headed young man then held up another cup of beer he grabbed off a nearby table in a saluting gesture. *"Prost!"*

He then gulped it down in obvious mockery of the advice that his erstwhile friend had attempted to give him.

Nick slapped the cup from Bog's hand. "Enough of that shit! Are you listening to me?"

In response, Bog simply staggered for a second. "I'm gonna fuck her after Gunther does, alright? Is that okay, or can I go first?"

Nick lost both any last erg of sympathy he had for Bog's illness and any for Anika's problem with his out-of-control machismo. He balled his fist and struck Bog in the face, smashing the cartilage comprising the shape of his nose and sending him falling on the table behind them. A fountain of blood spurted out of his now re-shaped nostrils as the crashing sound accompanying the destruction of the table was nearly heard over the booming sound of Tchami's "Untrue."

Several pre-filled cups of fine *Spaten* beer doused the fallen young man's shirt and pants as they slid off the broken counter. Bog's head could only quiver in pain as he sneezed out a messy spurt of blood to add to the size of the crimson stain that had already spattered on his clothing.

"Hey, what the fuck, man!" the pink-haired guy filling the bear cups shouted.

But Nick wasn't listening. Both his business with Bog and any further concern with enjoying the rave were finished. Now his only concern was Anika, and he ran towards the woods to find her. He made sure to follow the general direction he saw her walk towards minutes earlier, having a good idea of what trail she would be taking into the darkness of the trees.

***

Gunther dropped Nadja's lifeless form to the grass upon hearing the footsteps coming through the clearing behind him. Her skin was now as pale as his own, her eyes and mouth widely agape in a countenance of supreme horror; twin trails of blood flowed out of two visible puncture wounds marring the flesh of her throat. With his demonic hunger now slaked, Gunther could focus his full concern on the werewolf.

Gunther morphed into a cloud of etheric mist and swiftly trailed the currents of the wind to settle behind a local clove of trees. There he re-congealed into humanoid form and peered out from the concealment of the thickets. He wanted the element of surprise on his side again, especially in the event the oncoming human footsteps turned out to be the werewolf in human form.

What Gunther saw instead was a tall, striking young woman with blue spikey hair emerge from a path to the east and into the clearing.

"Eduard, where the hell did you get off to?" Simona queried. "Why the fuck did you take off on a side path like that?"

Gunther grinned. *Well, well… what have we here?*

It was a second later that Simona looked onto the grass in front of her to spot her bestie's dead and emaciated form. She was far too startled to yet notice the much more horribly mutilated corpse of Anika just a few meters further towards the towering birch tree.

"Nadja!" she screamed as she ran to her fallen friend.

The whitish pallor, bluish lips, and look of extreme horror on her friend's unmoving face made her condition all too clear to Simona.

"No! No! Baby girl, what happened to you?"

You are going to find out now, as the same fate is about to befall you, Gunther mused as he started to emerge from behind the cover of the thickets. He paused when he detected yet another set of human footsteps approaching, these from the western trail that led into the clearing.

Simona heard the rapidly approaching steps too. "Eduard? Is that you? Nadja is dead! She's dead!"

But it wasn't Eduard who suddenly emerged from the tree line into the clearing. It was Nick. He didn't recognize the woman he saw crouched on the ground who cried profusely as she cradled another, albeit unmoving girl in her arms.

"Anika?" he said. "Please, no…"

"No, that wouldn't be our dear Anika," Gunther said as he moved out of the thickets into full view. A sardonic grin was on his face, and this time his fangs were fully displayed. "Neither of us know that girl whose blood tasted so good. Our Anika is actually situated a few meters yonder."

The vampire pointed towards the large birch tree in the center of the clearing. Nick turned in that direction and his eyes widened with horror at what he saw lying torn and broken there.

"You… killed Nadja?" Simona asked as she glared at Gunther.

"Was that her name?" the vampire sniggered. "And yes, I did indeed kill her. It was quite fun, not to mention tasty, as well."

Nick ran to Anika's gruesome remains and the horror he felt was beyond description. He, too, only recognized her from what remained of her face. That the girl he came to truly love had met such a truly agonizing and nightmarish end was all too evident.

The despondent young athlete turned towards Gunther. "You did this to her? Like you killed that other girl?"

"Actually, no," the vampire said. "I know you're upset, but do I like look I am afraid to admit when I killed someone? Besides that, you should be able to tell that's not the handiwork of the same killer. Well, that of a vampire like myself, anyway."

"You mother fucking son of a bitch…" Simona uttered almost under her breath as her striking blue eyes remained fixed on Gunther. "You killed Nadja."

"No," a third male voice was suddenly heard from the distance. "Not Nadja. No…"

All three turned to the source of the voice that only Simona recognized. It was Eduard, who had doubled about and headed down a different path once he caught the scent of a vampire in the woods. A vampire he at last confronted. One that had taken something very precious from him. Even as he had unintentionally taken something equally precious from the vampire.

"That is the bastard that killed our Anika, Nick," Gunther said. "Tore her to pieces like the beast he is. The girl I killed had a much quicker and more pleasant death than the one that man inflicted on our girl. Something he is going to pay for!"

"Eduard…?" Simona said incredulously at Gunther's words.

Nick gave the newest arrival in the clearing an icy glare resembling the one Simona had given Gunther. "You. Did you… do this to Anika?"

Eduard took a deep breath as a crestfallen expression took over his face. "I'm… I'm sorry. I… didn't mean to. I didn't do it on purpose. Not like how that vampire killed Nadja on purpose. I need to make him pay for that. Please step aside, so…"

"You did this to Anika!" Nick screamed. "You fucking monster!"

Without another word the blonde-haired football player lunged at Eduard.

"Wait, please…"

But Nick wasn't hearing it as he waded into Eduard. The two young men fell to the ground rolling over the grass. They pummeled each other mercilessly as they grappled -- one determined to avenge the brutal butchering of the woman he loved; and the other determined to fend off this attacker so he could exact retribution on the creature that slew the girl that he loved.

"Hmm, this may be easier than I thought…" Gunther noted.

However, Simona was to prove otherwise as she suddenly bellowed, "You killed Nadja!"

The young woman suddenly pulled out a stiletto she had hidden on her person, extended it, and lunged at Gunther. The vampire was momentarily startled by the girl's unbridled fury as she plunged the steel blade into his chest. She then withdrew it and stabbed his upper body and neck repeatedly.

"Die, you fucker!"

Much to her consternation, however, Gunther barely displayed any pain. Steel was not a substance capable of inflicting serious injury upon a vampire. Instead of dying, Gunther grabbed the wrist of Simona's knife-wielding hand with one of his own and grasped her throat with the other in a vice-like grip. She was easily lifted off her feet and slammed hard against a tree located directly behind them.

"Very impressive! How feisty!" Gunther said as Simona kicked, struggled, and gagged to no avail against the vampire's incredible strength. "I think you will make a better inaugural member of my harem than Anika ever could!"

Gunther sunk his fangs into Simona's throat and drank deeply. Her eyes rolled back into her head and she let out a loud gasp as she felt everything vital being sucked out of her.

At the same time, Nick's fury enabled him to get the better of Eduard as they rolled and pounded each other. The former began punching Anika's butcher repeatedly, striking with blows that would lay low any athlete he had ever met. But he could not help noticing that his opponent's musculature felt as if it was becoming larger and harder as he poured on the blows.

Within a moment he saw the zippered front of Eduard's dark hoodie pop open as a gray furry chest of immense bulk expanded underneath the fabric. A second after that Nick's final thrown punch ended with his forearm caught in the jaws of what looked to him like the head of the largest, most fearsome canine he had ever seen. The football champion yelled in a combo of agony and terror as the beast's sharpened teeth punctured deeply into the flesh of his arm.

The werewolf then stood up to his full, impressive height, easily lifting Nick's hapless form in his muzzle as he did so. The athlete screamed again and began punching the head of the lycanthrope in a desperate bid to get the monster to open its jaws and release him. This noble effort failed, and the enraged werewolf simply grabbed Nick with both of his furry hands and flung him away, a toss that sent the man flying over ten meters distant.

"Get… off!" the lycan grumbled via a now only half-human larynx as he hurled Nick away. "Gonna… kill that vampire! Avenge Nadja!"

Nick's airborne body was halted when his right shoulder struck a tree across the clearing. Everything went black for the young athlete before he even hit the ground.

With a bestial growl, Eduard's human consciousness guided the lycanthrope into advancing towards what he considered his only true foe. The one his human half sought vengeance upon, and whose animal side sensed as a natural enemy. This desire for revenge from an inhuman creature feared throughout human history was not to be held by the man-beast alone, however.

Upon hearing the werewolf's snarl of rage, Gunther turned and released the limp body of Simona. It slumped to the grassy ground at the base of the tree with a deathly pale complexion and two bleeding puncture wounds visible on her throat.

The vampire bared his fangs to the half-lupine beast now confronting him, revealing incisors that were stained scarlet with Simona's blood. His blood-smeared mouth bore an expression that was partly anger, and partly a jeering smile.

"So, it would seem that it is down to the two of us at last," Gunther said. "You will pay for taking my Anika and interrupting my feast with this other lively girl!"

The werewolf growled a similar sentiment, with Eduard's partially in-control human half forcing only partly intelligible words out the creature's muzzle. "You… killed Nadja! Now I kill… you!"

***

With a vicious snarl the werewolf charged at the vampire on all fours like an enraged rhino. The lycanthrope leapt and slammed into Gunther with tremendous force, knocking the Undead predator against the birch tree behind him. Eduard's lupine form struggled to get his powerful jaws around Gunther's throat, but the vampire held the werewolf's large furry head with steel-fingered strength and a frenzied determination to keep those teeth away from their intended target.

Gunther attempted to push the werewolf's slavering jaws upwards to expose his jugular. If only he could sink his fangs into the beast's thick, furry neck he could not only savor the blood of a lycanthrope – a rare treat for a vampire – but he could end this battle in his favor. It was a big "if," however, considering what he was up against. But vampires weren't exactly a force to be taken lightly either; and these two types of monsters always knew they potentially faced off against the other to their mutual peril.

As the two creatures of the night nearly stalemated in their struggle the werewolf changed the game by pushing himself into a bipedal stance and slashing the vampire across the chest with his front claws. Gunther screamed as the pale flesh on his torso was raked and his vampiric blood began spilling out of the wounds.

"You stupid son of a bitch!" the vampire exclaimed as the pain fueled his rage. "I will kill you now!"

Gunther made good on his threat by delivering three amazingly swift punches to the werewolf's head and jaws. His supernaturally enhanced strength made these blows much more effective than those imposed earlier by the hapless Nick, and the lycanthrope was sent reeling. The massive head of Eduard's bestial form shook in an attempt to regain his senses, but Gunther wasn't one to allow him the precious seconds required for that. Instead, he executed a powerful leap and tackled the werewolf to the ground. He then grabbed the creature's muzzle with both hands, held the maw shut, and pushed it upwards to expose the beast's fur-covered neck.

Eduard fully understood the tactic his opponent was initiating, and the werewolf was determined to break free before the vampire would sink his fangs into his throat and drain his lifeblood. With his jaw contained the werewolf resorted to tearing into his adversary's back with the talons on all ten of his fingers. The sudden vicious wound caused Gunther to wail in agony and to soften his vice-like hold on Eduard's jaw. This enabled the werewolf to pull his head free with a sudden twist of the beast's powerful neck muscles. The lycanthrope then quickly struck again and raked Gunther across the face.

The vampire screamed yet again as over half the ashen skin on his right cheek was ripped away. The werewolf then lashed out with both of his massively muscled arms and slammed Gunther in the chest with the palm of each of his enormous hands. This stunning blow sent the vampire flying off Eduard's hirsute form. He landed hard on his back a few meters away, which greatly exacerbated the pain of the wound torn into his thoracic spine region.

"You stupid fucking beast!" Gunther keened as he struggled to push past the pain of these injuries and get back to his feet.

I... need to change tactics... and swiftly.

The werewolf was not about to let this opportunity go to waste. That was something both the human and animal sides of his psyche were in full agreement.

Sometimes the combination of human intellect and animalistic cunning truly worked to Eduard's benefit. *I have to press this advantage! The vampire needs to* die *for what he did!*

The werewolf leapt at the injured – but not quite debilitated – vampire, intent upon ripping him to pieces before he could mount any type of defense. The movement was swift and powerful – but fell short of lethal results when Gunther suddenly morphed into bat form and managed to take to the air just in time to evade the lycanthrope's pounce. The beast-man howled in rage and stood on two legs in a laudable attempt to catch the flying creature in his spade-like hands. The move was futile, however, as the vampire had frequently practiced his flight and was quite maneuverable in this relatively small, lightweight form.

Gunther pushed himself to gain altitude and circled his wolfen foe, looking for an opening or convenient avenue of attack. For his part, Eduard stood on his hind legs and moved his hairy clawed hands in gestures intended to taunt the vampire into attacking without a plan. He forced himself to speak in this form so his words could supplement the heckling of his movements.

"Yes, vampire! I... killed your Anika! I ate her! She tasted... like taco meat! Very yum!"

Had Eduard been more or less fully in control of the lycanthrope, he would likely have asked some deity to forgive him for exploiting his inadvertent slaughter of an innocent woman to lure the vampire to him. However, the animal in Edward was now head of the proverbial steering committee due to his level of rage, and no type of holy contrition was requested by the beast.

Unfortunately for Gunther, the baiting was successful. Nevertheless, before taking it he forced his now part chiropteran larynx to join the verbal assault.

"You insolent son of a bitch!" the circling bat uttered in a voice that sounded vaguely like Gunther's against the strained background noise of chalk being scratched across a blackboard. "I am betting your precious Nadja tasted much better. As did your friend with the blue hair. Their blood was like honey. I tingled as I sucked it out of them!"

The werewolf, undaunted, struck back. "Come… get me, vampire! Let's swap these stories… up close… you fuck—errrr…!"

With a loud angry screech, the bat dived towards the werewolf. The lycanthrope stood and prepared to grab the smallish animal-form by its leathery wings and shred them like tissue paper. However, Gunther had a different strategy worked out that Eduard failed to anticipate. He morphed into a human-sized bat with partly humanoid characteristics while in mid-drop. As a result, he landed on the lycanthrope with great force and the two chimeric monstrosities found themselves rolling across the grass while savagely biting and slashing at each other.

The two creatures finally rolled off each other to find themselves confronting one another less than two meters apart in crouching positions. Both had their furry bodies covered with visible slashes and abrasions, though Gunther still looked the worse for wear with the ghastly injuries perpetrated against the left side of his now inhuman visage (and just barely beginning to heal due to the supernatural nature of their source). The werewolf that was sometimes Eduard Russoff growled ferociously at his foe, while the man-bat once known as Gunther Radu released a deep hissing sound as his fangs were likewise bared.

It was then that they spoke their final words to each other before the battle re-commenced in all its bloody glory.

"Let's… finish this!" the werewolf grumbled.

"Yesssss…" the vampire hissed in agreement.

The snarling werewolf lunged at his foe, while the man-bat leaped to meet the attack. These monsters were enraged beyond any degree they had ever experienced in the past, either before or after their respective transformations into something simultaneously more and less than human. The ancient antipathy between these two types of monsters, despite their deep connection within the supernatural spectrum duly recorded in folklore, was intensified by deeply personal motives to make each utterly determined to destroy the other. Both had encroached upon the other's chosen hunting grounds this night, and both took something precious from the other. Neither foe would go down easily.

The no holds barred battle that erupted from that point on was beyond brutal. Gunther took the first offensive, using his now clawed bat-like hands to deliver two deep slashes to the werewolf's face. Eduard snarled in pain and rage as his left eye was sliced into by the assault. It quickly swelled and turned a reddish hue as it filled with blood.

This drove the werewolf into an even greater frenzy than before. The lycanthrope unleashed his full berserker rage, letting the animal side take complete control. The retaliation was fierce as the lycan slashed at the vampire mercilessly, tearing open partly healed wounds and inflicting several new ones. Gunther screeched in agony like he had never done before as the ichor that constituted his vampiric blood spattered about the nearby grass and thickets.

The werewolf then viciously pressed the attack by leaping forward and slashing at the vampire's torso again. The intent was clearly to rip out the nosferatu's heart and lungs; however, Gunther caught the lycan's wrists in his own steely hands, thereby barely preventing the planned evisceration. The vampire was now in desperation mode, which made the normally quick-thinking Gunther an even quicker thinker.

He twisted the werewolf's wrists with all his might in imitation of a sadistic game he used to play with his childhood peers called "Mercy." The lycanthrope howled as a result of the painful grip, momentarily moving his bulky neck upwards to do so, much as Gunther had hoped.

If I can just get at the beast's throat...

It was a good plan, but Eduard's human wrath combined with the animal fury he shared psychic space with was not to be contained for the invaluable two seconds this move would require. As the vampire moved his still bat-like head towards the beast-man's throat the lycan proved swifter and stronger by bringing his jaws to bear even faster. As a result, he caught the vampire's large-eared face in his vice-like teeth.

Shit!

Eduard bit into the vampire's head, piercing flesh and bone alike. This crushing force would soon prove too much for the nosferatu. However, the pain and terror drove Gunther to twist the werewolf's wrists even harder, cracking at least one of the monster's carpal bones. The werewolf held fast to the vampire's head despite the pain, but the muzzle's grip was loosened just enough that Gunther's adrenally fueled desperation enabled him to pull his skull free with a single almighty heave.

Unfortunately, much of the remaining leather-like skin that characterized his face in man-bat form was torn off and remained in the werewolf's blood-soaked maw. Needless to say, Gunther again screeched in extreme agony. Nevertheless, the vampire quickly returned to his feet and morphed into full human form. It was his intention to next morph back into full bat mode and take flight again. That was the plan, but the pain of his newest injury resulted in a failure to gain the required concentration fast enough.

It was a few seconds the enraged lycanthrope refused to give his foe. The werewolf likewise sprang up on two feet again and delivered another bloody slash to his enemy's upper torso, barely missing his throat. The lycan then lifted the dazed vampire over his head and threw his undead opponent against that same enormous birch tree in the middle of the clearing.

Gunther struck the dense botanical structure with great force and sunk to the ground unmoving. His head had conveniently rolled back, exposing his neck. This was exactly what Eduard had needed.

The vampire's throat is exposed. He enjoys biting people in the neck. Let us see him experience that himself when I rip out his fucking jugular!

The werewolf promptly dropped to all fours and ran towards the vampire, who was now situated several meters away. Picking up the required amount of speed, Eduard's lupine alter-ego executed a great ten-foot leap, his open salivating jaws headed directly for the vampire's exposed gorge.

The leap fell short in a most unexpected fashion, however, when Gunther suddenly thrust his legs forward and caught the werewolf's neck in an iron-gripped pincer hold. Those years I spent on the high school wrestling team have just proved themselves invaluable.

Eduard struggled with berserk fury to wrest his big wolfen head loose, and Gunther was thankful that the legs tended to be stronger than the arms, a trait carried over from human to vampire. Still, he knew he couldn't hold the werewolf this way for long, so the Romanian blood-sucker made a point to lash out with his fists again. He quickly delivered two powerful blows, one to each side of the beast's jawbone. The cracking sound he heard, and the beast's accompanying yelp of pain, indicated he was successful with inflicting injury. But he still needed to act quickly.

This he did by holding fast with his pincer grip, grabbing the werewolf's fractured muzzle in both hands, and using the combined strength of his legs and arms to pull the beast-man forward and directly over him. This slammed Eduard's massive lupine skull against the heavy bark of the tree Gunther was leaning back against for support and leverage (another concept he learned in high school wrestling). Taking advantage of the stunned lycan that was still held fast by both his legs and hands, Gunther yanked the beast's head upwards. He then finally managed to sink his protruding fangs directly into the werewolf's jugular vein.

Eduard's wolfen form whimpered and struggled with admirable force to break free, but his foe held him fast and his fangs had sunk deeply into his main circulatory tube. Gunther drank deeply, sucking out the lycanthrope's blood with the force of a black hole. The beast's formidable struggling continued but became increasingly weaker as the vampire siphoned the canid beast's life fluid into his own system. The werewolf's blood was invigorating in the extreme, and Gunther could feel himself beginning to heal from the horrible wounds inflicted upon him during the battle at a faster rate than before.

Several minutes later, the hirsute monster's struggles had ceased entirely, and moments after that there was nothing left in him for Gunther to siphon from his cardiovascular tap.

With a final heave of his vampiric strength, he tossed the heavy, unmoving bestial form off him. The vampire returned to his feet and watched as the werewolf's massive lupine corpse reverted back to the human form of Eduard Russoff.

If his lungs had still functioned as they did when he was human, Gunther Radu would have breathed a sigh of relief. He was nursing the many bloody and painful wounds that the werewolf had wreaked upon his person, but his consumption of several pints of lycan blood had reinvigorated him. Hence, he knew his full recovery was imminent.

"Anika, you are avenged," Gunther said quietly to himself. "That infernal beast is dead."

However, Gunther understood that this had been quite a close call, and he realized how much worse things could have turned out than they actually did. He knew it was time to leave the vicinity of the rave lest it contain any other unfortunate and potentially fatal surprises for him.

With much of his strength returned, Gunther willed himself into bat form and took to the night sky, departing the area towards the hidden coffin lined with Romanian soil where he would enter a recuperative slumber during the coming daylight.

Epilogue I

Loreley Scholz did not expect to find what she did when she left the perimeter of the rave to take a solo trek into the woodlands. Her only intention was to quietly relieve her bowels and then clean herself. She didn't trust those two mobile bathroom stalls at the rave, since they often had a line before them, tended to be less sanitary than the woods, and afforded too little privacy in her eyes. The last time she used one of those stalls its faulty lock enabled some guy to suddenly pull the door open and expose her seated on the toilet in front of a small group of leering young men. Well, never again.

Before she could find a quiet place in the clearing to do her "biz," however, Loreley ended up relieving herself in her jeans when her cell phone flashlight suddenly illuminated four bodies strewn about the area, two male and two female. And one of the latter was mutilated worse than those horrible coroner pics of the Jack the Ripper murders she once had the misfortune to stumble upon on the Internet.

After inadvertently soiling her jeans, Loreley fainted. Her boyfriend was thankful that when he came to look for her, she wasn't in the same condition as the other four bodies around her.

Epilogue II

Basement morgue of Saint Dumas Hospital, East Berlin, Germany; a few days later…

Coroner Dr. Hans Kern pulled open the drawer containing the chilled body of one of the young women found at what the newspapers and online journalists had been referring to as the "Secret Rave Massacre." He adjusted his bifocals and checked the records, and the name of this cadaver was identified as 20-year-old Simona Ionescu. Her short hair was still a dyed blue color, with dark roots just becoming visible due to the hair growth that often continues for a short time after death; her spikes were now largely matted down. The small round metal piercings so popular with young people (which Kern found inexplicable) were still affixed to her lips.

Kern turned his back for a few moments to pull on his medical gloves so he could begin the already delayed autopsy. Upon turning back he was startled when the young woman's arm suddenly moved upwards in a blur of motion and grasped his neck in a steel-strong grip. Before he could react further the again animate Simona pulled the coroner down to her and sunk two protruding fangs into his neck. He joined the other corpses in the morgue mere moments after she drained him dry.

Simona then rose to her feet, satisfied that this sudden new bloodlust had just been fulfilled. She wiped her mouth clean and looked disapprovingly at the dead medical professional she had just fed upon.

"Ugh. A fucking man," she lamented aloud. "Figures that was all that was available to me when I woke up."

Simona then looked around her for a bit before the obvious but rhetorical question came to mind.

"What the fuck have I become?"

Epilogue III

Second floor of Saint Dumas Hospital, East Berlin, Germany; also a few days later…

Nicolae Reicken was still in a state of shock after waking up in the hospital. He was told he was lucky to be alive after his ordeal. He was the sole survivor of the four victims who had run afoul of what were believed by local authorities and the press to be at least two serial killers working together. These killers had to be particularly nasty customers and were theorized to be part of some cult dedicated to Satanic ritual. This theory was formed due to the manner in which two of the bodies were drained of blood, whereas another was horribly mutilated while exhibiting signs of having actually been eaten by some large wild animal. Hence, the detectives on the case also had a working hypothesis that these serial killers may have been accompanied by a large attack dog under their control. The nature of the bite wounds suggested it may have even been an illegally captive Eurasian gray wolf.

Nick's broken shoulder blade and the horrible bite marks on his arm seemed to indicate that he was beaten after having surprised the cultists in the middle of their depredations, after which they evidently set their pet canine upon him. Why both men and animal didn't kill Nick as well as the other victims was as yet unknown, though it was surmised this may have been due to the fact that the attack on Nick had to have been made in haste.

What really startled the doctors, however, was how remarkably fast those bite wounds on his arm had healed; particularly since some of them went all the way down to the bone. His dislocated shoulder and surrounding torn ligaments were likewise coming along quite well.

However mysterious, that was the good news. The bad news was that Nick still appeared too traumatized to answer any questions, or even to speak very much. He mentioned Anika's name a few times, and the attending psychiatrists said it was natural for him to be emotionally debilitated with guilt and remorse over failing to save the girl he loved. That, along with witnessing the horrible ritual he evidently interrupted and the nature of the savage attacks perpetrated upon him, had taken their toll on his mind.

The authorities, his family, and the families of Simona Ionescu and Nadja Westhoff were told they had to be patient and understanding despite their firm and fully vindicated desire to bring these horrid perpetrators to justice. The identity of the other young man found dead at the scene had yet to be identified.

What the doctors were not yet aware was that despite not being wrong regarding the factors contributing to Nick's traumatized state, there was actually more to it than that. Much more, in fact. For his entire life, Nick Reicken was unaware of the historical significance of some branches of his lineage, and what he inherited from them; how an older branch of his family from Wales was known as Cornell.

Finally, there was the matter of his being beset by nightmares of a howling man-wolf. This creature wasn't the same one who had attacked and injured him during the rave, however. Somehow, he knew it was an altogether different beast of the same type. One he was on much more intimate terms with.

Opening his eyes after hours of restless sleep, Nick spoke aloud the identity of this dreadful man-beast that plagued his dreams. He said it to an empty room, but he had to say it nonetheless.

"That thing is *me.*"

END

CHAPTER 1: Charlie

Charlie ran for his life. He tore through the dark woods, dimly lit by the waxing half-moon in the cloudless sky. He did his best to ignore the branches whipping him in the face, arms, and body. *She* wasn't that far behind him; he could hear her giant feet as she tore through the underbrush after him.

He could almost smell her, that musky, yet feminine odor he had become more than familiar with. He could still taste it, as the room she had kept him in was reeking of it. It seemed to bleed from the walls and bypass his nose, going straight for his taste buds instead. She hadn't showered in a very long time. He was pretty sure she didn't cater to her monthly friend very well, either.

He had lived with a girl he had been duped by once who left her used items in the bathroom trashcan, exposed for all to see and smell. He knew most women took good care of themselves during that time of the month, but this skanky chick was not among any sort of respectable class of woman. She had more men over in those few months than he had had sexual partners in total. Charlie Griffin would never forget that smell. That rotten, dirty smell. This was that, but worse.

Worse because his captor and current pursuer also killed people. She butchered three in front of him when he had first woken in the basement hours earlier, sitting in an electric chair of all things. Those three people were his friends. Thankfully they were already dead, so he didn't have to hear the screams that most assuredly tore out of their throats while they still lived. He had awoken to the smell of guts and blood, his tormentor in the process of cutting off Laney's legs.

Charlie had cried out then. Laney was his current infatuation who kept him solidly in the friend zone, but never took his obvious interest in her with anything more than a grain of salt. He had then noticed Scott, her boyfriend he hated even though they were pretty much friends regardless, laying on the floor under the table. Laney's body was laying on top of it.

Well, part of Scott, anyway. The man's eyes stared at Charlie, accusing him of failing to save them from the she-hulk tearing Laney's left leg off and tossing it indifferently into a large plastic garbage bin. Given the sound when it landed, it was not the first body part inside. Charlie would be willing to venture a guess that the rest of Scott -- and likely all the pieces of Langdon -- lay in the bottom of the round container. Charlie looked at Laney, who was staring at him. For the briefest second, he saw her lower lip twitch and her mouth gasp a little bit.

Oh shit, she's still alive. Forget her, Charlie, she's too far gone to save now. Worry about yourself, son. That last thought was in his dad's voice.

The huge woman finished with Laney's legs, and then went to work on her arms. Charlie had taken that opportunity to notice he was not restrained to the chair he sat crooked in, and he bolted, ignoring the metal shish kabob skewer still protruding from his shoulder courtesy of the monster woman's much smaller sister. The sister who was the reason he was in his current predicament. Even now, his heart skipped a beat at the thought of her. Those dark brown eyes and red, flaming hair that she kept pulled back in a ponytail.

Eris, you evil bitch, I'll kill you if I ever get away from this ogre you call a sister, Charlie thought with confidence even he knew was bullshit.

In his crazed flight from the basement and warehouse, Charlie had failed to notice in his mentally traumatized state that he had reached the old building that marked the beginning of the twisted family's property. The start of their horrible day.

The brick and mortar building was falling apart, the windows boarded up with aging sheets of plywood, with the sign out front barely legible due to the wear and tear of the elements on decades-old paint. He and his friends had stopped here first, thinking it was the place they were looking for, his memory playing it back for him. When they realized it was abandoned, frustration led to fighting amongst them before his third friend, who had been missing from the basement of horrors, had suggested they smoke some weed before continuing.

After no protests were raised, Langdon had fired up a gigantic blunt. The rich kid from Minnetonka always had the best shit, even though he always ruined it by putting it in a blunt wrap. Charlie never liked the taste of tobacco and pot together. But he sure as shit wouldn't say no. They got incredibly stoned before the blunt was even half gone, which made the next moments even more surreal and confusing.

A black Ford F-150 from the late 1990s had pulled up to the aging building, high beams glaring at them. The door opened and a figure had gotten out of the truck. He could tell it was Eris as soon as she cleared the still beaming lights of the F-150. Charlie melted a little inside as he saw her, his lower region beginning to stir with arousal.

Then his crush spoke. "What are you doing here, Charlie? This isn't the right address, you dumb city fuckstick!"

The venom in her eyes was something he had never seen before in the five or six times he had interacted with the woman. He had first met and continued to run into Eris at the local fish stores in the cities, where she was a live aquatic plant distributor for the businesses who each claimed to have the best plants yet got them all from the same place.

"Whoa lady, what the hell is your problem?" Scott had stepped between Charlie and Eris, putting his hand out to stop her from advancing.

It worked, but only until she sucker punched Scott in the solar plexus. The unexpected punch launched by a deceptively slender arm felt like an aluminum baseball bat had been rammed into his gut. Needless to say, Scott went straight to the ground after being hit.

"Who the fuck was talking to you?" Eris had squatted down to Scott's face to ask him this last question in a gravelly voice, the woman's vocal fry grinding on her larynx with the hoarseness of it. "I was talking to Charlie, not you."

Langdon then tackled the woman, her angry cry of surprise telling of the rage she would unleash upon them. He punched her in the face, the closed fist's connection with Eris' face rewarded by a river of red gushing from her nose. The injured young woman screamed and stepped back, leveling a rigid, accusing finger at him.

"Your ass is grass, bitch." Eris grinned as she said this, blood flowing into her mouth making her words garbled a little. She never dropped her pointing index finger.

"Eat shit, you stupid c --"

Out of the trees to the left of the building, *She* exploded, tearing across the grassless lawn faster than anyone could react. Charlie had only a second to look at the charging brute before her giant cleaver was buried in Langdon's face. Long, dirty blonde hair ran down heaving shoulders, framing a thick face that would have been called handsome in a feminine way, like an attractive female bodybuilder in the super heavyweight class.

However, she had since been made hideous by a dozen scars that looked like claw marks. The huge woman now looked as if a mountain lion had made her mug into a scratching post, each healed wound having a deep line of scar tissue whose reddish color that made them look as if they were still wet.

One eye was mostly white, with very little iris pigmentation, giving it a cartoonish quality. A big, white orb with a black pupil in the middle. Her mouth, split by one of the claw mark scars, was wearing a fiendish grin as she pulled the buried cleaver out of Langdon's face, neck, and chest with an incredibly loud slurp. This move elicited a stunned peep from him before tearing his features in two. Langdon dropped to the earth, bleeding like a stuck pig all over the hard ground. His legs bucked and twitched spasmodically several times before lying still.

Charlie was mesmerized by the sight of this gory tableau. As his brain struggled to comprehend the events before him, Laney's screams as the huge woman came for her were not even registering in his head. He watched the blood find a small divot in the dirt, where it pooled up before overflowing and running down the slight hill towards his car. He suddenly became aware of a horrible sound, like a bird with a cackling call sounding off. His mind tried to rescue itself from the brain-numbing shock his body was experiencing in an effort to find the sound and stop it. It was going to drive him crazy if he didn't.

The GIF image of the cleaver burying itself in Langdon's face looped over and over in his head, distracting him. Something in Charlie's brain finally snapped together and he realized what the horrible sound was.

Laughter. The laughter of a giddy little spoiled brat.

Eris was laughing her ass off. He looked at the scene with a sense of reality once more.

Laney was underneath the huge woman, who was punching the shit out of Laney's face. Blood and bruises covered it as the wrecking balls the giant woman had for fists pounded the poor college girl's face like a meat hammer. Laney was unconscious, but that didn't seem to matter to the bitch beating her to a pulp. Charlie cried out, his dry throat cracking so bad it felt like it had torn open inside. The two murderous women's heads snapped to his position, a grin on each face. The big woman stopped pulverizing Laney and stood up to stare at Charlie. Turned to face him, eyes locked on his, death ever-present in them.

The ice crystal blue color of her irises was one of the prettiest he'd ever seen. This threw his mind into a tizzy. He acknowledged his murderer's gorgeous eyes, and then all he could do was scream until she struck him with the broad side of her cleaver and stars ushered him into darkness.

***

Charlie's brain focused on reality again, standing in the clearing by the old building, attempting to plot his next move. He looked over to where they had parked the car, completely forgetting they had even driven there, but found only tire tracks and the pool of blood that congealed where Langdon had bit the dust after receiving a cleaver to the face. In the moonlight, he could see a new set of tracks that indicated someone had driven it away, and he knew it wasn't anybody who had arrived in the Nissan Pathfinder his dad had given him as a high school graduation present five years earlier.

Dad. I need to get a message to Dad.

He was bleeding from several places all over his body and looked at all of them in contemplation. *Which one will be better for writing a message?* Then, he remembered the shish kabob skewer sticking out of his shoulder, the one Eris had stabbed him with during the single instance he had woken up during their rough transport of him and his friends to their secret chamber of Hell. They were trying to force him into an old electric chair, complete with the restraints, and he fought fiercely to resist. Then Eris produced the skewer out of seemingly thin air and plunged it into his shoulder. It pierced the flesh just in front of the clavicle on his left side, missing his lung by millimeters. He screamed and clawed at her eyes before the big woman punched him, returning the hapless Charlie to unconsciousness.

Focus. Write Dad a message before she finds you again, he thought, nodding once, Charlie tore the kabob skewer from his shoulder. He screamed, the long metal spike not wanting to leave the liquid warmth of its new home, and the young man had to wiggle and wrench on it to get it out. The pain dropped him to the ground before he was successful. Blood surged out of the wound immediately afterwards but soon slowed to a steady trickle running down his body. Charlie gasped and looked around, searching for evidence he had been heard and death was coming for him. There was no sign of either woman. He exhaled, not realizing he had been holding his breath.

Now, which side to write a message on? Charlie looked quickly at the empty building in front of him, thinking of his father a couple hundred miles away, and what the best place would be. He pictured his dad showing up there, searching for his lost son, the man's anger tempered by his unflinching determination to get what he wanted. Searching for something, anything that would lead him to his son. Then it hit him, and he made his way into the building.

Charlie walked past row after row of aquariums on multilevel stands. Their dusty, dirty glass tanks appeared to be pretty old by the frames on them. He walked past, his mind taking a split second to notice an old Eheim canister filter from like the 1960s or 70s, and his inner aquarist smiled at the antique underneath all of his terror. *Gotta keep moving,* he thought.

Seconds later, Charlie found the gender-specific bathrooms at the rear of the place. He burst into the men's room, and quickly entered a stall to begin writing a message to his dad. Sweat poured down his face as he scrawled with his own blood, having to dip it painfully back in the wound to get more improvised ink. Grinding his teeth from the pain of doing so, Charlie finished his brief message, took a second to look at it, and content with the attempt at code, left the men's restroom and entered the women's facilities. Now he climbed up on top of one of the toilets in the line of stalls and tried his best to not breathe loudly, or bleed… on… the… floor.

Shit.

Charlie Griffin looked down at the spots of blood that had followed him into the bathroom, and into the stall he was crouched in.

Shit! Shit! Shit!

He climbed down off the toilet, looking at the sliced-up shin of his right leg, with the blood running down over his shoe before it began to collect around his foot on the floor. Never mind the shoulder puncture that still wept blood constantly.

"Charlieeeeeeeee," a deep, feminine voice bounced off the walls in the main room outside of the bathrooms. "Come out, come out, wherever you are!"

Of course, I get the murderer who says cliché shit.

Charlie's inner monologue did nothing to assuage his barely contained hysteria. He was so close to squeaking in fright that his heart skipped a beat instead, the sensation of trading fright for a heart palpitation reminding him of plugging his nose to quell a sneeze. His body betrayed him anyway, as a nervous fart escaped his tightly clenched butt cheeks like the last bit of air let out of a balloon while stretching the lip. His heart sunk, his bowels threatened to give way, and icy blood filled his veins all at once. Suddenly, he knew he was screwed.

I hope you find my message, Dad, and get these sick fuckers for me, Charlie thought as he sadly resigned himself to the approaching doom that could be heard stomping his way.

The door to the ladies' room opened with a subtle hinge squeak, and as his mind silently screamed in absolute fear of the mountainous woman coming to kill him, he heard her whisper to someone that wasn't him.

"Husband, please accept this offering as proof of my undying love and save me from this mortal vessel you have banished me to. Your forgiveness means everything to me," she said, a slight hitch in breath at the end of her barely audible statement exposing her emotions.

Suddenly, the woman began yelling to her absent husband. "Hades! Come to me now! Let us take this little piggy to Hell together!"

The stall door buckled and flew forward at Charlie as the giant woman barreled into it. Before he could react, it hit him in the face, knocking him on his ass between the toilet and the wall to the stall next to him. He was wedged and couldn't get free, the door and his mangled body refusing to cooperate. With a rush of air, the door was suddenly lifted off of him and flung away, shattering the mirror over the sinks behind where his murderess stood. She was breathing heavy and licking her lips in anticipation.

"Why are… you doing this?" Charlie's dry, croaking voice sounded like a stranger's to his ears. "What the fuck did we do to you crazy bitches?"

A sob burst from his mouth as the woman towering over him replied, a hungry gaze in her hypnotic eyes and a grin on her scarred face. When she finally spoke, her words were smooth as silk.

"You had to go and look all tasty."

CHAPTER 2: Griffin

Two Weeks Later
Sunday

Persephone's Garden. That's the name of the place my kid went looking for. I finally cracked the password for his computer (Boobies00!, boy I raised a charmer), and searched his web browser history. Mostly websites for aquarium stuff -- that's what Charlie is into -- a few streaming sites, and his email. I had no luck looking into his email, can't get all the passwords right, I guess. I did, however, find the website for Persephone's Garden, an Aquatic Plants distributor and retail store supposedly located somewhere in central Minnesota.

Minnesota. Oh joy. From pronouncing the word 'about' like it was pronounced 'aboat', to saying 'ya know' a hundred and fifty times in a ten-paragraph conversation, I can't stand the way those almost-canucks talk. Canada should just swoop down and assimilate the whole damn state.

Forgive the vitriol, but I was born and raised in and on the outskirts of the Windy City. People talk normal there. That's where my lab is, as well. My son comes to stay with me once a month, per the custody terms set by the Ex Battle-Axe and her lawyer lover before they took half my savings and fled to California. He's twenty-three now, and still makes the monthly visit from Cali.

His new dad (who, humorously is not the lawyer anymore, (ha ha you bloodsucker) but a plastic surgeon out of Beverly Hills) does make a lot more money than I do. This sleaze ball will do whatever it takes to send my kid away so he can bang Charlie's mom without having to deal with him. He still does this even though my boy is old enough to live on his own. Charlie has made it perfectly clear he plans on spending as much of the asshole's money as he can. Sentiments like that tend to warm my cold, black heart a degree or two.

Yeah, I'm an asshole too, but in a completely different way. I've killed people, some of them undeserving. But when you are guarding the secret formula that has been in your family for generations from greedy fuckers of all walks of life, being nice isn't exactly a luxury you can afford.

Who the hell am I, you say? Secret formula, you say? What is this, a cheesy sci-fi story? Maybe, but that doesn't make it any less true. My name is Lionel Griffin. I am the current reigning genius from a long line of chemists, dating back to the nineteenth century.

Five years ago, a distant relative living in Europe somewhere died, and left his entire estate to me. Not having any realistic use for a large mansion in the English countryside, I packed up everything of interest, and bought a new house in Winnetka, Illinois. It's located a block over from where they filmed *Home Alone.* You know, the movie where one of the *Goodfellas* and the narrator voice of the kid from *The Wonder Years* rob a wealthy neighborhood during Christmas, but are foiled by a kid left at home by his terrible parents? He stops them with a bad attitude and a penchant for making homemade traps that should have maimed and/or killed the stupid crooks several times over. You know, *that* movie? Yeah, that's right, I live by *there.*

I'm not a millionaire or anything, as far as you know, but I do enjoy a respectable domicile. Charlie and his friends came to visit the day before he left on his little road trip. That Laney girl he is obsessed with lives six houses down from me. She always comes over when he is in town, stringing my boy along like a fish on a hook until she gets whatever she needs from him; then, she goes home to that Scott guy to get what she *needs* from *him.* If I didn't respect my son as much as I do, I'd have killed them both and chucked 'em into Lake Michigan a long time ago.

Then, last month, he showed up at my door, beaming like a teen who just got his first taste of second base. As soon as he gets his shoes off, he is showing me a picture of a girl he met up in Minnesota at one of those swap meet things he does for his aquarium hobby. My kid is obsessed with planted freshwater aquariums. Last he told me, he had a dozen at his mom's place in Cali, and even has two 55 gallons at my house. I cut him off at two, because I've become adept at the hobby myself from taking care of them in between his visits to Winnetka. I never signed up for that shit.

Fertilizing aquatic plants is a regular part-time job. Dosing the water column and substrate with nutrients, keeping the filters clean and compressed gas cylinders full of carbon dioxide is a bitch! Never mind the fish. The freaking lights annoy the shit out of my eyes, too. So many LEDs…

I'm an invisible man, mad scientist by default, I suppose, and here I am talking about aquarium crap. This is what happens when you have a kid and end up becoming concerned about its welfare and whatnot. I should be in the lab, trying to practice enough to still be considered a scientist, not an aquarist.

Anyway, he shows up last month parading a crappy cell phone picture around of this red-headed girl he met. His lens must have been dirty and his heart pounding because the blurry picture barely got the point across that she was good-looking. He told me her name was Eris, and that she was a plant distributor located just about halfway up Minnesota. The fact that he thought nothing about driving all the way up there to talk to a girl who didn't even know he cared worried me from the get-go. Then he informed me his not-girlfriend and her two boy toys were going with. I rolled my eyes but said nothing.

Who in their right mind would keep the company of a girl who kept him wrapped around her finger, her boyfriend she makes no attempts to hide that she is fucking, and the little yuppie turd they knew from the very state they were about to travel to? My dumbass kid, that's who.

That Langdon asshole was a doper, I knew it. He always smelled like one of those pot-filled cigars when I've been around him. Fine, to each their own, but when your parents' money pays for you to get stoned all day, every day, you gets no respect from me.

Sorry, I'm rambling again. They left to go find this distribution place. That was two weeks ago. No call, no email, nothing. Laney's mom even stopped by at one point to ask if I'd seen her daughter. Prick that I am, I said she was probably out fucking Scott and telling my son how inadequate he is at the same time. Laney's mom hasn't bothered me since.

I don't make a habit out of calling my son a cuckold, but that's the road he is heading down obsessing over that heartless bitch. I hate her, and my love for my son is the only thing that has kept her alive. So far.

Oh yeah, the secret formula I mentioned. Would you believe it is the honest-to-God, Invisible Man formula? Go ahead, laugh, I'll wait. Done? Good. I'm fucking serious. I can turn *invisible!* It's a fun little trick, especially since my relative somehow also conveniently perfected the formula that turns me visible again, something the others never achieved. I used to be a chemist for a certain biomedical giant, but we parted ways a few months ago due to... *ethical* differences.

So, I have to know-how to replicate the formulas with the notes I inherited from the deceased member of the Griffin family. I also developed a third formula that successfully turns certain materials invisible. Yeah, I'm that fucking good. It doesn't work on just any clothes, unfortunately, but I discovered that neoprene is very cooperative for a reason I haven't narrowed down yet. I'm not a great mad scientist, so don't expect some elaborate bragging session on how I did it.

Anyway, if I don't want to creep around naked all the time, I have a selection of wetsuits that I cram my junk into on cold nights. I don't creep around much in the winter, if you haven't figured it out yet. I've done a lot of messed up shit since I got my hands on the formulas, some of it mirroring the journal kept by my relative of unknown relation.

I had been out of town on business and had just gotten back home the day I realized Charlie was missing. I had just walked in the door with my suitcase when Kyle Brovlovski's mom from *South Park* shouted "What? What? What!" I dropped the suitcase and looked at my phone's screen. It was a text from Charlie.

"We're here but it looks like it's closed, text ya when we are on our way home."

This was followed by a picture message of a beat to shit sign that appeared to read, "Persephone's Garden." I could see the top half of Scott's dumb face at the bottom of the picture. I shook my head and closed the phone. I started walking towards the master bedroom to put my clothes away. Halfway there, realization hit me like a ton of bricks. I ripped the phone back out of my pants pocket, dialed in the password, and opened the last text from Charlie back up again.

I had to squint to see it at first, then I remembered the enlarging feature on the damn phone. I zoomed in with the reverse-pinching motion across the touch screen. Too blurry. I ran the picture through an app I had that could run it through a nighttime filter. My stomach felt like it was being repeatedly stabbed with an ice pick as I gazed at the blurry, enlarged image. A monster of a woman carrying a gigantic cleaver -- the kind you don't really think exists until you actually see one -- stood behind the sign in the picture. A sadistic rictus was plastered to her face like it was a mask. *Was it a mask?* I thought about it while I stared at this raging thing hiding in the woods.

I swore out loud in my big empty house, realizing what I had to do now. I was going to settle my affairs at my company, asking for some personal bereavement time. After all, the mother of my child had just died! Yes, my out of town business was indeed in California. That doctor widower of hers should be thanking me for all the money I saved him. Well, he should be if he can find his way out of the maze I put him in before he dies of thirst. See? I told you I was an asshole. And for the record, it *did* make me feel better. You know, *revenge?*

So, affairs settled at work, load up some… *supplies*, then it's off to… where the fuck am I going again? Shit. Sometimes I am really stupid for such a smart man. He never really divulged that information, other than central Minnesota and highway 65. A Google maps session and I have at least an inkling of where I am supposed to go. Going to take me a while, better get my ass moving.

Persephone. I don't know if that is the monster bitch's name, but as far as I'm concerned, it is. As I am preparing everything before I leave, the song "Shitlist" by the band L7 gets hopelessly stuck in my head, even though I haven't heard the song since the 90s, when I last saw the movie *Natural Born Killers*. I embrace this earworm, however, as the song is apropos for what comes next.

I got some Persephone hunting to do.

CHAPTER 3: The Fresh Wave Gang

Thursday Morning

"Joe, change the track, man," Tyler tapped the front seat passenger of Josh's Lexus LX sport utility vehicle. "Do you really like this old geezer rock? You should let Josh choose what we listen to, it's his Lexus."

Joe looked at Josh, who just grinned and continued watching the road ahead. "Don't look at me, I'm not playing D.J. while I'm driving," was all he said on the matter.

"Old geezer, my ass, Tyler! You're only five years younger than me, man." Jose wasn't taking Tyler's shit today. He usually let his elder Millennial friend's jabs on his musical tastes go, but he didn't take that shit when it came to Led Zeppelin. Just would not take it. He changed the track, purposely taking just long enough for Tyler to start to say something most likely along the lines of how it was about time, and he hit play on "Immigrant Song." The charging drums and guitar always made Joe think of a horde of Vikings going to battle with some interchangeable enemy army. Especially with Robert Plant's wailing war cry adding to the energy the song seemed charged with.

Tyler mumbled something from the backseat, and Joe heard Zeke laughing at Tyler. Tyler exchanged pleasantries and resumed staring out the window. They were almost to the address Jennifer had dug up on the Internet, and after talking to a lot of people she knew in the business. She didn't own her own top-rated fish store for no reason. She worked for it. Hard. Her husband had died in Afghanistan during Obama's presidency, and had left her a pretty substantial inheritance he had kept a secret from her during all their time together. This was the very same dark-haired woman who was ahead of them, driving the oceanic colored Toyota 86 GT, fresh off the lot a week prior. Her license plate simply read "MORAY," a vanity plate she got endless amounts of shit for but kept it regardless. Jennifer loved eels, and the moray was her favorite.

And that is exactly why Zeke was in love with her. The back-seat chuckler had worked for the woman for six years now, helping her, Joe, and Meghan, Joe's longtime girlfriend, build the Fresh Wave Aquaria store from the ground up. They had bought an old carpet store in an area mostly comprised of industrial warehouses and office strip malls. It was located in an otherwise rich suburb on the west side of Minneapolis.

First, they built their saltwater game all those many months ago, Zeke briefly reminisced. They next established awesome contacts all over the world and were soon carrying the supplies and capabilities to offer in-home delivery, setup and installation, and maintenance. Jennifer's contacts got her the prime specimens for the store, many of them overpriced and sometimes not as prime as they should have been. But business was good and the stored profited, a great deal in thanks to social media's digital word of mouth.

One day, a guy named Tyler had come into their store, looking at everything they carried and asking why they didn't have any freshwater aquariums. The response was that the other local stores had freshwater covered, to which Tyler laughed.

"I've seen those stores," he had said. *"They do have great selections, but none of them really cater to the planted tank community. Give me a month and this back room you are currently only using as storage, and I'll show you what I can do."*

And they did. They gave him a month and the back room. Jennifer even offered to foot some of the bill, which Tyler accepted a portion of, but mostly paid for out of his own pocket. In less than a month, Tyler had the entire back area dedicated to freshwater plants and shrimp. He set up a series of aquascaped tanks. Each one was hardscaped prior to planting and filling, and each was unique and amazing to look at. Especially a few months later when the plants had exploded to life and a large school of some kind of fish, usually a tetra, filled the open water of each aquarium. Their shrimp selection was getting better all the time, something Joe had taken to like iron filings to a magnet.

Tyler had dramatically increased their business, along with Joe's rapidly developing expertise with the small crustaceans that had become so popular in the industry the last decade or so. Things were looking awesome. Then Jennifer got an email from a guy who came into the store on occasion, almost always when one of their distributors would pop in with a shipment. The two women she always dealt with were odd duckies, one a sexually aggressive bitch, the other a freakish Amazon of a woman who looked like she would make Jason Vorhees her boot-licking lap dog. Plus, she had a scarred-up face to make Freddy Krueger jealous. Jennifer couldn't help but think of the Amazonian planet episode of *Futurama,* with the caveman-like giant women who punished men by 'snu-snuing' them to death, a.k.a., screwing them until the men's pelvises were crushed and they ceased to be.

That poor woman. I bet my cousin DeeDee could work wonders for that poor Neanderthal. Still, yikes.

But oh, the plants they had for sale. Joe and Tyler were drooling over them in a way that was all but sexual. They all were, really. The big woman -- Persephone her sister had called her -- busted out an array of Amazon Sword plants that got even Jennifer excited. And she was a saltwater woman. The leaves on their red rubin sword specimens were a gorgeous veined red and green with the vertically running veins looking healthy and strong. The leaves themselves were nearly three feet long! That was ridiculous, but certainly achievable. But there wasn't a local store within the five-state Midwest conglomerate that stocked such botanical specimens. You had to order them online. But if Fresh Wave could get their hands-on plants like that, oh the wonderful they could achieve.

A month after the sisters (she assumed) entered the store, Jenny was visited by a man named Minos. He came into the store and flashed a business card with a name she recognized.

He also came in with a cooler on wheels full of different plants in plastic bags. Joe had been nearby, cleaning out the Amano shrimp tank, and he quickly put the lid back on the Nano-sized aquarium and rushed over when he heard Jenny's audible gasp. Inside was a collection of some of the most colorful plants either of them had ever seen. There were several species of rare *cryptocoryne* plants they couldn't stock to save their lives; every species of *vallisneria* either of them knew of; more of the red 'rubin' sword plants, e*chinodorus 'Rubin'* -- although smaller specimens than the sisters' visit yielded. You wouldn't hear any complaints, though. They were just as gorgeous as the larger plants had been, the red and green contrasting together like the word's definition was matching instead of strikingly different.

But there were more plants in the apparently bottomless cooler. Mosses, floating plants, several prime species of *anubias, ludwigia, rotala, aponogetons*. The cherry on top was the smaller plastic tote in the cooler Minos pulled out. It contained some of the healthiest, most vibrant *bucephalandra* plants Joe had ever laid eyes on, including anywhere on the Internet. He whistled and quickly reached for the little tote.

His eyes bugged out like a kid on Christmas morning who awakens to a much larger haul than anticipated. *Bucephalandra* was all the rage currently, the little attractive plants grew similar to *anubias*, but looked quite a bit different, with many varieties of leaf shapes -- including one named *bucephalandra Godzilla,* which was an appropriate name for the spiny-looking leaves that resembled the famous *daikaiju's* back plates and skin color. It also seemed to grow fast in most cases and on top of that it was Joe's favorite.

Later, after Minos had arranged for them to meet near the actual site of Persephone's Garden and left for home, the cold, impersonal man's presence still lingered in the air. Jenny more than vocalized her distrust of him. Joe, however, used business to appeal to his employer.

"C'mon, Jenny, do you see this stuff?" Joe gestured towards the tank they had put most of the plants in, save for the *bucephalandra.* The buce that they were going to sell went into most of the aquascaping displays and shrimp tanks. Except for a large portion of the Godzilla buce Joe begged to have. Jenny harassed him for a while about it before relenting.

He lowered his gesturing arm and continued. "We can make a fortune selling their plants! This is the kind of thing that will draw in all of those freshwater people on the Saint Paul side of the Twin Cities Metro to our store, never mind the money we could charge for some of that buce." Joe's eyes glittered with hopes and dreams. "Call Tyler and have him come in and see. If he doesn't agree with me immediately, I'll drop it forever."

"I already called him," Jenny replied.

Less than an hour later, Tyler was drooling just as bad as Joe had been, but over some *fissidens fontanus* moss on 3D printed ledges. The plastic shelves had suction cups attached to stick the growing platform to the aquarium's glass. It was full and thick and already looked to be reaching out from where it grew on the ledges. He finally turned to look at Jennifer.

"Why are we not heading up there right now?"

CHAPTER 4: Griffin

Wednesday Night

After two days of driving around, I finally find the rotting building in the picture Charlie sent me, the one with the mean mama in the bushes. I spot the sign that used to read "Persephone's Garden" in large red italic letters painted on what use to be a green sign, now peeling and faded to look like it said, "Per hon 's Gar." I drive past the sign a little ways and find an old barn less than a mile further down the gravel road I turned down off of Highway 65. I keep the sign in my sight through the dust cloud kicking up behind my Jeep Compass Sport as I look for a good place to park my vehicle. An abandoned barn that was still somehow standing looks promising, and I carefully pull into the overgrown, rutted dirt driveway.

Looking up and down the road, happy for the lack of anyone, I walk up to the barn's doors and inspect their condition before trying to open them. Only one of the hinges on the left door looks really rusty and half of the hinge is corroded off, but otherwise the door seems to be in good enough shape to use, at least. Knowing better from previous experience, I fetch the small bottle of WD-40 from my glove compartment that I use on door hinges and frozen locks on occasion. I utilize it for that very purpose on the two doors, saturating the rust-colored metal of each hinge, and then let it soak in for a few moments before I try the doors.

The penetrating oil does its job and I am rewarded for my efforts with the tiniest of squeaks from the door with the half rotten hinge before it goes quiet. The right door gives nary a peep. And just like that, my vehicle is out of sight as I drive into it, the barn only being full of old hay and broken pieces of wood that I drive right onto and crush into the dirt floor. I get out and load up my supplies into a thin backpack I'll wear, and once satisfied with my armaments, I glance out the hole in the corner of one of the doors at the fading daylight. I look at my phone and verify the time. The sun should be going behind the trees in about an hour. I drink the formula and prepare myself for the slightly brisk 50s of the Fahrenheit scale that can be common on a May day in Minnesota.

Once my visage and form disappear from the normal range of vision, I strip down. The shrinkage is legendary as I pull out the wet suit chosen for the ensuing festivities. I am hopefully going to set in motion sooner rather than later. I slide into it fairly easily, only having to hop up and down twice to get in all the way and zip up. I pull on a pair of neoprene boots, as well, and stash my backpack in the Jeep, loading the items I will need from here on out in a different bag, this one made of neoprene and invisible as well. Sometimes I can't even find it, save for the tag still looped around the zipper pull.

Tonight, I will need to cut that off. I don't need to get busted because of a price tag. How much of a jackass invisible man would I be? Before I do, I pull out the sword I brought with me, an honest-to-God *katana* from Japan. Not a damn show sword, either. This was not some mail order weapon with *The Walking Dead* inscribed on the blade, or some dumb shit like that. I acquired this particular item myself.

I took a trip to Japan last September, to visit Tokyo and have some *me* time, if you know what I mean. Wink-wink. Nudge-nudge. I decided to steal some things while I was there, testing out my abilities to sneak into secured places. A foreign country isn't the best place, admittedly, but I was having way too much fun fucking with the citizens of the most populous metropolis in the world. I was losing interest in the standard deviances I commit whilst invisible and decided to break into the Japanese Sword Museum. It was pretty easy, I just waltzed in before closing and found a place to hide. I lifted a Mumei signature *katana* from its display, which of course set off all kinds of alarms. The cops showed up and let me out unknowingly as they stormed the building looking for a suspect. It was hard to not laugh.

I slice the tag off of the backpack and pull it on, hanging the sword's scabbard over my right shoulder and across my chest so it hangs down at my left side. The very visible scabbard seems to levitate around me, and I frown a little at the annoyance of my visible weapon. It doesn't matter, though. I'm very good with this sword. Minutes later, I set off down the road, comfortable with the wet suit's dry warmth capabilities as I walk down the side of the road, heading back to the deserted building. Dusk is in full bloom, bordering on night when I reach it.

I head inside the place, breaking a window to gain access. Confident no one is around, I don't care about the loud shatter of the glass, and crawl through the large opening with ease. I glance around the place and see old aquariums from yesteryear coated with all of the maladies of age where they rot on old wood stands that would probably not hold them if they were they full of water. Old filter devices and light fixtures sit on another shelf, and I notice one of them looks like it was moved recently, its awkward placement on the shelf catching my attention.

Charlie would have lost his shit over this, there is no way he wouldn't have at least picked it up, I think, staring hard at the antique canister filter. My night vision isn't the greatest, so I pull out a headlamp from my backpack after setting it along with the sword down first. I don't put it on my head, but instead just point it like a normal flashlight, using the blood light setting made for hunters. In the faint red light, I see footprints and blood trailing into the men's bathroom. Swallowing hard, I enter.

The place smells like it hasn't been used or cleaned in a decade. The lingering smell of decomposing urinal pucks in the three wall-mounted pissers assaults my nose, as does the coppery smell of blood. I follow the trail to the stall and open the door slowly, dreading what I will find within.

A pool of blood surrounds the toilet bowl on the floor. Streaks of it run down the side from smaller pools congealing on the seat. A clear ass print seems to be the squish factor that made the blood run down to the floor, as well as a major drip from somewhere on whoever's bleeding body sat in this stall. Being thorough, I step in and close the stall door, which groans with displeasure. The breath hitches in my chest and I thank whatever god helped me get to where I am at this particular moment. It's a note. From Charlie.

46°02'56.3" N
93°13'20.1" W
There's 3
help me

It wasn't all neat and organized like that; it was dripping and sloppy, written in his own blood, but I could still recognize the writing. I don't know how the hell he got the coordinates, never mind how he memorized them. Unless he somehow had his damn phone still. *Operative word is* had, *asshole.*

A slowly burning rage started burning hotter inside of me, making me anxious for the fucks to show up so I could track them down and murder them once I found out what happened to my kid. I followed the trail further, curious where he went after writing the message that was somehow overlooked or ignored by his pursuer.

It led out into the small hallway for the restrooms before turning into the women's. *Did he not realize he was bleeding all over the floor? How messed up was he?*

My wonderings reached a horrible conclusion as soon as I opened the bathroom door. There was no body or anything, but one of the stall doors had been obliterated by someone knocking it off the hinges and into the stall itself, where it lay bent and broken atop the also broken toilet. A flood of water had prevented the blood-tinged stains from mixing with bodily fluids before drying on the linoleum tiles. My eyes got watery for the briefest of instants before I left the bathroom to find a good place to sit.

And wait.

CHAPTER 5: The Fresh Wave Gang

Thursday Afternoon

"This is the place. Turn in here."

"*This* is the place?" Jenny was incredulous, questioning the beat-to-shit structure Meghan was telling her to turn into.

The black-haired owner of Fresh Wave Aquaria glanced over at her blonde-haired friend of eleven years. Meghan grinned and nodded, giving up even trying to talk over the blaring "Caravan Palace." Electro swing, though not the only type of music Jen listened to, was her current obsession. Meghan liked the energetic French group but was starting to get sick of them.

"Okay..." she said and turned the Toyota into the sand-covered parking lot, completely disregarding the faded yellow lines of the ten-car lot.

Josh followed her in with the Lexus and parked parallel to her crooked park job, taking up half the lot just for the two vehicles. Both engines were silenced, and the occupants exited their respective rides. Candy, one of the new employees at Fresh Wave who was quickly becoming their friend, crawled out of the back seat with a groan and stretched her cramped muscles. The back seat was not all that spacious in the zippy little car.

"Oh damn, Jenny, nice car, but I call shotgun on the way home," Candy said, chuckling.

She pulled out an E-cig and puffed away. There was a strict "no-vaping" rule in Jenny's car. She hated the sickeningly sweet clouds of still completely undetermined toxicity. She didn't give a crap what arguments were thrown in her face about how they were different and less harmful, blah, blah, blah. To Jenny it was still smoking.

Candy had a few puffs before they left, and it had only been a couple hours or so, but vaping came with increased usage thanks to the ease of getting your fix, thus making the need more urgent. Unlike the dragon people with their giant tanks that sounded like a blowtorch when they fired them up, Candy was a respectable vaper, fairly discreet and never blowing her cloud in anyone's face intentionally. And she never whined about the car's "cloudless" rule.

"What the hell flavor is that, Candy?" Meghan sniffed the air loudly as she closed the passenger side door. "Smells like cotton candy. But then again, most of them do."

"It's called 'Citrus Sports Drink'. I nicknamed it 'Brawndo', after *Idiocracy,*" she said.

"'It's got what plants crave!'" Josh shouted as he climbed out of the driver's side of the L X, closing it a little harder than was probably necessary.

Zeke laughed behind him, exiting the back-driver's side door. "'Go away! 'Batin'!" The curly orange-haired man laughed heartily as he closed the door.

"Sadly, that movie is becoming reality," was Tyler's first comment upon getting out of the back-passenger's side. "Ever since Pumpkinhead took office."

"Tyler!" Jenny yelled at the aquatic green thumb. "What the hell did I tell you about calling *him* that?" She had a stern look of deep annoyance on her face.

Tyler ducked his head down a little bit before replying. "It's insulting to *Pumpkinhead*, one of your favorite movie monsters, created by Stan Winston, and starring Lance 'Bishop' Henriksen. The android guy with milk blood from *Aliens.* Yes, I know, but I'm still breaking myself of that habit, toots. Sorry."

Joe and Meghan laughed from where they had met each other, exchanging a kiss before leaning against the front end of the Lexus's passenger side. Tyler stood by them, checking his phone. There were no bars and he didn't recognize the name of the carrier that had replaced T-Mobile in the corner.

"Of course not," he muttered to himself, and sighed. *Hope these people aren't some freak cannibal family*.

"So, when is this Minos guy supposed to get here?" Josh asked this as he pulled a beer out of the cooler in the back of the L X.

Jenny made a face at him guzzling the Grain Belt Premium Light like, well, a light beer.

"Sometime between now and eight o'clock tonight," she said.

"That's not for another three hours! What the hell are we supposed to do until then?" Josh was clearly annoyed, burping up the last word of his question. Jenny's face crinkled in disgust.

"I don't care what you do, asshole. Go jerk off in the woods for all I care," Jenny spat.

He didn't work for her, so the fear of getting fired was not present. Josh was a friend of Joe's, and he'd known the guy since they were eleven, when Joe moved to Minnesota and Josh was the first friend he had made in his new school. If not for her deep respect for Joe, Josh would not have been invited along. Well, that and his sexy Lexus SUV. They *had* needed another vehicle for the trip, and his was there so she decided to put up with the impulsive weirdo.

"Fuck you, lady, you ain't my boss!" Josh flipped her off and stuck his tongue out like Gene Simmons from KISS.

Jenny was up in his face in three seconds, her bacon and ranch choice of snack foods for the drive torturing his nostrils. The shorter woman had flames in her eyes.

"Excuse me, needledick?" She was inches from his chin, the extent of her attempts to get in the taller man's face with a height of only five feet.

Zeke pulled back on her gently, and she miraculously allowed him to. Then he stepped between them and looked directly at Josh. The latter glared at Jenny through squinting eyes, his teeth grinding visibly through parted lips.

"Dude, what's your problem?" Zeke used a tone of voice reserved usually for girlfriends when he pissed them off and had to kiss ass for forgiveness. "You know this is her party, man. She's paying for your gas, food, and lodging if necessary. You could at least not be a prick to her."

"Yeah, and you aren't going to have to wait much longer, anyway," Joe said, pointing at an approaching vehicle. "I believe our mystery man has arrived."

The F-150 pulled into the parking lot behind both of their vehicles, blocking them in. A warning siren went off in Tyler's head, but he kept it to himself.

The dark-haired man named Minos got out of the truck, accompanied by a grinning red-haired woman. Both looked very Greek to Tyler, who fancied himself an amateur expert on determining a majority of nationalities in people from their appearance. The woman's red hair, not so much; but their features seemed Mediterranean at least, if not Greek. Minos sported a thin, dark mustache, soul patch, and the eyes of a man who was a hard read, either from lack of anyone being home upstairs or from excelling at hiding his true emotions from others. Either way, Tyler was skeptical of him. And of the woman with him.

She was beautiful in a dangerous, exotic way. More than just her red locks gave her a fiery demeanor, even though at present she was smiley and bubbly. Tyler could see the hellcat within her. He hoped they wouldn't see her pissed off. Minos either, but not as much as the woman, who Minos introduced as Eris. Something about their names rang bells in his head, but he couldn't nail the names down.

I know I've heard those names before, he thought. He looked back at the newcomers, who were discussing the plan.

"Pleased to meet you all," Eris said through her smile. "We will just lead you guys to our place. Be sure to follow us close, because the turn comes up out of nowhere." Eris's grinned dropped. "Make damn sure you stick close to us, there are a lot of rednecks living out here, and I wouldn't want you to run into some of our neighbors. They are avid firearms aficionados, and I imagine they dream for the day someone trespasses on their property… especially city slickers like youse."

The woman's almost blatant use of the word 'youse' made Zeke chuckle inside. He stifled the laughter quickly. He caught a dirty look from Candy standing by Jen's car. She shook her head once. He just smiled and turned back to Eris, who was looking at him.

"Something funny, guy?" She had an eyebrow raised up at him, waiting for his answer.

"What? N-no, sorry, please continue," he backpedaled. "Sorry."

Eris stared him down a minute longer and turned back to Jenny.

"Okay, Jennifer, right? So, you guys just follow us to our warehouse and we'll give you the grand tour, and after that we can talk distribution terms," Eris said as she turned the smiling charm back on full force. "Sound good, folks?"

"That sounds perfect, Eris. I apologize for my people, we're a little squirrely from being cramped in the cars for a couple hours." Jenny held out her hand to Eris, who looked at it suspiciously. She then seemingly decided to err on the side of trust before and shook the offered hand with a steely grip that nearly made Jenny wince. The strange woman giggled a little as she squeezed hard, then released her vice grip after several seconds. Eris then turned around and got back into the passenger side of the F-150 without a further word.

"Okay, ladies and germs, load up and follow me," Minos announced in his nearly emotionless voice.

Once he was satisfied that his message was heard, he jumped back in the truck, fired it up, and tore out of the parking lot. The vehicle raced down the road, swerving and kicking up rocks and dirt, before slowing down to wait for its accompaniment to catch up.

They drove down the dirt road for about a mile and a half, passing a dying barn built by the side of the road that probably hadn't been used for decades. Finally, the car turned sharply on a muddy road and followed the F-150 for another half mile.

They came out of the woods that the dirt road ran through and into a grassy clearing. They immediately saw a peeling white farmhouse, a large pole barn just behind that, and an incredibly long building that was most likely their growing operation warehouse. A sign that was an exact copy of the business card decorated the double door entrance to the warehouse.

Kind of primitive, but still promising, Joe mused to himself. Jenny's thoughts mirrored his from where she sat in the driver's seat of the Toyota. They followed the little pickup down to the one lane that made up the parking lot for the dark-colored brick of a warehouse. Minos settled his F-150 into a choice spot, and he and Eris waited by the front doors while they all parked and disembarked from their vehicles. Both of them frowned at Candy vaping on her way to the door.

Bite me, she thought, blowing out an extra big cloud right before she turned her device off and put it in her little travelling purse that she only used on road trips. The seven people walked up to the entrance, and Minos and Eris both made a show of opening and holding the double doors for them. The visitors were then motioned inside like they were being allowed into Willy Wonka's chocolate factory as the first outsiders ever to be allowed inside, creepy smiles plastered all over the faces of their hosts.

As they sauntered in, their hosts followed quietly behind them, still grinning. The double doors swung shut unimpeded, slamming shut with a loud bang. For majority of this party of seven, it would be the last time they would see the outside world.

CHAPTER 6: Griffin

Thursday Afternoon

I wake up the next afternoon to the sound of parking automobiles. A little sporty Japanese number and a frickin' Lexus SUV. Seven people get out, ranging from their late thirties to early forties, but all come off at first glance as younger than that. The ladies are all smoking hot, and I catch myself licking my lips. As for the thoughts that come to my mind, I will spare you the details. Whoever the hell you are.

They go from getting their nicotine fixes to talking about movies, Trump, movies, and then something about a guy named Minos.

Minos.

Persephone.

Eris.

I loved Greek mythology as a kid, and conveniently I took a more in-depth class in college. I won't bore you with the details, but you should look them up yourselves and discover that they all have the names of characters from the myths. Oh hell, quick rundown.

Minos was the first king of Crete and a half-human son of Zeus and Europa, a Phoenician woman. He's the horrible king who sent equal amounts of children of both genders to the Minotaur's jaws within the depths of Daedalus's labyrinth every seven years. Nice guy. I bet the current Minos isn't much better.

Eris is the goddess of strife and discord. She is the sister of Ares, the god of war. Not much more needs to be said about that name. Who would give their kids these names? I can't imagine that any *sane* people would.

Persephone, however, is a little different. She was the goddess of vegetation. Vegetation. Let that sink in. My son is a plant nut. If that doesn't both annoy and creep you out at the same time, I'm explaining it wrong. This shit screams of a trap to me, but I am a mean man and I'm distrustful of everything. Persephone, by the way, was also raped, apparently, by Hades, the god of the dead, and taken down to the realm of Hades, the Greek version of Hell named after the god who rules it. Zeus got her out again, but she had to still live with Hades in the Underworld for a third to half the year, depending on the source. Ain't that bitch? Might drive one a little crazy, don't ya think? It's like having to go to prison and get raped by the same guy for half the year, and the rest of the time you are free to be far away from the fucker.

Sorry, I got a little carried away there. I just can't believe some of that crap. Thank whichever god is *really* in charge that the Greeks were off their rockers in the Bronze Age or whichever, I forget. It's been a while. If they were right, life would suck so hard.

I'm not convinced those are the plant people's real names, but I also don't care. I have coordinates, names, and other people I can follow to find the place easier. While they are arguing about when Minos was meeting them, I climb up onto the Lexus as quietly as possible, hoping nobody will notice. I'm just about to check my stealth, sweating heavily in the neoprene and worrying about the odor besides, when a little Ford pickup pulls up behind both of their rides. This provides me with the distraction I need to change my mind and jump in the back of the pickup, instead.

Perfect. Now I don't have to walk. Shit. I look down. I see nothing at my left side. *No sword.* Then I hear her name. Eris. I look up and see the back of her red head on the passenger's side of the truck. The dark-haired driver, who is Minos, introduces her to the people from the Twin Cities. She starts talking to them and I can hear the smile in her voice. And in that moment, when I hear Eris begin to speak, I know my son is dead and she or her brother probably killed him. My rage boils under the surface and I scream at myself inside my head for not making a *neoprene* scabbard for my sword. Gee, ya think that would've helped? Dumbass.

I climb out of the truck and quietly walk back inside to retrieve the object I needed to end the lives of those prime-time serial killer drama wannabes, as I'm sure they did to Charlie and his friends. By the time I snagged it and my bag, they were all tearing out of the lot.

Shit.

I am *walking.*

CHAPTER 7: The Fresh Wave Gang

Thursday, Early Evening

The front entryway of Persephone's Garden was nothing special -- lots of new and used equipment, planted aquarium substrate, lighting, and animal related items like nets, hidey hole decorations, driftwood, medicine, and many different kinds of fish food. Then they walked into the fish room next door.

Four walls of tank stands ran like a library down the center of a huge room, at least seventy feet long. It was hot and humid, and the air was thick to breathe. The walls on the sides were filled with aquariums as well. Freshwater fish originating from all over the world filled the tanks. From the Amazon to Africa to India to Australia to the Great Lakes, a variety of species could be found. The seven guests dropped their jaws at the sheer quantities of fish they saw: brilliant blue neon tetras, bright red cherry barbs, and gorgeous golden yellow and blue Australian Boesemani Rainbows all swam carefree in tanks three times larger than the standard fare they offered for their fish at Fresh Wave.

A whole row of tanks that had to be 300 gallons or more housed arowana species, discus, gar, snakeheads, and even freshwater rays, all active and healthy-looking. One of the side walls was all invertebrates and gastropods. Shrimp, crayfish, and snails aplenty, of all kinds and colors. Joe was slack-jawed and dumbfounded.

"Look at these cherry shrimp! I've never seen any so red before, not even my best," he mumbled, mostly to himself, as he looked in on a forty-gallon breeder-size aquarium full of little tiny red shrimp buzzing about a lush, carpeted tank of *bucephalandra* on a bed of driftwood.

Suction cup ledges lined the back of the tank, and moss tumbled down from each, looking like a mock waterfall of vegetation. The miniature shrimps milled about on this too, all of them grooming the plant life like the caretakers of their little garden world. The rest of the entourage had to tear Joe away with promises to return later.

The next room was the plant growing house. It was humid and hot, like the fish room had been but worse. The whole left side wall was all immersed plant growth and tissue cultures beginning to sprout. Hot lights provided nutrients to the rooted plants growing out of the water. These were becoming more popular because of their snail-free nature. They lacked the possibility of snail stowaways on their plants, unwanted pond snails and others that bred quickly and asexually in some cases.

But then there were the submerged grow tanks that made up the rest of the even larger room. Huge sword plants, gigantic *anubias*, vallisneria that reminded Tyler of the guy with the world record for longest fingernails the way the leaves curled on themselves at the surface. One tank was full of *cryptocoryne* plants that were the biggest they had ever seen. That was when Tyler's brain caught up to him.

Persephone was the goddess of plants! Now I get it. Minos and Eris weren't nearly as nice, though. I can't remember...

"Earth to Tyler!" Jenny's voice brought him back to the tour as she looked at him with pursed lips. "You okay, buddy? Did you hear me? I asked you what size tank you would need to grow this at our store." She pointed at the aquarium in front of her, which was full of colorful plants that were decidedly *not* green. Reds, purples, and greenish blues were present throughout the entirety of the tank, reaching for the lights above the surface with impressive growth.

Tyler was speechless as he looked at the same aquarium. He made sure to note the steady stream of carbon dioxide coming out of the diffuser, which brought a certain question to mind. He turned to look at Eris and Minos.

"How do you run CO2 to all of these tanks?" He looked up above the tank racking after asking, then back to the two tour guides.

Minos spoke first. "We have it piped throughout the warehouse. I have a few friends in the compressed gas industry, and they helped us put in the system. We have four bays of four 100-pound cylinders. One bay is for the entire front fish room's plants, which you might have noticed was a little less planted than what you see back here, eh?"

Minos smiled as he spoke, pointing occasionally to indicate which directions the things he was referring to were. "The other three are for this entire room." He gestured to the expansive section they stood in. "We have a delivery service stop every two weeks to swap out empties."

"How do you know when they are getting empty? I can't imagine you check them individually all the time," Tyler's face scrunched up at his failure to understand. Minos chuckled softly, the man's very mousey demeanor making Jenny's skin crawl. Something was… *off* about him.

"We have them on digital scales, 24/7. They weren't cheap to put in, but so worth it for keeping an eye on the agent left in the cylinders." He turned to Eris. "You would know a bit more of that end of things, Eris."

"I can get you in contact with our CO2 distributor, she responded to Minos's prompt. "They will be able to get you a quote to install the same setup for you. It's worth it. It pays for itself after a few months."

Eris smiled and winked at Tyler as she said the last part. A quacking noise brought her phone out of her pocket. She read the information, a text message it seemed, that popped up on the screen. Her eyes widened a little as she smacked Minos and showed him the text.

"Dammit," he said. "We better go see."

Eris nodded and turned to their guests. "Our sister, *the* Persephone, needs to see us in her workshop. I apologize, but we must leave you to your own devices for a little while. There is a bevy of vending machines by the office in our front retail area. You may feel free to check out the fish and plants, and you will notice the coordinates system we have on our racking system. There are item lists you can fill out at the end of each aisle. We can fill this order for you before you leave, after we talk distribution contracts. Please do not leave this building for the time being. My brother and I will return shortly."

Eris flashed another beautiful but extremely cheesy smile at them before she and Minos left them. The duo departed quickly, as if there was an emergency they weren't telling them about.

Once the two hosts were gone, Zeke commented. "That was kinda weird. I wonder what's going on?"

"I don't know but these people give me the creeps," Candy said, pulling out her vape pen.

"Candy, don't you fucking dare," Jenny warned her friend.

Candy's lips disappeared into a straight line of unhappiness "Fine. I'm going to look at the fish again," she said, tucking her e-cig back into her tiny purse.

Then she walked out into the front room again, Josh following her.

Zeke laughed when they left. "He's got it so bad for her."

"Well, they can have each other," Jenny grumbled. "Between his mouth and her douche flute addiction, I'm looking forward to this trip being over. I hope our hosts finish whatever business took them away, because we need to get something figured out, so we don't have to find a place to stay up here tonight. There isn't exactly a lot of hotels around here, and I've never been one for staying in motels."

"True dat," Tyler said quietly from where he stood staring at the greenless planted tank. "I would definitely need a better CO_2 setup at the store for something like this, Jenny."

He looked at her, and she shot a questioning look back, before realization dawned on her face. He was still answering her earlier question.

"Yeah, I kinda figured we would," Jenny replied. "Draw up some plans when we get back. I will get their supplier's info and we can get service set up through them."

Jenny wandered over to a shelf full of old filters, mostly the hang-on-the-back variety. A lot of them looked really old, dust covering more than a few. She saw one that looked familiar and pulled it out of the pile. The one she picked was apparently holding back a flood, and the whole shelf full of HOB filters fell on the floor. The face she made at her *faux pas* was almost humorous, and Zeke secretly laughed at her behind her back, while Joe and Meghan were getting their own snickers in.

Jenny heard the giggles. "Shut up, you assholes!"

She was laughing, but so red-faced it was obvious she was incredibly embarrassed. Jenny blushing was a rare thing, and this was sometimes a precursor to her wrath if you teased her too much. This time, however, she seemed to be maintaining her embarrassment. She picked up the filters one by one, inspecting them for damage, as well as wiping some of the dirt still on them off on her jeans. When she got down to the one that had caused them all to fall, she looked it over again.

"This was the first filter I ever bought for a planted tank," she said, turning the curvy HOB filter around in her hands, studying the object as if seeing something like it for the first time. "This is an old Proquatics. They were great filters, and I never did find out why they quit making them. The flow was awesome for a HOB, and you could put your own filter media in it no problem, not like those cartridge slot pieces of crap from you know who."

"We don't speak of their filters, remember, Jen?" Joe pointed his finger up in the air for some reason as he said this.

"Yeah, that's my rule, remember? I just haven't seen one of these since I had to throw mine away years ago," Jenny replied.

Then she tried unsuccessfully to put it back on the shelf, attempting to fit it in like a puzzle piece atop the haphazardly stacked equipment. The filter kept falling out wherever she tried to stuff it back in, and this made her frustrated. Jenny swore under her breath and shoved it in on top of a filter made by the very company they didn't speak of. This act of shoving rocked the entire shelf.

"Whoa, easy, Jen! You're going to knock the whole shelf –"

There was a loud click, and then the shelf opened up towards them, its secret job as a hidden door no longer secret. Meghan gasped as she and Joe walked over to the now revealed open passageway leading to stairs. Rotten air hit them in the face, and Jenny began gagging.

Jenny covered her mouth before uttering a muffled but still discernible question. "Oh my god, what *died* down there?"

"Holy shit, I don't know if we should find out!" Zeke replied. "I don't think we should be here anymore." He looked scared as he said all this. "Don't you dare go down there, Jen."

But Jen didn't listen, and the oldest of the ensemble proceeded into the passageway with her ears open. She put a finger up to her lips to stifle Zeke from whining due to his fear. Then she heard it, very faint but very much there.

"*help…me…*"

"There's someone down there!" Jenny kept her exclamation at an incredibly loud whisper, pointing down the stairs in front of her.

Tyler's mind had identified the odor of blood as soon as the door opened, and he shook his head vehemently. "Nononononono! That is congealing blood we smell. We need to get the hell out of here, right now," he decreed.

"I'm not leaving someone down there if this is some kind of fucked up, serial killer kidnapping shit," Jenny rejoined. "Someone come with me, *now.*" She said that while trying her best to order her employee-slash friends into a potentially dangerous situation. Zeke's bowels shifted uncomfortably when she leveled her dark brown eyes at him. They quickly softened into bedroom eyes, and he knew he was screwed. "Zeeekkkeee. C'mon, sweetie, I know you don't want to abandon some poor soul down there! *Please?*"

The honey in her voice was dripping, and Joe rolled his eyes at her obvious taking advantage of the guy. It was no secret among any of them that he was hopelessly in love with her. And she used it to her advantage whenever it served her best. It was the one thing about his boss and friend that he absolutely loathed.

Unsurprising to no one, the lovestruck man followed her like the loyal crushing fool they all knew he was. The look on his face said it wasn't a surprise to him how bad he was stuck on Jen. She smiled and put her hand on his shoulder, mouthing 'thank you' up to him. Joe's annoyance bubbled up to the surface, and he was able to displace the reason for it.

"Jen, you shouldn't go down there; let's get out of here," Joe pleaded. "Before they come back and see what you've done."

"Fuck that, Joe! I'm with Jen," Meghan said as she entered the landing to the secret stairwell and stood by her intrepid friend. "What if there is someone down there who needs help? We might be the only chance they get for freedom! Where's your balls?"

She gave him the look that he knew meant no sex for a while if he didn't get his ass in the stairwell next to her in the next five seconds. Profanity exploded silently in his head, and he walked over to his mate.

"Fine, but if we get killed, I'm going to be really mad at you two," he stipulated.

The small group started down the stairs as soon as Joe crossed the threshold of the mystery stairwell. Tyler stood there for a moment, unsure of what to do. Finally, instead of joining the others in their trek down into the dark unknown, he walked back out to the fish room to tell Josh and Candy what happened.

CHAPTER 8: Griffin

Thursday, Dusk

I hate walking. Always have. Running is slightly better, you get there faster, but I don't like doing that for very long either. I have an elliptical in my lab that I use periodically during my work, to break up the extended hours of sitting at microscopes and computers, but I'm not going to sit here and tell you I run five miles a day. Five miles a week if I'm feeling ambitious. Not usually though, and I must be the laziest invisible man ever when it comes to regular exercise.

Hopefully, I will make up for that in the next few hours with viciousness. I'm going to gut those people like fish for what I am certain they did to my kid. Charlie's dumb grin fills my imagination, and my eyes tear up. I'm going to make them suffer more for making me cry.

I finally reach the property, the sign on the giant warehouse tucked into the woods verifying this for me. For some odd reason, the song "Come as You Are" by Nirvana suddenly pops up in my head. That early 90s grunge song is an old favorite of mine, despite being horrendously overplayed on the radio.

The earworm this time helps me to take stock of the situation. One farmhouse, a pole barn, and the huge building with the Persephone's Garden sign on the front. I see the S.O.L.'s vehicles parked in front next to the F-150. Yeah, I called them S.O.L.s. You don't think they're shit out of luck? Well, you're a helluva lot more optimistic than me if you do. I think they're all screwed like my kid probably is. My blood runs hotter as I approach the warehouse, taking cover as I do to hide the katana that must appear to be floating in the air.

I'm glad I do, because just as I duck behind a stack of plastic pallets stored up outside the main doors to the warehouse, Eris and Minos come out, walking like they have a purpose. Minos is bitching about something I can't hear because he talks like he has cotton in his mouth, muffling everything. They pass me without revealing anything useful. I slip in through the doors just before they close, one of them clipping me a little as I slide between them.

Inside are the vaper girl and the nerdy guy who drives the
Lexus. They don't see me and my sword as I quickly duck behind
a shelf full of aquarium decorations. Suddenly one of the other
guys comes out of the next room, looking upset.

"You guys, Jen opened some door to a stairwell," the guy says.
"There was some switch in the wall she must have activated on
accident." Judging by the looks on their faces, his friends aren't
buying what he's selling. He persists upon seeing their reactions.
"I'm serious! It smells like death down those stairs, and someone
down there was begging for help!"

"Tyler, don't fuck with us, man! This place already gives me
the creeps. You serious?" The Lexus driver looks about one joke
away from laying out the skinnier guy, Tyler.

The girl pipes up.

"What? Is she fucking crazy?" Vaper girl takes her device out
and hits it a few times. Neither of her friends protest. "We need to
get out of here. This place is giving me bad vibes, and I don't
believe in vibes."

The doors open like something crashed into them and I look
towards the entrance. Minos, Eris, and the big hulking bitch I saw
lurking like Leatherface in the back of Charlie's cell phone picture
enter. The giant woman has to be damn near seven feet tall, I'm
guessing about six foot, eight inches or so. Her wide shoulders
have to be close to three feet across from side to side. Long, dirty
blonde hair frames a mannish face that would be 'handsome' in the
womanly way, were it not for the slashing scars covering her face,
and her ripped, exposed arms.

Hot damn, this bitch has some muscles. This is going to be
harder than I thought. Especially with the giant cleaver she holds,
an ancient-looking weapon with a curved handle to assist with
swinging. It is still red from the last time it was used. And it looks
wet.

These people are up shit's creek without a paddle. I was going
to help them if I could, but it looks like they're almost dead
already, and I'm not giving myself away until I'm ready to strike.
Not for people I don't know from this horseshit state. I'll never
understand why Charlie and the lousy excuse of a woman that his
mother was liked this damn state so much.

I look towards the doors to the next room for a split second, but it's too long. I see it happen out of the corner of my eye but hear it first: the sound of a large blade hitting meat. The vaper girl screams. I look back to see the giant cleaver buried in the skinny guy's face, his arms flailing uselessly as he drops to the floor. Vape girl runs towards the back rooms, leaving the Lexus driver behind. He pleads with the psychos standing in front of him.

"No! No, wait, please –"

Minos pulls an old looking revolver from his windbreaker and levels it at the guy's head. The barrel flashes as he pulls the trigger, and a bloody hole tears into the nerd's forehead before the back of his skull explodes out behind him in a shower of blood, brain, and bone. His body drops unceremoniously to the floor, where he twitches next to the skinny guy's bisected form for a moment, then lies still.

Crap. I hate guns. I've been shot before, while invisible. It's kind of a downer, obviously because it fucking hurts, but also because it ruins the camouflage. My blood is *very* visible. The science of it baffles me, and I cannot figure out how to make *it* invisible, too. So, I try to stay far out of gunshot range when someone thinks they're going to shoot the invisible guy. But as the three whack jobs run after the vaper girl, I leave my position by the decorations and follow them into the next room before the door finishes closing.

We pass through a room dedicated to fish and other aquatic critters, but I waste no time leering as I stay right behind my quarry, the katana in my hand, the scabbard abandoned in the front room. I move as silently as possible, praying neither of them looks back and sees the magical sword flying through the air. My pulse is racing as I enter the next room.

I'm momentarily distracted as I take in the sheer amounts of aquariums full of plants in this part of the building. Persephone stalks down the side aisle towards an open doorway, Eris and Minos not far behind. Eris seems to have obtained a hunting knife from somewhere between the retail space and where we are now.

I hear screams emanate from somewhere that sounds either closed off, or on a different level -- I'm guessing from the open doorway framed by what looks like a false wall. The monster woman and her sister run down the stairs, Minos right behind them. Just after the women are out of sight, I whisper a word just quiet enough to qualify as a whisper.

"*Motherfucker.*"

Minos stops in his tracks, and spins around, looking everywhere for me. I'm standing right by him, the sword tucked behind the end of the racking I'm standing near. He trains his revolver all over the place, not saying a word. Listening for me. Not as stupid as I thought, but it doesn't matter.

I run at him on my toes, reducing the noise I make and propelling me faster to his location. His eyes register the sword seconds before I lop his head off like we're playing *Highlander.* Blood squirts everywhere and his head bounces three times before laying still in the secret entryway's landing. It comes to a stop with his surprised eyes seeming to look right at me, as they quickly glaze over with death.

I move slowly down the stairs, picking up Minos's head before I do. It's hard to hold because of the blood and his short hair, so I give up and jam my left index and middle fingers, along with my thumb, into the gory end of the head, holding it like a bowling ball. It's gross, but it's the best way to grab the severed cranium for what I'm going to do.

I reach the bottom of the cement stairs and can't believe what I'm seeing.

The basement level is a chamber of horrors. First thing I see is a gigantic tank, set partially into the cement floor. Five-foot-high walls of thick glass, or maybe acrylic, are lining the oval-shaped enclosure, with about a twenty-foot diameter at its longest point. There is a rock island in the middle of the water-filled pen, and the biggest turtle I've ever seen is munching on a fucking *arm* in the middle of it. This thing has to have a shell that is at least three feet across and five feet long, with lots of pointed scutes and jagged edges.

I recognize the species from watching Animal Planet back in the day when it was about animals instead of people who are 'animals.' I always thought it was deplorable how they turned an educational station into more redneck reality show garbage. This was what started us down the dumber path humanity has decided to take lately. Reality TV. MySpace, then Facebook, then Smart

Phones and everything else only added some pretty flammable fuel to the fire. But that's just my opinion.

While I was busy musing on the alligator snapping turtle and the horrible transformation the good cable channels have taken since the turn of the century, I missed the guy named Joe getting jumped by Eris, who was raking his face with her not-so-fake-looking fingernails while screaming like a wild animal. His girlfriend, I'm guessing, runs up to help him, but Persephone is faster, grabbing the woman by her head and throwing her to the floor, where she buries what looks like the biggest pair of tweezers I've ever seen into the poor woman's eyes. She screams for a second, then the monster bitch rips the tweezers out in a spray of eye and head fluids and the instantly dead girl drops like a bloody sack of potatoes.

Joe screams her name, "Meg-ahhhhhn!" He doesn't grieve long though, because Eris shreds his eyes as well, and his screams increase in pitch for a minute more, then cease. I see her pulling her nails out of his eyes like she's dipping a brush into red paint and wiping the excess off on his cheeks. Then she claws his face some more, all the while making this low angry growl, like a cat who is getting ready to attack.

That's when I notice the Toyota driver and the guy who obviously thinks her farts smell like Roses backing away from their aggressors, unknowingly approaching what looks like a mortician's badly kept embalming station, complete with a body fluid drain underneath. A dead guy lays chopped up under the slab, and the dismembered body of a woman lies limbless atop the table with blood surrounding her. Her face has a freshly dead look, and I'm guessing that's who these S.O.L.s heard begging for help.

Next to that are more giant fucking aquariums, and these ones are full of all sorts of huge, mean-looking fish. I recognize a couple; snakeheads; arowana; arapaima – *River Monsters* fare. Geez, Animal Planet again. This is getting annoying to narrate for you. Pretty soon I'll be spitting out 80s pop culture references and quoting Jeremy Robinson books.

Then, I see him. My son. And my heart breaks as my mind snaps.

His head is being gorged on by a tank full of snake-like things. They latch onto his face and twist their bodies until they come away with some meat, leaving a circular hole in his face each time.

Fucking lampreys are eating my dead son's severed head. These fucks cut his head off and fed it to those horrid fish with a meat grinder for a face.

Without trying, a painful wail escapes my lips, rising in volume and intensity, as I run at Eris, the katana held behind me, ready to swing. Everyone looks around suddenly, unsure of where the god-awful sound as a result of me crying over my son's desecrated head in a fish tank full of lampreys is coming from. Persephone seems to figure it out, and I know the sword has been spotted. She forgets about the last two people, who intelligently run for their lives the second her back is turned and high tail it the fuck out of that horrid basement.

The big bitch growls, watching them run but too late to stop them. She then turns back just in time to watch me whip the sword around from behind my back and embed it into her sister Eris's face, slicing in between her screaming mouth as she still claws at Joe's dead face. The sword sticks and my swing stops. Eris's eyes look at the weapon that is cleaving her face at the mouth, tracing up to the hilt and somehow realizing what is happening.

I swear she looked right into my eyes at that very moment, her hatred for me burning within until the very last second when I ripped the sword out of her face. This motion snaps the little bit of the top half of her head that was still attached to the bottom. I laugh as it tumbles away and stops by someone's lower body that was severed at the waist. I recognize the shoes.

"Eris! No!" Persephone screamed. "Goddamn you, whoever you are! I can smell your rotten man-stink!"

Persephone's emotions are running high at this point, having watched an invisible foe cut Eris's melon in half while she watched, and I get it. But I'm a little bit more upset. Especially since she just called me out on my B.O., which has gone unchecked since I put the damn wet suit on. Didn't think that one through, did I? At least I think I'm more upset until she plucks the one fire extinguisher off the wall and sprays me with the purple powder inside.

And just like that, Persephone can see me.

Before it fully registers in my head what just happened, her meaty paws are around my throat, choking the life out of me. Stars twinkle in my vision as I stare into the eyes of a human monster hellbent on avenging the siblings I killed, one right in front of her. I gasp for air, her grip constricting my neck like an anaconda does a capybara.

This is where my story ends, true believers. No, I'm not sure how I'm telling you all of this if I'm dead, but it is what it is. I bet you thought there was going to be some big *Freddy vs. Jason* deathmatch, huh? Yeah, so did I. The real world isn't that climactic, I guess.

I feel the strength leave me, the sword clattering uselessly to the ground. I take one more look at my dead son's head, the son whose mother I just got back from cutting into pieces along with her newest beau, and then went chumming on the ocean to get rid of. I told you, I'm an asshole, but I still loved my son, and my last regret that I try to acknowledge before I lose consciousness is that I wished that I could have saved him. The irony of the last thought from a hell bound soul like mine being one so unselfish and loving certainly doesn't go unnoticed by my oxygen-starved mind.

Then I hear Persephone giggle like a little girl with her deep, throaty guffaw, a disorientating sound that makes the encroaching darkness more surreal. Then she says one more thing. But not to me. Before I slip from consciousness and this reality -- an invisible man, choked to death by a backwoods freak -- the last thing I hear just confuses me more.

"For you, Hades, my love. For you."

END

CYCLOPS VS. DRAGON: JASON'S LAMENT

The sun was slowly rising over the sea, as Jason held Medea in his arms. He could hear their newborn son stirring at the foot of their bed. It had been nearly a year since the hero had sailed with the Argonauts to Colchis and retrieved the Golden Fleece. Jason had faced numerous monsters, undead warriors, and threats from the very earth itself, but he had succeeded in his quest. The hero had brought the fleece and Medea back to Thessaly with him. Jason then regained the kingdom, which was rightfully his, married Medea, and fathered a son.

In addition to this prosperity, Thessaly had enjoyed the protection of the Golden Fleece. As the fleece was a gift from the gods, there were few creatures who could challenge its power. Foreign armies, monsters, even natural disasters were all warded away from Thessaly by the power of the fleece.

Jason rolled over to kiss Medea, when something caused a tremor to shake his palace. The King stood and walked over to his window. In the distance, he could see a colossal figure with a club in its hand walking towards the city. The creature was so tall that it was blocking out the sun.

Not since his encounter with Talos had the warrior king seen a being of such massive proportions. At first Jason thought the creature to be a giant, who would sense the power bestowed upon the fleece by the gods and then turn and leave. As the sun slowly came up behind the beast, Jason gasped. With the giant figure no longer obscured by the sun's light, the king could now see the creature's face. Instead of the human-like visage of a giant, Jason saw a single bulging eye in the center of the beast's face with a sharp horn protruding out of the flesh just above it. The king was also able to see that the monster had a lower body similar to that of a goat, with fur covered legs and cloven feet.

Without hesitation Jason ran to his bed and woke his wife. "Medea, quickly take our son and leave the city! There is a great danger approaching!"

Medea smiled at her husband. "Jason, we are protected by the power of the fleece. Nothing short of a god could defy its power."

Jason pointed to the window at the towering cyclops heading toward the city. "The cyclops are older than the gods; older than the titans. They were among the first children of Uranus who locked them away in Tartarus for their hideousness. Zeus freed the cyclopes, during his war with the Titans so that they could help him overcome Chronos's forces. In addition to their freedom, Zeus agreed to not interfere with the actions of the cyclopes so long as they did not threaten his rule." Jason looked again to the window to see that the cyclops had entered the city. "The fleece will afford us no protection from this creature. Zeus cannot deny the cyclops the ability to feed!" He pointed at the monster as it reached down and grabbed a handful of the citizens of Thessaly.

Medea screamed in horror as the beast stuffed the terrified people into its mouth. Her scream woke her son, who began to cry.

Jason pulled his wife out of bed. "We will have to defeat this creature on our own. Now take our son and go! Ride to the southern wilderness and hide there. I will come for you when this beast has been dealt with."

Medea grabbed her son and glanced out the window to see the cyclops devouring another handful of people. "Jason, how will you defeat such a creature?".

"With cunning, and with the knowledge that the enemy of my enemy is my friend," Jason replied as he donned his armor.

He then grabbed his sword and shield, kissed his wife and son, and ran out of his bedroom.

As the warrior king was sprinting through his castle, he came across the captain of his royal guard. When Jason saw the captain he yelled, "Gather as many of the palace guards as you can! Attack the monster from the eastern side of the city. We need to draw his attention to the guards and away from the people! When your forces engage the cyclops, stay as far away from him as you can by attacking him with spears and arrows!"

The guard ran after his king. "My liege, what of you and your family? How shall we protect you?"

Jason turned toward the royal stables and exclaimed, "My wife and son are already fleeing the castle. As you are distracting the cyclops, I shall acquire the means necessary to defeat it."

Before the guard could ask what those items were, the warrior king mounted his horse and rode it out into the city.

As Jason's horse bolted out of the stable, he could see the cyclops devouring another mouthful of his people. The kind-hearted king felt the death of each and every one of his people whom he saw killed by the cyclops. He looked briefly to the west, at the mountains in the distance. The only possible means to defeat the cyclops resided in those mountains. In order to access those means, Jason would have to attack the cyclops, ride up to the mountain, and commit an act for which he would never forgive himself. As he was attempting all of these tasks, he would have to hope that enough of his people would survive the attack to make his actions worthwhile.

The hero turned his head back to the rampaging cyclops. He could see his royal guard taking up a position in front of the beast. The captain of the guard raised his arm into the air, and as he did so dozens of archers aimed their arrows at the monster. Jason drew his sword from its scabbard. He had almost reached the giant monster when the captain dropped his arm, thus signaling the archers to fire.

Dozens of arrows embedded themselves in the cyclops's chest, causing the creature to roar in pain. The monster looked down at the arrows sticking out of his torso and with one swipe of his massive hand, he brushed the weapons away. The monster took a step toward the massed archers, and it was at that moment that Jason charged toward the creature.

The great warrior king wanted to scream as he rode toward the giant in order to empower himself, but he knew that in this instance he needed stealth more than power. He quickly looked at his guards to see the captain moving his men backward several city blocks away from the approaching monster before ordering them to stop. When Jason saw the captain raising his hand to order the arches to fire again, he dug his heels into his horse's ribs to urge the animal into galloping even faster. The king knew that for his plan to be successful he would need to strike the monster at the exact moment the archers unleashed their second volley. The king had nearly reached the cyclops when the archers commenced the assault.

Once more the arrows struck the cyclops in the arms and chest, causing the beast to roar in pain and take a half step backward. At the exact moment that the giant's back foot touched the ground, Jason reached the enormous heel and plunged his sword into the giant's foot while holding onto the hilt as tightly as he could. The blade was so deep in the monster's foot that by holding onto the weapon Jason was pulled off his steed. The king was hanging several feet off the ground as he watched his horse riding away.

Jason saw the cyclops's lone eye glaring down at the source of the pain, followed by the monster's hand coming toward him. The king knew that he needed to act fast if he hoped to survive this encounter. The hero twisted his sword, causing blood to spurt out of the cyclops's foot and cover his body. He then pulled his sword out of the cyclops's foot and fell to the ground as the giant's outstretched fingers brushed over his head.

The blood-soaked Jason then sprinted away from the now enraged giant beast. The warrior king was whistling for his well-trained horse when a shadow suddenly fell over him. The hero didn't even bother to look up; he knew what the shadow meant. He responded by quickly shifting direction to his right and pushing his legs to the limit. A second later Jason was knocked to the ground by the force of the cyclops's foot crashing down behind him. Before he even attempted to stand up, the hero king rolled back toward the giant and slashed open another wound on the cyclops's foot. As blood gushed out of the of the wound, he moved his body beneath it and let the crimson liquid splash onto his body.

Jason saw the monster's foot rise into the air in preparation to try and crush him once again. The warrior then heard a galloping sound coming toward him and he tilted his head back to see his horse sprinting toward him. The hero knew he didn't have time to stand up. As the steed came near him, Jason reached up and grabbed the bottom of the horse's saddle. The blood-soaked warrior king was dragged away just in time as the cyclops's cloven foot again came crashing down into the earth.

Jason pulled himself onto his horse's back as his royal guard fired another annoying, but ultimately ineffectual, volley of arrows at the cyclops. While the attack didn't hurt the monster, it did draw the beast's attention back to the guards. The giant roared and ran toward the gathered soldiers. Jason saw the cyclops's foot come crashing down onto the front row of archers and his captain of the guard. The rest of the soldiers were bravely holding their positions as they fired arrows and hurled spears at the rampaging behemoth. Jason made a silent promise to honor the bravery of his guards by providing for their families after this crisis had passed.

The hero then turned his thoughts to his people who were hiding in their homes. Jason was determined to make the sacrifice his guards had made worthwhile by saving as many of the citizens of Thessaly as he could. The king urged his horse to run through the city while he shouted, "People of Thessaly, this is your king! Neither the Golden Fleece nor your homes can offer any protection from the cyclops! Flee into the forest! I will come for you when it is safe! I know it is difficult to flee your homes, but they can be rebuilt, whereas you cannot!"

When they heard the commands of their beloved king, the people of Thessaly took to the streets. A mass of men, women, and children ran out of their houses and took off for the forest which bordered the southern edge of the city. At the sight of his people escaping, the blood-covered warrior king rode back toward the cyclops. He watched in horror as the colossus ignored the never-ending wave of arrows assaulting him, reached down, grabbed several more guards, and stuffed them screaming into his mouth. The shrieking Jason heard was soon drowned out by the grizzly sound of bone being crushed in the cyclops's slavering maw.

The king yelled at his soldiers, "You men have done all that can be asked of you! Flee for your lives into the forest! Find your queen and the infant prince! Protect them and I will come for you when the time is right!"

Jason then turned his horse north and directed the animal to run to the mountains in the distance. Without the protection of the gods or the Golden Fleece, there was only one force capable of defeating the cyclops and Jason was determined to lure the creature into battle with the one-eyed horror. The king decided that it would take him nearly an hour to reach the cave near the top of the mountain. Behind him, the hero heard another building being crushed by the rampaging cyclops. The Argonaut closed his eyes and uttered a brief prayer to Hera that there would still be something left of his kingdom when he reached the cave.

Jason took a deep breath as he crept to the edge of the vast cavern. He could smell the rancid odor from the material the beast consumed wafting out of the cave entrance. The hero shook his head as he neared the cave. He took no pride in what he must do. On his quest for the Golden Fleece, he knew that taking the glittering pelt from the people of Colchis would be detrimental to their land; but for the good of Thessaly, he took the treasured item anyway.

As Jason stood in front of the massive cave, he considered the great pain he was about to inflict upon another innocent. The dragon that lived within the dank grotto had never posed a threat to him or his people. Now in order to save his kingdom, the King of Thessaly was about to commit an unspeakable act of horror on the reptilian creature. Jason reminded himself that he served many roles -- including king, husband, and father. All three of those roles meant that there were other people he had to put above himself. If he needed to feel personal shame and remorse for the actions, he was about to take to protect his people, wife, and son, he was ready to accept those consequences.

Jason looked to the river that ran alongside the cave and then down the mountain to the city. He felt fortunate that the great beast had chosen a cave that was so close to the river. The greatest of the Argonauts estimated that he could reach the water in ten seconds from the cavern's entrance. The same river that quenched the dragon's thirst also served as the city's water supply. Today it would not only serve as a water supply to Thessaly, but also as a highway for what Jason hoped was the city's savior.

If Jason had any hope of saving the city and his own life, he would have to hope that ten seconds would be enough time. The king took a deep breath and drew his sword. As he entered the cave, Jason recalled the history of the dragon.

It had been three years since the dragon had first appeared in the mountains outside of Thessaly. When the beast had first been seen outside of the city, the people of Thessaly were terrified of the beast. They demanded that the creature be slain before it started attacking the city and eating people. Jason reminded his followers that the Golden Fleece protected them from such threats and that they had nothing to fear from the dragon.

To further calm the fears of his people, Jason took one third of the palace's cattle and had them moved to a ranch near the mountain. The cattle were placed there as easy prey for the dragon. To the surprise of the people of the city, the dragon did not feed on the livestock. Rather it seemed to prefer to feed on the foul-smelling substance which emanated from the depths of the Earth. The fact that the beast did not eat flesh appeased most of the citizens of Thessaly, and at the behest of their king the people agreed to let the monster live in peace.

The dragon's exact origins were unknown. The only suggestion offered about the monster's genesis came from the priestess of Venus, goddess of love. Days after the dragon had appeared, the priestess came to Jason and told him that she had a dream in which the goddess told her that she had brought the creature to Earth from the sphere that bore her name. It seemed that Golden Fleece had been guarded by the Hydra for so long that it felt as if it needed a dragon nearby for protection. In order to ensure that the Fleece's needs were met, Venus took the dragon from across the stars and placed it in a stream on top of the mountain. Since the goddess of love herself had delivered the dragon to Earth, it was decided that the reptilian beast would be known as the Venusian.

Jason's thoughts returned to the present when he saw what looked like two oblong fluid-filled sacs laying on the floor of the cave. Despite their odd shape, the hero knew exactly what the objects were. Roughly a week ago, a horrible wailing was coming from the Venusian's cave. Jason, a few of his guards, and the priestess of Venus rode up to the cavern to determine why the dragon was wailing and what it meant for the people of Thessaly. When the party reached the cave, the warrior king peered into the cave entrance to see the Venusian standing over the two fluid-filled sacs. The monster was gazing down at them with the same love that he looked upon his son with. The wise king immediately understood that the sacs were eggs of some sort, and the wailing was the sound of the Venusian giving birth.

As Jason stood above the eggs he prayed for the gods and goddesses of Olympus to forgive him for his actions. The king of Thessaly knelt down and rubbed the blood of the cyclops on the eggs. He then drew his sword and sliced the sacs in half. With each egg that he cut open, a smaller version of the Venusian slid out and screamed for a brief moment before it expired. When the wailing of the dying infants echoed through the cave a deep guttural roar exploded from the depths of the cavern. When the warrior heard the roar, he ran to the cave entrance and then sprinted for the river.

As Jason reached the portal, he could feel the ground shaking beneath his feet. When he heard a roar behind him far louder than the first, the king lowered his head and ran even faster toward the river. Upon reaching the edge of the river he dove into the water head-first. Jason then stripped off his clothes and allowed the current to drag them back towards the city. While underwater, the hero quickly used his hand to scrub every particle of cyclops blood off his body.

Jason swam to the surface of the river where he heard another roar of anger, followed by a brief silence from the cave. The quietude lasted nearly a minute before an anguish-filled wail echoed over the mountain. In that time, Jason swam to the far side of the river and did his best to cover himself in mud.

As that wail faded into the distance, a roar exploded out of the cave. It was so rich in hatred and anger the warrior could feel it in his bones. Jason rolled over in the mud and looked back toward the cavern's entryway. A second later, the Venusian burst out of the cave.

The monster was huge. It was nearly as large as the cyclops itself. The dragon's appearance was horrifying to behold. It was green with knobby bumps covering its body. The reptilian monstrosity was bipedal with a human-like torso, arms, and legs that ended in powerful claws. The creature's head was shaped like that of an ape with the exception of a scaly whisker-like appendage above its mouth, and a fin that ran down the middle of its head. The dragon's tail was thick and nearly as long as its body. At its tip, the tail forked off into two smaller appendages.

Jason watched as the Venusian sniffed the air. The dragon roared as its head snapped in the direction of Thessaly. The monster then turned and ran towards the river. The beast was able to determine that the odor of the creature who had destroyed its eggs was coming from the nearby city, and the Venusian was determined to tear the giant apart for what it had done.

Jason did his best to stay perfectly still as the dragon dove into the water. As soon as the beast entered the river it swam towards the city with a speed unmatched by even Mercury himself. As he watched the Venusian swim toward the city and the cyclops Jason felt a great swell of pity for the creature. He had slain the dragon's family in order to save his own. As the king pulled his body out of the mud he wondered if he was just as monstrous as the cyclops that was feeding on his people.

Jason pushed the thought aside and swam out to center of the river. There he let the current carry him towards the quickly moving dragon. The king's actions had been successful in sending the Venusian into battle with the cyclops. His plan had given his kingdom and his people a chance at surviving the cyclops's attack, and Jason was determined to see his plan through to the end.

As the dragon swam toward the city, rage coursed through its body. When the reptilian reached the section of the river that bordered the city, it exploded out of the water and roared at the rampaging cyclops.

The Venusian's resounding cry caused the cyclops to turn around and see what had challenged him. The cloven-hooved brute took a step back when it beheld the dragon. The cyclops had walked the Earth for vast millennia and had seen all manner of titan, god, monster, animal, and even dragon but he had never beheld a creature such as the entity that now stood before him. The dragons which the cyclops had come across in the past had the same hunger for human flesh that he did. The one-eyed giant had slain those dragons in order to protect his food and he was determined to do the same to this creature. The cyclops snorted at the strange dragon before he lowered his horned head and charged.

The swift moving current carried Jason to the shores of his city just in time to see the cyclops plunge his horn into the shoulder of the Venusian. The dragon roared in pain as the cyclops pushed his horn deeper into the reptilian creature's shoulder. The Venusian was forced back several steps before it wrapped its claw around the cyclops head, pulled the horn from its shoulder, and then tossed the ancient creature to the ground.

Jason climbed out of the water as the dragon stepped over the cyclops and began to deliver a series of punches to its face. The king noticed that the wound on the Venusian's shoulder was not bleeding. Jason thought to himself that the dragon's internal system must be far different from any creature which had been born on Earth.

The Venusian was raining blow after blow on the cyclops, until the one-eyed horror placed its cloven foot on the dragon's chest and pushed it backward, thus causing the Venusian to stumble and fall to the ground. The cyclops then stood up and began walking toward the downed monster. The one-eyed giant had almost reached the dragon when the Venusian sprang to its feet and wrapped its arms around the cyclops.

The two beasts grappled with each other for several seconds before the smaller but stronger dragon threw the cyclops to the ground. The Venusian bent down to start pummeling the cyclops when the giant rolled over onto its hands and knees and charged the dragon. The cyclops drove his horn through the Venusian's leg. The reptilian creature wailed in pain, but once more no blood or any other fluid escaped from the wound. When Jason saw the dragon rake his claw across the cyclops's back and draw blood, he knew that there was no doubt as to which of the two beasts was going to win this encounter.

After using its claws to create several more deep gashes across the cyclops's back, the dragon punched the one-eyed horror in the back of the neck. The blow forced the cyclops's horn free from the Venusian's leg. The cyclops stood up as the dragon limped back a few steps from the giant. The cyclops roared and rushed at the dragon, slamming into its chest and knocking it to the ground. Jason watched as the two monsters rolled across his city crushing homes, streets, and carts as they clawed and bit at each other. With each movement the two creatures made, Jason could see more red blood covering both them and the battleground. The hero knew that with each drop of precious blood, the cyclops was growing weaker. The battling monsters rolled around for several more minutes, and with each passing second the dragon continued to gain the upper hand.

Finally, the dragon forced the cyclops onto its back and the reptilian monster latched its jaws around the cyclops's throat. The monstrous giant stuck the Venusian over and over again, but he was unable to force the dragon to release his hold. The cyclops uttered one last blood-filled gurgle before it expired. With its enemy defeated, the Venusian stood up. The dragon did not unleash a roar of victory, however. Instead, the sad and heartbroken monster turned and silently returned to the river.

As Jason watched the Venusian slide back into the water, he uttered one final prayer. "Venus, I know that what I have done today was an unforgivable affront to the Venusian. Please understand that what I did, I did out of love. I slew the dragon's offspring so that my family and my people might live. Faced with the same situation again, I would make the same decision without hesitation. Still, if there is anything you can do to bring some solace to the creature I would be forever in your debt, much as I am in the debt of the dragon that bears your name." Jason then turned and started walking towards the wilderness to retrieve his family and his people so that they might begin repairing the damage done to the city.

When the Venusian returned to its cave, it found the goddess Venus holding the remains of its offspring in her hands. The goddess turned toward the dragon and said, "When I speak you shall be granted the ability to understand the meaning of my words."

The Venusian said nothing but simply gazed at the goddess. Venus then began to mold the two slain infants into a single being. The new creature created from the combined material of the deceased offspring had the overall appearance of the Venusian, with some notable changes. The new creature now had four arms instead of two and its two-pronged reptilian tail had been fused into a thick fluke, like that of a whale. The goddess breathed on the newly formed creature and it began to stir.

She then turned to the Venusian. "You have done a great service to a king who is highly thought of by the gods of Olympus, and as such great Poseidon has decreed that a service shall be done in return for you. Your offspring will not only survive but now that they are fused together it shall grow to be the largest and most powerful creature on the planet. Since it was a human who slew your children it shall now be a slayer of humans should they displease us. I shall take your offspring to the sea where it will grow to the enormous size I spoke of, and from this day on it shall be known as the Kraken."

END

MOTHMAN VS. THE JERSEY DEVIL: THE BATTLE OF PINE BARRENS

Three days. That's how long Frank's squad had been chasing after their target. Three days of hunting a fugitive of a rather unique variety, although maybe that wasn't the best choice of words for what they were hunting for; considering that would insinuate that the squad's target was human, and that was by no means the case. If you were to tell the twenty-six-year-old corporal that he and nine other men would be chasing after a winged creature, he would think that you were stoned out of your skull.

Despite being born and raised in Point Pleasant, he never put much stock into the stories he heard about the so-called Mothman. Franklin Ryan wasn't the type of person to believe in monsters; if he couldn't see it for himself, then it wasn't real. Now the Viet Cong he had spent days and nights battling in the deep jungles of 'Nam, those were monsters he could believe. This was especially after seeing his childhood friend, Ronnie Lincoln, having his head explode from a sniper's well-placed bullet, leaving Frank's face covered in a mass of blood, bone, and brain matter.

Frank had heard tales of the mysterious winged creature that stalked the lonely roads outside of his hometown from the letters he received from his younger brother while he was serving in Vietnam. While his platoon was either intrigued by the stories of the winged monster, Frank thought it was all some sort of massive hoax to get some decent tourism for the little Virginia town. Once he his nine-month tour overseas had ended, Frank returned to Point Pleasant and could hardly believe the amount of talk there was about the Mothman. No matter where the solider went, almost every conversation he could overhear was about that blasted winged freak of nature.

To make matters worse for Frank, his brother, Jeff, has been doing his own investigation of the monster that had become the talk of the town. At this point, Frank had had enough of this nonsense and stormed out of the house and into the cold December night. It was the soldier's hope that he could just take a walk that and be free from any talk about that blasted winged creature for at least a few hours. How wrong he was going to be…

As he continued his walk, Frank heard a sound that would be forever ingrained into his mind for as long as he lived. It began as a low, grinding, groaning sound that immediately made the corporal think of how the tanks tried to move through the rugged jungle terrain with little success. The horrendous sound grew louder, thus drawing Frank's attention toward it. The closer he got to the source of the crunching sound, the more he could hear another sound beginning to mix with the grinding: screams. Frank's training suddenly kicked in as he now raced toward the noises as the horrific cacophony of screams and grinding metal grew louder like some sort of twisted choir.

Suddenly, the grinding noise was silenced by the sound of a loud splash that only made the screams grow louder. When the solider finally reached what was the cause of the all the panic, he was caught in an instant state of horror.

There, lying broken before him in a mass of twisted metal and concrete was the Silver Bridge. Frank was awestruck by the sight before him, like a young boy caught in the middle of a nightmare. All around the corporal was panic, terror, and absolute confusion, and Frank was among the frightened masses. In the river that had now consumed the bridge, he could see several flashes of the car headlights that were immersed within the river. However, he could not see the people who were no doubt trapped inside of those vehicles --something that Frank couldn't bear to even imagine.

As the terrible night went on, the young solider could only watch as rescue parties went below the river's dark, cold waters and extricate both the pulverized cars and the twisted bodies within them. In the end, forty-six people went into the river and never resurfaced, including two of Frank's old friends from high school, one of his neighbors, and his middle school gym teacher. But the biggest loss the corporal endured that night was his brother, who had gone out to look for his elder sibling in order to try and reconcile with him.

In the days following burying his younger brother, Frank's life spiraled downward into a whirlwind of self-loathing and anger. He had been having trouble enough with being unable to sleep without being plagued by the nightmares he endured during his time in Vietnam, but now he was enslaved by his self-hatred for being the reason his last surviving family member was now eternally resting beside their parents. He swore that he would never let any harm come to Jeff, a vow that he had single-handedly broken due to his own anger towards a creature that he didn't believe existed.

Frank's rage boiled over one night when he instigated a bar fight with another man after overhearing him telling his friends his theory of how the Mothman was the one responsible for the bridge's destruction. Drunk and full of fury, Frank not only fought with the man over the idiotic idea about how that blasted creature was behind something what was clearly the fault of men, but also with the police who had come to try and calm down the situation.

After being thrown in jail for assaulting an officer, Frank was visited and subsequently bailed out by his platoon's leader, Captain Mitchell Wallace. Wallace was a rugged, thirty-four-year-old battle-hardened solider that had saved Frank from an early grave in Vietnam more times than the corporal could count. He had now saved him once more from the fray. Frank was grateful to his captain for his latest save but was confused as to why he was here in the first place, considering that he was supposed to be still serving in 'Nam at the moment. Once they left the police station, Wallace explained to his war-buddy that he was doing this as more than just a favor for a friend.

As it turned out, Wallace had arrived at Point Pleasant in order to recruit him for a special assignment. At first, Wallace wasn't quite specific on the details of the mission, only telling him that it was a manhunt. Obviously confused by that statement, Frank asked as to why the Army would be undertaking a task normally left for a homeland security organization such as the FBI or CIA, but Wallace refused to tell him anything further.

When the two soldiers returned to Frank's house, the corporal found that they were not alone. Upon entering his home, Frank discovered two men dressed in black suits with dark sunglasses covering their eyes. The two men were busy destroying any and all leads and evidence Jeff had on the Mothman, instantly throwing Frank into a rage at the sight of his late brother's work being thrown away like trash. But before Frank could even so much as touch either of the agents, Wallace stopped him and explained that these were two heads of the mission at hand.

Once Frank had calmed down, the two men introduced themselves as Agents Baker and Maryland; names that Frank was quite certain were to be false. They also insisted that they were from the government, but they refused to say which one when the young solider asked. The agents also ignored Frank's pleas to leave Jeff's work alone, claiming that it was "dangerous material."

At this point, Frank had more than enough of all this madness and demanded to be given some answers. Agent Baker gave a nod to Captain Wallace before returning to destroying Jeff's work. Wallace then told him that the mission was one of top-secrecy and that he was to never disclose any of the details of this assignment to anyone from now till the day he died. After Frank agreed, Wallace revealed the what -- or better put, *who* -- they were being sent out to hunt for.

The corporal was caught completely off guard when Wallace told him that they were being ordered to search for and either capture or kill the Mothman. At first, Frank was in disbelief and thought that this was all some sort of sick joke at his expense. But Wallace insisted that this was no ho and that the monster that haunted the shadows of Point Pleasant was in fact a being made of flesh and blood.

It was then that the agents returned and confirmed that the Mothman was indeed a living creature. They showed the young man a series of top-secret photos that had been confiscated by their agency from citizens, though they didn't say what had happened to those they had gotten evidence of the mysterious winged beast from. It was like being hit by a tsunami. In one moment, Frank Ryan's beliefs had been swept away and were replaced by a new world of uncertainty. What the young man still knew to be true, however, was that his brother was dead, and it was still his fault. If had been at least only a little open-minded about the monster, then perhaps his brother wouldn't have been crushed to death inside his own car when the bridge plunged into the river. Frank asked the agents if the Mothman was truly responsible for the collapse of the Silver Bridge, but they merely said that they were unsure at the moment; they had a strong suspicion, however, that the creature had at least some form of involvement in the bridge's destruction.

That was all Frank needed to hear to convince him to sign up for the mission, although he was pretty sure that he couldn't opt-out even if he wanted to. If he could put a bullet into the monster that took his brother away from him, then he'd gladly take it. He knew that it was still his fault for Jeff's death and that being a part of this mission wouldn't bring his younger sibling back, but he'd feel a hell of a lot better seeing that creature either in chains or lying dead at his feet.

That very night, Frank Ryan was redressed in his combat uniform, carrying an M16 and ready for another fight. Once he was prepared for combat, Frank was brought to a nearby military installation where he met the rest of the squad that had been gathered for this unique assignment. While there were several people within the ten-man squad Frank knew from back during his tour in Vietnam, there were a few others among them that were hand-picked from other squads by Wallace himself to hunt this monster. All of whom the Captain told the corporal were other soldiers he trusted to undertake this mission like he did with Frank.

For three days, Baker and Maryland lead the Wallace's squad on a long hunt for the Mothman. Apparently, shortly after the destruction of the Silver Bridge; the squad's target had fled northward, and weather it was scared or merely looking for a new town to haunt was difficult to say. In those three days, all Frank could think of was if he was truly ready to face the monster that been cast over him like a shadow. True, all he could think about was hating the beast, but there was a big difference between hating your enemy and facing your enemy. This was wasn't some Viet-Kong screaming words the corporal couldn't understand while spraying a volley of bullets at him, this was a true to life monster that would more than likely fight back against his would-be captors like an animal backed into a corner. Frank was even fearful at the idea that the bullets from his rifle would do little to harm the Mothman should he be face to face with the beast.

Corporal Ryan would soon get his answer. Hours ago, Baker and Maryland had received word that a hiker in New Jersey had reported to the local authorities that he had seen a large, winged creature that flew over his head during one of his walks through the woods. The agents and their accompanying squad set out to the last known location where the target was sighted: The Pine Barrens. Now the team was here, preparing to enter the vast and foreboding woods of the Barrens to face a monster that could easily kill them all before they even had so much as a chance to fire off a single round.

It was a little past midnight when the squad arrived at the forest. As the soldiers disembarked from their transport vehicle, they felt almost a collective chill crawl up their spines as they looked upon the darkened woods of the Pines Barrens. These ten battle-hardened warriors had faced the depths of a war-torn jungle without the slightest hint of fear, but they couldn't help but feel a sense of trepidation here that they had never felt on the battlefield.

"Gentlemen," Agent Baker began, "this forest is the last known location of our target. We will split into two groups and search every inch of this area for any trace of the creature. Agent Maryland will take five of you and search the northeastern perimeter, while Captain Wallace and I will lead the rest of you in our search through the northwestern perimeter. Once both areas are thoroughly searched, both teams will then move further southward in our pursuit.

"Should you encounter the target, your first option is to capture it alive. But should it come to it, lethal force has been authorized. "We cannot let the animal escape under any circumstances"

Maryland then gestured over to Captain Wallace.

"Captain Wallace will further brief you," he said to them

With that, the two agents stepped aside and allowed the captain to step forward.

"Thank you, sir," he regarded, fringing respect the best he could.

Corporal Ryan, his captain and the rest of the squad didn't care much for the two agents that they had been assigned to assist with this mission. Aside from the fact they were secretive about further information on the Mothman, they had a tendency to treat the troops more like servants than soldiers. Needless to say, the troops weren't too keen on these two men.

"Our target is capable of flight at high-speeds and is believed to be intelligent," Wallace stated. "We will have low-visibility in these woods. The creature, however, will not. Both teams will keep a tight formation at all times. If you set eyes on the target, call out to the others within your squad and engage it as a unit. Do not try to face this thing alone, boys, or it'll fuck your world up faster than my ex-wife."

The troops let out a unified 'yes sir!' before the group of would-be monster hunters readied their weapons and cautiously entered the dark and seemingly endless woods of the Pine Barrens. As planned, the squad split into two smaller groups and headed into the forest. Frank was a part of Wallace and Baker's team, which also consisted of two other men Frank had served in Vietnam with. Their names were Colten Gamble, a private from Denver, Colorado; and Sargent Willis Freeman, a former boxer turned solider from Gatlinburg, Tennessee. The squad's formation had Agent Baker in front while Captain Wallace and Frank stayed close behind him, with Gamble and Freeman covering the rear.

They stayed in a tight group, carefully scanning every inch of the surrounding area with what little illumination they had from their flashlights and from the Moon. The squad especially kept their eyes on the tree line above their heads, fearing that their target could swoop down out of the dark skies and decapitate them before they could even register that their heads had been removed from their shoulders.

"This shit is insane," Gamble mentioned to the others. "Whoever thought we'd be monster hunters?"

"I'm not trying to think about it like that," Freeman replied

"Well, how the fuck are you thinking about it then?" Gamble questioned

"Like a bug I gotta squash," Freeman said simply "A *big* bug."

"What about you, Ryan?" Gamble asked his teammate. "What do you think about hunting the freaking Mothman? I mean, the damn thing destroyed the bridge in your town and killed your brother. Shit, you gotta be looking for some payback, am I right?"

"I'd love to put a bullet in that bastard's head, but I'm going to follow my orders first," Frank informed his fellow squad member. "But honestly, I'm hoping we can kill it."

"You will only do so if I give the order, Private," Agent Baker reminded him sharply. "If the target is killed without my say-so, then I will hold you all personally responsible."

Frank and the other soldiers glowered at the agent but quieted down regardless. They hated the idea of having someone on the federal level calling the shots. Baker and Maryland had no right to order the men around like a bunch of hunting dogs, but there was hardly anything that the squad could do about their commanding officers for this mission.

"So, can we even hurt this thing, Captain?" Gamble inquired.

"It's hard to say," Wallace answered. "There's no report of anyone firing on the target before."

"Oh great, so we could just be pissing it off," Gamble said with an eye-roll. "I knew I shouldn't have signed on for this shit!"

"Do you ever stop complaining, Gamble?" Frank chided. "Seriously, I didn't think you could bitch more than you did in 'Nam."

"I'm just saying that maybe we should think this through a bit more before going after a thing that can destroy a bridge?" the fellow soldier shrugged off before adding. "Just a thought."

"Can it, Gamble," Wallace ordered in a firm voice.

"Alright, I guess we'll all die then," Gamble mumbled under his breath.

Frank gave Gamble a quick, but stern look to get his squad mate to finally shut his mouth. However, it wasn't even a full minute before someone else spoke up. This time around it thankfully wasn't Gamble.

"Maybe Gamble was onto something, Cap," Freeman said to his C.O. "Maybe we should reassess the situation."

"See, Freeman's got the right idea," Gamble added before Frank shot him another look

"I don't mean we should cut and run, Captain," Freeman clarified. "I mean that maybe we should be prepared to engage two hostiles out here."

"What *do* you mean?" Frank asked, now curious.

"You mean you don't know, Ryan?" Freeman asked back. "Come on, man, this is the Pine Barrens! You can't tell me you haven't heard the stories about the Jersey Devil?"

"I didn't believe that a seven-foot-tall flying bug man was real until three days ago, Freeman," Frank reminded him. "So, what the fuck makes you think that I thought whatever dumb shit you're talking about was real?"

Well, that wasn't entirely true. Frank faintly remembered hearing a story about the Jersey Devil from his uncle who used to live in New Jersey before moving down to West Virginia to be closer to the rest of family before he blew his brains out after catching his wife with another man. From what little Frank remembered of the story his uncle told him, it was a tale about a woman named Jane Leeds who had twelve children, was pregnant with her thirteenth, and cursed the child in her womb, saying that she wanted it to be a devil. Shortly thereafter, Mother Leeds gave birth to just that; a true to life devil. Moments after being born, the monstrosity killed the midwife and scurried up the chimney, where it then flew out into the darkness of the Pine Barrens and has stayed there ever since, or so the story goes.

"It's just a story, man," Frank disregarded. "It ain't real."

"That's funny," Freeman replied. "Didn't they say the same shit about the thing that killed you brother?"

Frank growled at Freeman but said nothing in response. The corporal didn't want to say it out loud, but his teammate had a point. In no less than three days, Frank Ryan's perception of the world had been completely shattered. No longer did he exist in a world where the paranormal was something to be scoffed at as some hoax; now he lived in a world where nightmares were made real.

The corporal tried his best to keep calm with the knowledge that he was now aware of. This was difficult to do, however, since he always thought such things like the Mothman as nothing more than a delusion brought on by mass hysteria. It made Frank wonder if tales of monsters, ghosts, and other strange phenomena were as real as the winged lifeform that they now hunted. If that was the case, were Heaven and Hell real as well? If that were true, then perhaps it could give him some sort of comfort knowing that Jeff was back with their family.

"I bet Agent Baker knows if the Jersey Devil is real or not," Freeman continued in a sly, mocking tone. "Don't you, sir?"

Agent Baker turned to face Freeman, but before he could say anything in response to the soldier's accusation, the sudden sound of distant gunfire rang out through the darkness, making the small team collectively jump it surprise as it did. The gunfire was soon followed by the sounds of men screaming. But among the cacophony of bullets and bloody cries, Frank and the rest of his team could detect another sound rising through the horrific noises the squad were hearing. The noise was ungodly, unlike anything the men had heard before. The closest thing they could describe it as was a bizarre mixture of the wails of a police siren and the yowls of a mountain lion.

While he didn't show it on his face, Frank couldn't stop the fear from spreading inside his mind like a wildfire. He glanced over to Captain Wallace, who, while keeping up a strong and stern expression, couldn't hide the small tinge of terror in his eyes. Gamble and Freeman were visibly shocked by the sounds that were coming from the shadows of the forest. As the chorus of chaos continued, another noise began to be heard within the flurry of horror the men were hearing: the sound of flesh being torn, which in turn made the screams grow even louder and the gunfire to slowly die down.

"Maryland, come in!" Baker spoke into his radio. "Have you engaged the target?"

No answer.

"Maryland! Come in dammit!" the federal agent demanded in a more panicked voice.

Again, no answer came from the other end of the radio. The squad could only stand there and listen to the screams of their teammates being slaughtered by what could very well be the monster they had been tracking; or, as Freeman had mentioned earlier, something much worse.

"Captain, we're going in!" Agent Baker ordered.

"Are you fucking crazy?" Gamble nearly shouted in disbelief. "Can you not hear what's going on out there?"

"You were given an order, Private!" Captain Wallace reminded his junior officer sharply. "Now do your job or so help me God I'll put a bullet in your head!"

Gamble instantly shut up upon hearing that. Baker then drew his sidearm before leading the team toward the direction of the horrendous sounds they had heard. Following the low light of their rifle-mounted flashlights, the squad struggled to move through the pine trees that surrounded them as fast as they could. Captain Wallace called out to the other team while Baker continued to try and contact his partner via radio but with no response. Frank's mind began to race with what scene they were about to come upon once they reached the other team. He hoped that they could reach what was left of the others, but from the dying sounds of gunfire and screams that hope seemed a slim one at best.

Finally, they reached the source of screams and found exactly what Frank had imagined. All that remained of the team members were a pile of severed parts. It wasn't until Frank looked down to see that he staring at what was left of Sidney Jacobs, a man who had dragged him out of a fire fight during the battle of Pleiku.

The corporal tried to keep the bile that was rising in his throat down but failed to do so. He was unable to stop himself from vomiting on the corpse of his friend that was under his boots. He had seen his share of friends in a pile of blood and gore back on the battlefield, but the sight before him was different. It was if Jacobs had been torn apart by an animal, only at the same time, it seemed to be an animal that knew where to attack. Sidney's stomach had been not only torn out, but the contents of what he had eaten had been spilled out as well.

The right side of his face was covered in three deep gashes that resembled claw marks. This attack had ripped his face apart, tearing away his cheek and eight eye by the looks of it. His left arm appeared to be ripped, or more accurately, *bitten* off at the elbow and tossed five feet away from his corpse. It also appeared to be gnawed down to the bone, leaving on parts of the hand and some strips of meat as the only remnants of flesh. He pulled his flashlight away from the mangled mess of his friend's body as he stepped off of it.

However, as Frank moved his light upward, it fell upon the body of another solider, which had been impaled on a tree branch (well, the upper half of his body, at least). The soldier's lower half was left at the base of the tree with his legs bitten off at the knees and his intestines strewn across the ground.

"I... I think I found what's left of Agent Maryland," Gamble called out to the others, his voice cracking from the horror he was witnessing.

"So did I," Freeman, standing ten feet away from Gamble, glumly mentioned.

It was then that Wallace let out a rage-filled cry as he suddenly spun around and struck Agent Baker in the chest with the butt of his rifle, knocking him to the ground in doing so. Wallace then kicked away the agent's sidearm before aiming his M16 directly at Baker's face. The rest of what remained of Wallace's team also gathered around and aimed their weapons at the man who had essentially sent their brothers-in-arms into a slaughter.

"Start Talking," Wallace gritted through his teeth. "Now."

"You and your men put your weapons down immediately, Captain!" Baker commanded.

"Not until you tell us what exactly the fuck we're fighting!" the Captain demanded.

"You all knew damn well what we were up against from the start!" Agent Baker shouted back.

"You didn't tell us that this thing could do this!" Wallace scolded the agent like a child.

"This isn't the target's M.O," Agent Baker said. "All of our sources say that the asset is a non-hostile -- it was supposed to be an easy capture!"

"Well, it doesn't look like a fucking non-hostile to me!" Frank snarled. "I knew some of these men -- and you just left them to die!"

"My partner is also dead!" Baker reminded the squad. "Maryland was torn apart just like the rest of your team!"

"Can't say that I feel sorry for him," Gamble sneered.

"I'm telling you that it wasn't the target that did this!" Baker stated. "This was something else!"

"Then what the fuck could've...?" Wallace's voice trailed off.

It was then that everyone remembered Freeman's story, and with that, these men -- who had seen years of horrid combat in a godforsaken jungle halfway around world -- felt something that they hadn't when they battled the Viet-Kong: fear. Suddenly, the wailing sound could be heard again, only this time it was much closer. Acting on their training and instincts alone, the soldiers turned their attention away from the agent and onto the coming fight.

The five men spread out in a tight-knit defensive position, scanning every inch of the bloodstained area with what little light they had. The wailing continued, seemingly drawing closer as it did. Agent Baker also regained his composure before picking up his weapon and joining the rest of the men in facing the unknown assailant that had slain his partner. He would have them all buried in a nameless shallow grave for assaulting him -- assuming, they all made it out of the Barrens alive, that is.

"Do you see anything?" Wallace called out to his team.

"I can't see shit, Captain!" Freeman replied. "It's too dark!"

"Well, whatever it is, it sounds weird and pissed off," Gamble commented.

"Wait, do you hear that?" Frank asked the others.

The squad quieted themselves to listen to whatever it was the corporal was hearing. Accompanying the wailing and screeching of the unknown creature was another sound in the background: the unmistakable whoosh of wings flapping through the night's air. Everyone instantly aimed their rifles high and began to carefully search what little of the darkened treetops they could see. Even though the soldiers tried their best to keep their composure, the terror was slowly welling up within them with each screech of the monster that was hovering somewhere above them. Was it the Mothman, or the creature from Freeman's story? Whatever it was, it sounded as though it would be on them soon.

"Steady, boys," Wallace told his men. "Don't fire until you see it."

"Well, it ain't gonna have any trouble seeing us," Freeman retorted.

Before the captain could say anything, there was a sudden *'whoosh'* through the air, sending a huge gust of wind around the group of armed men. The soldiers collectively jumped with a fright. In a panic, they darted their eyes all over the area around them. As they did so, Frank saw Captain Wallace standing still; however, there was one problem: the top of his head was missing.

The rest of the squad saw what Frank had already seen and let out gasps in horror as the Captain's tongue twitched sporadically, as if it was looking for where the rest of the head had gone. All the while, it spurted up small fountains of blood. Wallace's body stood in place for several more seconds before falling backwards on the ground.

Frank then caught something in the treetops. At first, he assumed that it was it was an owl, but that thought quickly left his mind when he noticed the sheer size of the winged being that was looking down at him. Then he saw them: *the eyes.* They shined a bright red and seemed to be looking directly in Frank Ryan's very soul. There it was, the monster who had murdered his brother, staring back at him almost in a state of curiosity. There was no thought that was going through the corporal's mind as he raised his rifle up toward the creature except for one: kill it.

"Contact!" he shouted to the others before pulling the M16's trigger back.

Even though they couldn't see what the corporal saw, the other soldiers opened fire in the same direction as Frank, thinking that he had caught sight of the monster who had slain their captain. Even Agent Baker fired alongside them. Before the bullets struck it, the Mothman quickly spread its massive wings and flew off in a circle away from the gunfire as the remaining troops tried to shoot the winged beast down. The Mothman flew deeper into the Pines Barrens, apparently unharmed by the bullets.

Frank still had no other thought than seeing the creature dead despite claiming that he would follow his orders. He quickly reloaded his rifle and took off after the Mothman, leaving his fellow troops behind. He did not mentally register the calls from his teammates as he raced into the darkness after the monster that had taken away the last member of his family. What did make him stop, however, was the sound of Gamble, Freeman, and Agent Baker screaming like the other squad had done before they had been brutally slaughtered.

Realizing his error, Frank spun around and ran back toward the others, thinking that the Mothman had somehow managed to double-back without himself noticing. When he came back to where he had left his remaining brothers-in-arms behind in a fit of rage, he found the bodies of Gamble and Freeman lying on the ground in a mass of blood and gore. Despite that, Frank's line of sight was drawn toward what was currently standing over their corpses. Holding Agent Baker in its bloodstained claws was the creature known as the Jersey Devil.

Standing at an imposing six feet tall, the flesh and blood demon was muscular with a green-scaled upper body and a dark, reddish-brown lower body with a pair of large goat-like hooves that supported its body on a park of bent, almost stork-like legs. Two massive, leathery wings like those of a bat adorned the beast's back, looking as though they could stretch out to about eight feet in length if the monster chose to unfurl them. Its face was elongated like that of a horse. The creature had sharp fangs that were currently being bared at the solider, while two curved horns sat atop the monster's head. A length of tufted hair ran from the back of its head down its long, camel-like neck to the center of its back, finally ending at its furry torso. It's long, serpent-like tail ended in a fork that was also covered in the blood of those it had killed recently.

As Frank stared into the Devil's yellow reptilian eyes, the terror inside his heart reached a fever pitch. So much so that he dropped his rifle as the beast snarled at the new intruder to its home, snapping its jaws at him as he did. Agent Baker had been slashed across the chest and down his face, but he still drew breath... albeit barely at this point. The corporal was overcome with fear; he was unable to speak or move, and he could hardly think of anything other than the thought of being torn to shreds like the others before him had been.

The Jersey Devil then let out a cry that pierced Frank's ears before suddenly taking Baker by the head in each of its clawed hands and splitting it open right down the middle, an act that spilled blood, bone, and brain matter all across the already gore-covered ground. The living demon then took its tail and impaled it through the dead agent's chest and tossed the body aside, now focusing entirely on its next victim.

The demon-like creature slowly advanced toward the now helpless corporal, taking one slow step with its hooves at a time. It seemed as though it was savoring the fear it was projecting onto the human, as if it knew that it struck fear into Frank's heart and was relishing every moment leading up to the inevitable kill. As the soldier continued to stare into the monster's wicked eyes, he could almost swear that he could see a glimmer of sick joy highlighted within them.

But just as the Devil had started to approach Frank, it suddenly took a step backwards, letting out another ungodly screech as it did. At first, the corporal was confused as to the creature's sudden trepidation. That is, until the solider turned around to see what had landed behind him. There, standing an imposing seven feet tall was the Mothman.

The newly arrived winged monster was pitch black all over, save for its two luminescent red eyes. It stood upon two long legs with three clawed toes at the end of each foot. Its hawk-like wings that sat on its back appeared even larger than the Jersey Devil's, clearly more than able to provide the lift which the monster needed to get off the ground and into the skies. Its arms were long and muscular with clawed hands at the end of them. But the strangest feature of the creature was that it appeared to have no head per se, just two red eyes sitting on its oval-shaped body.

At this point, Frank was in a state of near-madness. In no less than twenty minutes he had encountered two creatures that he believed to be nothing more than hoaxes. Yet here they were standing before him like living nightmares.

Before Frank could even move so much as his finger, the Mothman suddenly swung one of its arms at the solider who had been hunting it. The force of the impact sent the young man flying sideways into a nearby tree, slamming into its wooden husk with the force of a crashing car. Frank could feel his spine crack like a twig on impact. His mind was in a clouded haze, a clear indication of a severe concussion. While the solider now lay on the ground in a broken heap, he was left to witness a battle that none would believe should he live to see another day and tell the tale.

The two monsters stared one another down, neither backing down from the fight that was sure to come. The Jersey Devil let out another screech as it flared out its wings in an attempt to make itself look larger. Its posturing, however, did little to faze its opponent, who stood unmoving like a statue before the Beast of Leeds. Enraged by the newcomer's unwavering stance, the horned fiend let out a rage-filled roar before charging toward the Mothman with its claws and fangs at the ready. The monstrous interloper from Point Pleasant spread its wings and flew toward the other monster a with quick burst of speed.

The two beasts smashed into one another in a mass of fury and violence. The Devil had the first strike by slashing across the chest of its enemy. In in response, the Mothman struck the demonic beast directly in the face. The Devil let out a hiss before lunging again, this time stretching out with its elongated neck and striking like a snake. It bit into the arm that the Mothman had hit the horse-headed beast with and clamped down on it in a vice-like grip. Even though the creature of Point Pleasant didn't make a sound to illustrate its agony, it did wince in pain.

Using its free hand, the bright-eyed monster started to furiously pound on the Jersey Devil's horned head. Rather than let go, however, the Devil of Leeds only sank its teeth deeper into the other cryptid's arm until the Mothman punched its equally monstrous opponent in the eye. The Devil yowled in pain as it stumbled back, clutching its bruised eye with one of its clawed hands as it did so. Blackish, slug-like blood oozed out of the wound left from the bite wound on the Mothman's arm, but if it was difficult to determine if it actually hurt due to its emotionless, faceless façade. With the Jersey Devil still reeling from the strike to its eye, the demon's opponent saw its opening and flew forward for a tackle that sent them both to the ground.

The Mothman managed to pin the Jersey Devil to the ground with a foot planted on its chest, while the other winged cryptid snarled and snapped wildly up at the bright-eyed beast. Still holding its rival down with the sheer weight of its leg alone, the Mothman began to deliver punch after punch directly at the Devil's face, not relenting for even so much as a second. The creature from Point Pleasant was seemingly aware that if it let up for even a split second, the tables would be turned on it.

The merciless pummeling continued until the Mothman felt a sharp, stinging sensation shooting through its leg. The beast of Point Pleasant glanced down at the source of this sudden agony to see that its Jersey Devil had stabbed the sharp end of its tail clear through the its leg. The temporary distraction was all the ruler of the Pine Barrens needed to kick the other monster in its torso with one of its hoven feet, knocking the Mothman off its person and giving it enough time to stand up once more.

With a furious screech, the Jersey Devil rushed toward the other monster, thinking that it had a shot at ending this fight in its favor. But just before it could so much as sink its claws into the Mothman's flesh again, the eyes of Point Pleasant's winged terror flared a bright, hellish crimson that was so blinding that even Frank hand to force himself to look away. The blazing flash of light from the Mothman's eyes hit the other monster directly in its own line of sight.

The Jersey Devil let out a pain-filled shriek as it backed away from the other cryptid, clutching its head in its claws as it did so. At first, Frank assumed that the Mothman had managed to temporarily blind its enemy with its surprise attack. As he looked on at the demonic resident of the Pine Barrens, however, he noticed that the horned fiend was starting to snarl and swipe wildly at the empty air around it. The fallen corporal was confused by this strange behavior until he remembered something that Agent Baker had mentioned during a briefing about a rumored ability that the beast of Point Pleasant possessed.

There had been some reports that the Mothman could project illusions into the minds of others, a power that had not been fully confirmed by the agency Baker and Maryland had worked for. As Frank watched the Jersey Devil continue to attack the air around it, the corporal could only assume that that was what the demon was experiencing at the moment. As the Leeds demon aimlessly attacked images of things Frank couldn't even begin to imagine, the Mothman spread its wings once more and flew back up toward the treetops to make an escape. Shortly thereafter, the demonic cryptid had managed to shake off the effects of the Mothman's mental assault, and from what Frank could see it looked seriously pissed off.

With a hideous screech, the Jersey Devil unfolded its wings and took off after its now fleeing opponent. Frank was unable to see what was about to take place in the dense treetops of the Pine Barrens, but he could still hear the sounds of battle between the two monsters. What was then happening in the trees was that the Devil was following the scent of the Mothman's blood. While it couldn't match the speed of its opponent in flight, the horned creature could still track it with its excellent sense of smell and nocturnal vision. The Jersey Devil wasn't built for long flights like the Mothman due to the latter's heavy build, so it had to occasionally grab onto a tree and proceed to jump from one to another until it had the strength to fly again.

From the strong smell of blood in the air, the Leeds Devil could detect that the bright-eyed beast was close by. While the Mothman was indeed built for speed in the sky, the close proximity of the trees made it difficult for the winged denizen of Point Pleasant to maneuver in. This gave the Jersey Devil the chance to keep up with its fleeing rival. The Mothman was so occupied on trying to navigate through the dense tree line that its pursuing adversary had managed to swoop close in and kick it into a tree with a swift strike of its hooves. The bright-eyed beast collided with a nearby tree back first, but quickly corrected itself in mid-air and flew straight toward the ruler of the Pine Barrens.

The two-winged terrors then engaged in midair combat. The Mothman took a swipe at the Devil's throat with its claws, only for the other monster to snake its neck to the left before slashing at the destroyer of the Silver Bridge's eye.However, the Mothman brought its arm up to shield the most vulnerable part of its body, which caused the guarding appendage to receive the damage that was meant for its eyes. The Jersey Devil kept up the assault by shooting its head forward like a venomous serpent, sinking its teeth into its rival's shoulder before spitting out the foul-tasting meat to the ground below. It then pulled its head back, ripping a chunk of flesh from the other monster's body.

In a fit of anger and pain, the Mothman reached out and took hold of the Devil's tail. Holding onto the forked appendage tightly, it used every ounce of its strength to hurl the horned creature back toward the ground below. The demon from Leeds landed only fifteen feet away from where Frank was laying when it crashed to the earth. The creature broke one of its wings upon colliding with the ground, making it release a screech of agony as it felt the bones crack. The Jersey Devil was so focused on the pain that it nearly forgot that its enemy was cavorting just above it. Seeing an opening, the Mothman suddenly began to rapidly descend toward the other monster with the talons on its feet ready to put an end to this fight.

Just as the Mothman was about to crush the Jersey Devil's skull under its talons, the demonic cryptid rolled out of the way at the last possible second before jumping back onto its hooves once more. Despite the major wound it received to its wing, the lord of the Barrens's rage was overshadowing the pain that coursed throughout its body. Frank could see it in the two monsters' eyes that this was it, this was the final round. Only one of the winged beasts was going to walk away from this fight and the loser would be nothing more than a pile of meat for the other to consume. If Frank could find the strength to run, we would've done so long before, but the pain in his broken spine forbade him from moving from the spot that the Mothman had thrown him into.

At this point, the seriously wounded soldier knew that he was going to die. But whether that death was by his injuries or at the claws of the winner of the battle between the monsters remained to be seen. He tried to reach for his rifle which had been knocked a few short feet from where he had been thrown, but his broken back kept him from even moving so much as a finger. Despite the agony that the solider was in, there was a far greater sensation that he was feeling, one that seemed to block out the pain he was in: fear. As a solider, Frank had to accept that death was only a half-step away from him every time he went out on a mission, But seeing these two titans about to kill each other -- and then subsequently him shortly thereafter -- made him feel only sheer terror at the idea of being consumed by one of these titans as a snack and then forgotten.

The Jersey Devil let out another furious cry before the two monsters charged at one another once more. The lord of the Barrens ducked under another swipe of the Mothman's talons before taking both sets of its own claws and slicing deep into its opponent's torso in an 'X'-shaped pattern. The bright-eyed beast retaliated by grabbing the other monster by the horn and slamming it head-first into the nearest tree repeatedly. In order to stop this beating, the Devil used the end of its tail to slide downward until it reached its opponent's feet. The forked appendage then slashed open the tendons on each of the Mothman's legs, causing the terror of Point Pleasant to immediately collapse to its knees.

Knowing that it could no longer stay in the fight, the Mothman released its grip on its enemy and quickly unfurled its wings in an attempt to make a quick escape. But before it could flee, the Jersey Devil managed to take hold of one of its opponent's now lame legs and slammed it onto the ground. In a last-ditch effort to get away from the demon of Leeds, the Mothman unleashed another flash from its eyes.

However, rather than feel the confusion sheering through its brain, this time the Jersey Devil fought through the illusions and reached out with its claws to tear out one of the Mothman's iridescent red. Acting on the mortal wound it had given its rival, the lord of the Barrens slammed the invader from Point Pleasant into the ground. The horse-headed monstrosity then lifted one of its hooves high over the equivalent of the other monster's head in the center of its chest before bringing it down crushing whatever its face skull underneath it.

With a triumphant screech, the Jersey Devil declared its victory to the wilds of the Pine Barrens. Frank would almost be amazed by the sight he had just witnessed had it not been for the fact that he knew what was coming next. With the Mothman dead, the Devil from Leeds turned its attention on the last human who had dared to wander into its domain. The creature slowly moved towards Frank, its fangs bared and ready for another kill. Within moments, the Devil's maw was mere inches away from the soldier's face. Rather than give it the pleasure of hearing him scream, Frank instead spit a mouthful of blood at the beast's horse-like face in defiance of his death.

"I hope you choke on me, fucker," Frank declared.

The last thing Frank Ryan saw was the Jersey Devil's mouth engulfing his head.

END

OGOPOGO VS. GIANT EEL: WRATH OF THE OKANAGAN LAKE GOD

The semi-trailer truck lay still in the two and a half meters of glassy water near the peaceful and pebbly Antlers Beach. The truck looked like it was on the verge of turning into a derelict as small waves rippled between the barely closed cargo-trailer doors. The light overcast sky held impressions of the sun trying to decide whether it will show itself. The mix of light and cloud projected an almost whitish glow onto the area.

Okanagan Lake reflected the light as the lake silently watched the clouds echo the smooth watery surface. However, beneath the lake's surface the murkiness and deep depths suggest concealment of a mysterious lost world. This steep underwater realm was dark, unexplored, and suggestive of another presence that found a perfect home in such a mysterious domain.

This and other thoughts plagued Chad Armand Chubb, age 49, as he lay shivering on the beach. Covered in a towel, he watched several RCMP officers directing a tow-truck to the semi-submerged truck in the lake.

In truth, he was the driver of the semi that now lay in the water. Long story short, he was carrying a piece of cargo that two mysterious individuals wanted him to get to Vancouver as quickly as possible. Being forty-something years old and a practical guy, Chad suspected these two guys to be part of the black market but couldn't be sure. Pulling out of the cargo holding area and hitting the highway, Chad felt all questions concerning the men beginning to bother him.

Why were they so in a hurry to get the cargo on the truck?
Couldn't they have waited for another, better trucker?

These and many other questions assailed his conscience before becoming too tired for his own good -- until he nearly ran into a car. He turned hard to the right before hitting the water. The things he remembered vividly were getting out of the truck with water pushing against him and finally breaking free before he swam towards shore. He recalled nearly conking out before having the mind to find help.

Chad sighed as a wave of guilt washed over him as he stared at the truck lying still in the water. Despite his stupid choice to not pay attention to the road, he felt he had a responsibility to own up to his actions and he was pretty sure he would get fired after the recovery was complete.

"Sir, can you come around here?"

The officer who called to him seemed to be heading toward the cargo holding area of the semi. This officer was focused on the rear doors of the truck, both of which were open, strangely.

Chad snapped out of his thoughts and waded into the water as a new question popped into his head. As he trudged through the water, all five officers craned their necks at the opened cargo doors. When Chad approached, none of the officers moved in the slightest. He also noticed then that the doors were ajar, which was odd because he was sure he had closed them. Chad began to feel uneasy. None of the officers seemed to be the kind of people who spook easily, yet they were reluctant to go any further.

As he got closer, a jolt of uneasiness shot to his heart as he began to get a clearer look at what the officers were looking at. When the doors opened, Chad's heart dropped, and he began to regret taking the cargo.

In the containment area of the truck sat a large glass aquarium, badly damaged from the accident and half submerged in the water. The most frightening part, however, was not the aquarium itself. It was what it had sustained that made all who saw it uneasy.

Chad and the officers saw the front of the aquarium and the large, jagged hole in the glass. *Something alive* had ruthlessly broken through the glass -- and escaped into Okanagan Lake.

At that point, Chad felt his knees turn to Jell-O.

***

The dark underwater dimness of Okanagan Lake slithered past the shadowy creature which broke the glass of that crammed aquarium. Its glowing light blue eyes coldly pierced the dense green murk and scanned the underwater ridges which rose out of the silt like small mountain peaks.

The creature silhouetted in the darkness was 29 feet long with a torso about 2 and a half feet wide. The eyes shone a light blue through the murk. The face of the monstrosity was round and blunt not unlike a wolf eel, but slightly more humanoid. Its jaws wrapped around near the back of the creature's head, where two pairs of four gills breathed in the oxygen of the lake's underwater scape.

The creature's hue was greenish charcoal gray with a lighter underbelly. The dark coloration was punctuated with two sets of fins thrusting into the water on either side. The huge aquatic beast possessed no other visible extremities, though the jaws hung open in carnivorous anticipation.

As the shadowy serpentine thing glided through the water, its body undulating side to side, it caught movement out of the corner of its unfeeling eyes. It glanced up towards the surface. A shape 15 meters above it was moving, with a strange rectangular piece covering the eyes and objects that resembled duck-feet were thrusting up and down. It had a covering which was black with green streaks going down its length and a strange oblong-shaped oddity on its back. The eel-like enigma could see an apparatus on the mouth area, and it could hear a hissing sound emitted from the newfound creature.

While it continued to observe, a pang of hunger shot through the long serpentine body and the beast turned to look upwards at the strange-footed, long-limbed being. It hadn't eaten for a while and if it had possessed salivary glands, streams of the oral digestive fluid would have glided down its jaws. The temptation to devour and slaughter caressed it with a seductive thrall the underwater beast hadn't felt in a while.

It turned slowly towards the flippered beast. Moving slowly but ominously, it tried to make itself a mere shadow to the unsuspecting creature above.

***

"Topside, I haven't found any sign of the subject from the broken aquarium yet," said lead diver Bill Melnyk as he continued to swim slowly while carefully scanning the waters. "I'm requesting ten more minutes to stay down and continue searching."

"Permission granted, but don't be down there too long," replied the lead diver.

Bill could hear a cautionary edge in the leader's voice and honestly, he understood quite well. The Chad Armand case was already very disconcerting for the RCMP to investigate on land, but in the water, it was even more so.

Bill's dark diving suit with green stripes brushed past pieces of tiny algae as he swam past the large underwater ridges offshore from Antlers Beach. He felt his heart beat faster than usual. As a diver who had 27 years of experience in navigating the dark waters of the Great Lakes, not to mention working for the RCMP, Armand's broken aquarium indicated something able to bust through the container's extra-thick plexi- glass. And now he's tracking that same something in *murky water.*

Even though I'm a damn well experienced diver, this assignment gives me the chills. Bill was sent into the Okanagan depths to do some reconnaissance of the offshore waters to see if there were any traces of what could have broken through the glass.

Suddenly, he caught a glimpse of a shadow coming up underneath him. He looked down, albeit timidly, and squinted.

The shadow was faint in the murky water, but it was heading towards him quickly. As he watched, the shadow grew larger with each foot of distance closed, thereby upping the fear level in his chest. Instead of a solid shadow, glowing light blue eyes and the almost wolf-eel-like mouth were seen with terrifying clarity.

The long, dark, greenish-gray body slithered right towards Bill, its speed frightfully increasing with each passing second. He was unable to radio topside and doing it while that thing was clearly eying him up was an idiotic idea anyway.

Bill tried booking it for the surface, the green underwater scape becoming a blur as he jetted through the water as fast as he could. Right before he tried reaching for the surface, the veteran diver felt a piercing pain shoot through his leg, as if every vein was simultaneously boiling and bursting.

He didn't want to see it, but Bill knew that serpentine thing had latched onto his limb! The man screamed, and he could hear the leader yelling for other people to get into the water. Bumps, equipment being moved, and shouts from the lead diver were all heard through the radio.

Bill swiftly looked to see the creature beginning to chew off his calves. Each bite went deeper into the diver's flesh, with every inch making the pain more unbearable.

He tried kicking it, but all it did was distract the enormous eel temporarily before its glowing eyes snapped back and glanced at him. Bill then looked into the eyes of this newfound creature, staring at its soulless orbs for a heart-stopping moment.

Bill didn't know why he looked, but after doing so he couldn't turn away from those eyes.

Then, the Giant Eel lunged toward him. Bill's screams radioed through the comms like a knife piercing through a steak. Though no one saw what actually happened, the reports said a thick stream of blood came to the surface.

That blood was the last part of Bill Melnyk that the crew would ever see.

***

The Eel continued its bloody feast as a pair of eyes watched from below in territorial repulsion at the new invader. Slowly, the shadowy creature's body stealthily went back into the murk as the Eel began to move once again.

The mysterious creature began to shadow the Eel's movement as it headed toward the North end of the lake, planning something for this very unwelcome visitor to its long-time domain.

***

"*Jeezum crackers*! At least, he doesn't have to go through any more pain," said Chad after being told what happened to Bill Melnyk.

The body was hauled onto an ambulance at Peachland, a small town on the Westside of Okanagan Lake. A news crew was reporting on the gruesome incident. Nothing unusual was likely to be mentioned in the local papers, however.

"It's an ugly scene, isn't it?" The voice asking the question sounded not too old, yet not too young.

Chad spun around to see the source of the voice. Who he saw behind him was quite unexpected.

A young man, no older than 22, stood a bit stunned but more in apology for shocking Chad. His physique wasn't striking, but he looked to be in pretty good shape. The shoulders, while not broad, seemed quite strong and the legs suggested someone who observed a routine regimen of walking, running, or jumping. The face was oval-shaped, with brown eyebrows distinctly making their mark. He possessed ocean blue eyes which silently yet attentively watched for Chad's next move.

The man wore a t-shirt with "BCCIS" printed on the back. On the front it had a sasquatch, a camel-headed serpent creature, and another snake-shaped entity possessing a horse-like head with a greener color tone, all holding the British Columbian flag. The jeans he was wearing seemed in good condition save for a small tear beginning at the upper right leg. The running shoes he wore were white and all navy blue inside. On his right wrist was a silver analog watch. Completing the young man's distinctive look were a pair of black sunglasses with white ends adorning his forehead.

"Sorry, didn't mean to scare you, mister! The diver looked like he had a real bad day," said the new arrival on the scene.

The young man seemed nice and cordial at this time and place. At least, Chad didn't have to worry about lack of manners with this one.

"It's alright, kiddo!" Chad replied. "I think what happened here has disturbed everyone." He wore a solemn scowl as he looked towards the ambulance pulling out of the scene.

"Okay sir," said the young man. Before anything else was said he asked, "by the way, did the diver see something?"

Chad twisted his head to his youthful interlocuter and cocked an eyebrow. Usually, young people would look at the scene, then go about their daily routine as if nothing happened. But this man was different. His ocean blue eyes fixed onto Chad and in an instant, the would-be truck driver felt the receiving end of the kid's focus. It was as if he was being interrogated by police.

The young man slightly twisted his head with a questioning, perceptive look in his eyes. "You saw those bite marks, didn't you? They weren't from any ordinary animal. You know that, right? Did this have something to do with the crashed semi-truck up ahead?"

At this point, Chad felt he should explain what happened and he realized this young man knew something he may not.

"Well kiddo, here's all I know. And I guess I should tell you how the poor guy got injured in the first place!"

Chad started his tale, not knowing that tragedy had struck twice.

***

The Giant Eel ripped a piece of flesh off a dead water skier, thus demonstrating how truly hungry it had been. The water skier, a man of thirty years of age, had eyes wide in silent terror. The last moments of his life were entirely silent due to the fact that the Giant Eel leaped out of the water and tore out his windpipe.

The serpentine invader gulped down another piece of flesh. The throat portion moved provocatively and sharply, as it attempted to digest the freshly torn piece of human meat. The creature had then eaten its fill for the time being.

Now returning its attention to its aquatic environment, the elongated beast's eyes slowly scanned the immediate area and soon spotted something in the distance. A snake-like figure stood silently on a yonder ridge, like a sentry guarding some unspeakable Lovecraftian city. Out of instinct, the Giant Eel swam towards the oddball shape. Its glowing light blue eyes twitched in curiosity as it got closer -- at last, it was there!

As it turned out, the thing on the ridge wasn't living, but merely life-like. It was a statue of some serpentine creature with a head vaguely like that of a dragon (but cartoon-ish), with two front fins and a fluked fin running from its head and down its back. The eyes were wide and cutesy, giving the impression of a friendly creature. Its mouth had very rounded teeth on it and the snout was long.

Before the Giant Eel could get any closer -- *WHAM!* An impact from behind the elongated predator drove it into the statue as well as the rocky ridges surrounding it. The serpentine invader shook itself from the impact and turned around, its maw gaping with teeth ready to bite the aggressor. What it saw next took it off guard and had it crouch down in intimidation.

Set against the bright green murk, a serpentine *something* looked down at the invading Eel. The large round eyes, which were the size of grapefruits, stared at the rival monstrosity with murderous intent. The snout of the creature would remind humans of a cross between a horse and plesiosaur, except with teeth jutting out of its upper jaw. On the top of its head was a menagerie of small horn-like protrusions that covered it like a reptilian mane. The neck possessed a single row of spine-like ridges crested over the neck and down the nearly 50 feet of winding bone and muscle.

At the end of the tail were three splits that had separate rows of ridges. The body itself was snake-like, but all muscle. Every time the newcomer twitched, the movement was strong and smooth, yet lordly, as if it had a purpose. As the Giant Eel quickly glanced down from the eyes, it could see four, jointed legs. Each such limb ended in three-digit clawed toes. The body to which the strong legs were attached was round but very lithe.

The lake serpent growled a challenge at the beast below it. Its eyes contorted in rage and anger at the invasive predator. The Giant Eel responded by opening its mouth wide and snapping it at this formidable-looking challenger. It was angry yet desperate and thus not opposed to fighting.

Seeing this blatantly rebellious display, the opposing serpentine creature -- the one that humans call *The Ogopogo* -- lunged towards its rival with a speed that would turn the face of a motorboat owner pale. It opened its mouth as it did so, revealing every one of its fearsome teeth and a clear intent to *kill.*

***

The Giant Eel barely had time to react as the impact of the Ogopogo hit its opponent's smaller body. The massive collision reverberated through its body and rattled all the creature's senses. The Eel thrashed wildly after its ropey form was ground into hard granite rock at a painful speed.

At last, the Eel bit down on one of the legs of the Ogopogo. The lake creature cried out in pain and retaliated by latching its massive jaws onto the Eel's neck, attempting to wrench the opponent off its limb. The Eel sunk its razor-like teeth even deeper into its opponent's thin but sinewy arm as the Ogopogo thrashed about. A crimson cloud of blood billowed from the limb and wisped into the column of water like a red cloud omen signaling doom to a younger world.

With a vicious swing, the Okanagan Lake creature knocked the Eel into a hard piece of granite. The impact sent a shock through the lengthy creature's body. Instantly, the Eel's grip loosened, and the invasive species spiraled downward into the silt. In a second, the Eel suddenly saw the Ogopogo rocket down towards the serpentine fish with its maw open and ready to kill the miscreant intruder.

The Eel dodged the attack as the Okanagan lake cryptid was about to land its next blow. The Ogopogo's claws slashed the silt where the Eel was sequestered -- but the giant serpentine fish was nowhere to be seen! The lake monster looked around carefully, the green murk making visibility ambiguous even to a creature used to living within its depths. Shadows rippled in the aquatic gloom, provocatively tickling the Ogopogo's heightened state of awareness and territorial intent.

Nothing further occurred for a few minutes --

The silt beneath the great lake monster suddenly stirred. Before the Ogopogo knew it, the Eel exploded out of the sediment and quickly wrapped its huge, elongated body around its dragon-like opponent. The Ogopogo thrashed in shock as it as it began to be pulled down towards the depths.

The Okanagan lake creature bared its teeth in determination and anger. This was its home! *It, not the Eel,* was the dark lake's *ruler*!

The natives here called the creature's kind N'ha-a-itk, the Sacred Creature of the Waters. Its marine ancestors had ruled the deep oceanic depths for centuries before they migrated up the Columbia River and settled in the lake. Its ancestors, older than the dinosaurs, had survived more dangerous threats than this. Not even the humans who populated the area and built mini-skyscrapers in the valley could attest to such a durable existence.

As the Ogopogo struggled, it heard a faint rumbling in the water. It turned out to be the obnoxious, familiar sound of a motorboat. Moreover, it could hear the voices of a young man and the ex-trucker who started this mess in the first place.

***

"I'm positive the reports said the guy went missing under the surface -- errmmm, right here," said the young man as he scrutinized the area, based on reports from boaters.

He pointed towards the middle of the lake where a water skier went under. Piloting the motorboat, Chad seemed unsure of the situation as he looked rather uneasily around the lake. Long story short, right after the young man had introduced himself as Erik

Halverson, reports came in on the radio of one police car that a man on a water-ski fell into the water after something bumped him from underneath.

Without warning, Erik quickly turned to Chad and told him they needed to check out the scene ASAP. Chad asked why, and Erik's response was not what he expected.

"Because I think I know what you carried on your truck."

Chad turned to Erik. "You sure about that, kiddo? You've been spot-on so far, but how can you be sure?"

Erik shrugged. "I don't know, sir, but what I can tell you is that when something invasive is released into a habitat, things will get ugly for the native creatures. And believe me, this lake beneath us has seen that already. Look at the weeds! They're milfoil weeds. They came from China, but some Chinese tourist didn't check the bottom of his boat, plunked it in the water, and *voila!* If weeds can harm this lake's ecosystem, I'd really hate to see it sink any further."

Chad glanced a little closer. Obviously, Erik was holding something else back too. "Yes, and?"

"I guess it's because I respect the mystery beneath us, thanks to a childhood experience I had. To make it short, I was eight years old and I was with a wildlife art class at the time. We were at a beach near Westbank -- well, at least it was called Westbank before changing it to 'West Kelowna.' Anyway, our art instructor decided to shake things up by having us go canoeing for a while -- not far from the beach, mind you! Forty-five minutes later, the instructor decided it was time to return to the beach and have lunch."

Erik paused. "That was before something underneath bumped my boat and capsized it. All I remember is seeing a huge, dark serpent-like shape whiz past me and into the murkiness. Since then, I guess you can say I've wanted to know what I've seen ever since, and no 'expert' will comfort me *until I know.*"

Suddenly, a huge fountain-shaped blast of water erupted right in front of them. That occurred just before a huge, monstrous head blasted towards them. Before Erik or Chad could do anything, the Giant Eel collided with the latter and knocked him off his feet. The 20-foot-long serpentine fish writhed in the motorboat like a living, algae-covered whip, thrashing with an intensity that could slice through a man's leg.

Shocked, Chad landed on his back and frantically crab-walked backward as the Eel slithered in his direction. The terrified ex-trucker's eyes widened as he came face-to-face with the creature he hauled in his truck, and instantly beads of sweat rained down his forehead.

Chad's fingers frantically searched for something to hit the slithering beast with. The only thing he found was a glass water bottle that was in a holder, but he felt the monstrosity's slimy body slither onto his leg before he could put it to use. He turned around to see the Eel practically on top of him, its eerie light blue eyes staring directly into his own. A flash of hunger gleamed in its eyes as it opened its snout to reveal needle-like teeth glinting in the afternoon sun.

Chad raised the glass water bottle, ready to strike down the nightmare he unknowingly brought upon Okanagan Lake. The Eel pulled back with its needle-filled mouth gaping open, the recesses of which Chad could only see the darkness of. It was as if a cave had come to life and it just happened to pick him as lunch!

Suddenly a blur struck the Eel hard enough for it to hit the left side of the boat. The Eel snapped out of its trance and turned its head to see Erik with his hands raised up. He was in a ready stance, his body facing sideways with high guards ready to block any attack. But the Eel was focused only on Chad for some reason.

Erik lunged forward and grabbed the creature by the gills, trying to pull it off Chad. But the creature was solid muscle and was not moving anywhere! Instead, the Eel twirled around and almost bit him in the face. Erik dodged the creature in time, the needle-like teeth almost touching his flesh and face. He literally just escaped with his face intact.

"Hang on, I'll get him!" Chad yelled as he got up to run and grab the Eel's head with the same intent.

"Let's get this thing to the port side, put a tracker on it, and dump it!" Erik said, trying to keep his grip on the writhing creature.

The slimy body was on the verge of slipping through his hands. Erik felt his grip tighten in vain as the creature began to slide out of his grip. Chad clamped both hands over the top and lower parts of the head as he and Erik began to shuffle awkwardly toward the boat side. A thought passed on how comical this whole scene might look to another person if they're not in the fight of their lives. Erik snapped out of that trance and hauled the Eel onto the side of the boat with a simultaneous heave of strength combined with Chad's.

Just as they were about to push this thing out into the water, Erik came to a sudden realization and yelled, "Wait, that thing could be what killed the two people!"

"What? You mean *this* thing?" Chad queried in disbelief. The creature was beginning to writhe in their hands more easily now and was on the verge of slipping through their hands and into the water. Chad realized Erik could be right, but the grip tightened even more as the thing began to slip through the grip. He could feel his own hands beginning to submit to the smooth yet powerful movement of the creature and swore every liter of sweat was pouring down his face.

"We have to get this thing to people who know how to handle dangerous --" Erik started to say before being interrupted by sudden eruption of spraying cold water that came roaring from behind.

A long, serpentine shape leaped from the water and slammed onto the motorboat. Chad quickly drew back and tried to reach for any sort of object to use as a weapon. He found nothing, but the creature slid onto one of the boat seats. In that time the vessel began to tilt into the water and before Eric knew it, the boat was almost partway into the water.

But those thoughts were shattered as a sound that resembled a cross between an alligator's snarl and a roaring bull broke the water. Erik turned around.

The damn creature -- which he saw was an Ogopogo -- had bitten onto Chad's left leg in a frenzied state. The enraged water beast was so preoccupied with tearing *anything* apart it forgot about its real target.

"Oh crap!" Erik exclaimed as he frantically looked around for anything to hit the creature with -- only to look down at his own hands with a frustrated grunt... "I really hate to do this!"

In no time flat, he flew onto the creature and tried hitting it in the nose.

Didn't work!

Erik next tried grabbing onto the nostril to get the creature's attention to focus on him instead of the injured Chad.

Didn't do Jack, even if he tried.

Erik tore a can of bear spray out of his coat pocket, aimed directly into the creature's nostrils, and pulled the trigger. The stinging spray of pink jalapeno oil and whatnot jammed down the Ogo-creature's nostrils like water from Hell.

The creature roared in pain as it felt the mini-waterfall of stinging sensations run down its sinuses. With unparalleled viciousness, the Ogopogo lashed out with its tail as it rocked the already tilted boat. The cold lake water began to splash up, obscuring Chad's and Erik's vision.

In response to the bear spray assault, the creature bit down further on Chad's leg, still not knowing where the Giant Eel was at that point. Chad began to feel the teeth cutting through the muscle and reach right down to the bone.

"Get off me!" Chad yelled as he kicked the creature in the snout, adding injury to the already stinging pain the Ogo-creature felt.

The lake monster let go of Chad's leg but ripped its teeth out of the man's calves in the process. As a result, torn pieces of flesh went flying in all directions --

Only for the Ogopogo to yowl back in pain.

Erik and Chad looked surprised and confused as to why the creature yowled -- until they saw another, very different-looking tail whip up from behind the Ogopogo.

***

The Giant Eel's teeth had a firm grip on the tail of the Ogo-creature, refusing to let it go this time. The Eel played entirely on the defensive, but the Ogopogo was now on the motorboat and it wasn't about to let this newest opportunity slip. The huge serpentine fish tugged the legendary lake monster off the vessel and into the depths to re-commence their bloody fight.

The Eel hesitated for a minute. A wound on its left side was beginning to open up; a nasty dermal would from the Ogo-creature's clawed feet began to bleed even more. The pain ran up its elongated body and began to bother the Eel as it loosened the tight grip it had over the lake monster's tail.

In an instant, the Eel thrashed wildly as the Ogopogo's posterior appendage began to lash the water about. Up, down, and a myriad of other directions whipped past the unsympathizing eyes of the Eel as it gripped its opponent's tail ever harder. The enormous predatory fish's teeth began to shake as the thrashing became increasingly intense.

Soon, the tail lifted the Eel out of the water a full seven feet and smacked its elongated form onto the water several times. The impact with the water's surface felt like hitting concrete. Consequently, each blow knocked the Giant Eel's senses out of whack. The friction against the monstrous fish's smooth skin stung like an attack from a thousand wasps, except synchronized to less than a second.

The final blow knocked the Eel off the Ogo-creature's tail and the former swam off, dazed and confused after the hard-hitting barrage.

What the Eel did not realize was that it failed to hear the Ogopogo submerge behind it. The splash of its abrupt submersion reverberated through the water, yet the Eel was too dazed to react as it retreated into the depths.

This would prove to be an unwise decision, even for a cold-hearted aquatic predator.

***

"Chad, are you alright?" Erik yelled at the truck driver as he got up after just dodging the very irate Ogo-creature.

Chad's leg was bleeding badly after the lake monster had unceremoniously ripped its teeth out of the limb and whipped the Giant Eel around like a toothy ragdoll. To make matters worse, the boat was half full of water.

"Yeah, I-I'm fine! It just hurts like *el diablo*," grimaced Chad as he tried to get himself up onto one of the boat's seats.

Blood trickled from his badly injured leg, with the crimson-brown liquid dribbling into the clear lake water that had partially filled the boat. Chad was struggling to stand-up without rocking the vessel.

"Here, let me give you a hand," said Erik as he provided Chad with a boost, carrying him over to the nearest seat.

Sighing, Erik put his hands up to his head. He tried to figure something out amongst the slowly filling water. This was easier said than done, of course. The multitude of unanswered questions surrounding the circumstances was beginning to wear the young man down. Trying to go through all of them one by one was proving near impossible. Questions like, *why is the Ogopogo creature acting so aggressive? Why is it battling the Giant Eel?*

Many more such queries filled his mind, much like Hercules cutting the heads off the Hydra -- only for two more to grow back in their place. It only took a few more seconds until something hit Erik like a proverbial monster tail-whip to the stomach.

"Wait a second," Erik said under his breath as he realized what might be going on.

"What is it, young-un?" Chad asked in a world of pain as he tied a tourniquet from the first aid kit around his torn leg.

"I was just thinking that the Ogopogo creatures -- based on the research and reports I've read -- are very docile. All the research I've done into purported stories of "the lake demon" were actually not a part of this creature's legacy in First Nations' lore. And there has not been one confirmed report of the creature attacking anyone. But that doesn't exclude -- "

"Boy, what are you trying to get at?"

"What I'm trying to say is, up until that Giant Eel got into the lake, the Ogo-creatures haven't acted intentionally aggressive. But now, that one Ogopogo is suddenly trying to fight like the Devil, hellbent on ridding its territory of that Giant Eel. It's as if..." Erik trailed off as if a sudden revelation bit him in the throat like a viper.

"Like what? Tell me, boy."

Erik took a deep breath and before Chad's eyes widened in terror and confusion, Erik finally replied.

"It's as if the Ogo-creatures are watching for *something else.*"

And something down in Erik's gut told him it was not the Giant Eel that the Ogopogo was arming itself against.

In one motion, Erik scooped up a bucket and began to haul water out of the boat. The splashing became more frantic as the rhythm of water being dumped back into the lake began to go quicker. Erik can't see the panic in his eyes, but he could feel it racing up his veins and into his heart.

Before Chad could comment again, Erik fired another comment. "We've got to do something. First, let's get all this water out of here!" Stunned but unwilling to drown with a wounded leg, Chad began to help as best he could despite his condition.

As he did so, he muttered, "This kid... knows more than he lets on."

***

The Ogopogo turned and lashed at the Giant Eel, ferociously. The Giant Eel dodged the blow and tried to retaliate with a vicious tail-whip. The creature of Lake Okanagan likewise dodged and blasted through the water toward its elongated opponent. The collision hit the Eel like a boulder-sized hammer and the marauder was blown back onto the muddy bottom.

The impact with the silt was akin to a mini-explosion. The resulting cloud of sediment expanded rapidly until it encompassed the whole area. The Giant Eel tried to see through the thick haze of deposit cloud, stringently attempting to catch sight of its implacable reptilian foe. The cloud of silt became frustratingly profuse, and the Giant Eel began to bite around in various directions within it, hoping to grasp its enemy in in its jaws. Nothing.

As the Giant Eel was caught in the dust cloud, the silt that was not stirred up moved very slightly. At first, the huge predatory fish was unable to detect this bit of motion through its frustrated efforts.

Then the silt moved again. This time, the Giant Eel detected it slightly. The Eel was becoming more aware of the muddy sediment which had settled to the bottom. The view it had was clearer than before. It swerved its massive head, its coal black eyes growing wider. If the marauder was human, it would have sworn that something had just moved beneath the silt.

Just before the Eel could get close to the sedimentary bottom, the Ogo-creature burst out from under the silt. Its eyes were furiously focused, with teeth bared and ready to tear into the Eel's body with the ferocity of a rabid grizzly bear. Hitting the Eel with the force of an SUV, the lake creature smashed its adversary into the hard earth of the lake bottom.

The Eel was stunned from experiencing the full force of being slammed into the hard, jagged rock. The sharp edges were beginning to bruise the Eel's rounded head, and to make matters worse, the wound on the side of the Eel's body had opened up once more.

In an act of desperation, the Eel bit onto the nose of the Ogo-creature, driving its teeth into it hard. It could hear the underwater caterwaul of the Ogopogo as the lake monster struck back with its clawed hand. In one swift motion, the Ogo-creature's foot slammed into the side of the monster Eel and sent it into the mid-water column.

The Ogopogo then lunged at its tubular adversary -- but failed to see that it wasn't moving out of the way. Instead, the Eel gurgled in predatory satisfaction. This was *exactly* the situation it had been hoping for.

Just before it noticed, the Ogo-creature spotted a small whitish glow near the bottom of its foe. Then, it felt a slight charge in the water -- *like static electricity.* Before the Ogopogo could react, the electric charge spiked into a powerful shock. The reptilian lake monster suddenly went limp; though still alive, it began falling towards the bottom. Panic set in as the Ogo-creature realized that it was unable to move any of its limbs, including its tail. Needless to say, the lake monster's heart rate spiked up a tremendous level.

The Eel closed in, its cavernous maw open to tear the flesh out of its victim. Its razor-sharp teeth gleamed in the late afternoon sunlight that pierced the otherwise dark waters. Its eyes became visibly excited as it ominously approached the now weakened Ogopogo.

As it drew closer, the Eel opened its jaws at the lake monster's throat – when without warning, a harpoon-like arrow was shot at the elongated giant fish. The sharp weapon hit directly into its open wound, blood clouding the water like crimson silt from the lake bottom.

The Eel let out a bloody croak and retreated lower into the Okanagan depths. The serpent-shaped beast looked in the direction where the arrow was shot to behold a brown-haired young man with light blue eyes and wearing goggles standing back. In his hands was a firearm that was built more like a miniature harpoon gun.

***

Gotcha! Erik triumphantly thought as he saw the blood flowing off the Eel's wound. This was his last-minute plan and luckily it was right on the mark, as the monster fish's wound was opening even more. Unfortunately, he was too focused on this small victory to notice what was coming next. Put short, Erik knew the battle would get ugly fast, so he decided to use one of his self-defense tools and formulate a crack plan: to distract the Eel *and make himself the target.*

The Eel, sensing the young man's arrogance, lunged at him. Erik barely managed to keep up with the giant fish as it blitzed through the water like a man-eating torpedo, its teeth glistening like one-inch swords. Before he knew it, the creature bit into his shoulder and began to rip and tear pieces of flesh off him.

Erik screamed, though the sound of his shrieking was distorted by the water. Before he could do anything else, his right hand grabbed the Eel by the lower jaw. He tried to pry it off him before he realized he was getting too much water into his lung system.

Damn it! Get off me! Erik thought in desperation as the Eel kept furiously tearing into him. The young man's strength was quickly waning, and his vision started to go blurry. For a minute, the embrace of darkness rushed in to claim him… and Erik knew better than to deny Death its wishes.

Suddenly, something knocked into its chin and the painful sensation of teeth was released from Erik's shoulder. His eyes popped open in shock. The Eel was being dragged away into the water at an alarming rate. The eyes of the grotesque giant fish were bulging in horror and its clamp-like maw was biting all around as if trying to pry itself from the force dragging it down.

Why is the Eel being dragged into the water? Upon looking carefully, Erik spotted the cause. He felt his heart leap sky high when he saw what was dragging the Eel!

Only just able to continue moving and fighting, the Ogopogo heaved the Eel down into the depths. As one may have expected, the Giant Eel was thrashing wildly and biting at the Ogo-creature, trying its damnedest to break free!

But the Ogopogo simply carried it down further into the darkness, where no light would reveal the real victor of the fight to human eyes.

The Ogo-creature kept on swimming despite not having 100% of its speed with a determined expression filling whatever may pass for its soul. At last, the reptilian lake monster reached the spot where the final battle would be held and tossed the Eel into the muddy lake floor.

The silt cleared and the Eel looked up at its dragon-like assailant. For the first time in the fight, the Eel began to hiss in anger at the Ogopogo.

***

"Faster! Faster!" Erik screamed in excitement and sheer nervousness as the boat raced across the water. Chad was driving the vessel as quickly as possible towards the location of the fight.

Ignoring all questions posed by Chad, Erik concentrated on where in the heck the two watery enigmas might be battling. Every possibility ran through Erik's head like a volley of gunshots: Paul's Tomb, The Bennett Bridge, Gellatly Bay, Green Bay -- none of the following locations seemed to click.

That is, until Erik realized there is one possible location.

Squally Point! For some reason, Squally Point -- characterized by the sharp, jutting point just past a small islet -- has been pinpointed as the home of the Ogopogo creatures. Even the Native Americans had stories of something living offshore of Squally Point, and a handful of sightings place that as the home of the creatures somehow.

"God damn it, kid," Chad yelled over the motorboat, tired with all the cryptic actions. "What exactly are we doing now?"

"You'll see in a minute, damn it," Erik yelled.

Even he was getting impatient, but he simply couldn't let this battle go unsupervised! If there was a chance the Giant Eel could win, then the casualties on the lake could get out of control. Chad, he knew especially, would not want to see that happen, considering how he -- albeit accidentally -- caused the invasion.

"So, why? Why are you following the Eel's battle instead of reporting back," Chad was obviously more frustrated this time than before. "Why are you so concerned about the battle? What is making you act like this, especially when you might die?"

Erik fell silent. His heart leapt to his throat as he struggled to find a way to answer Chad's questions.

Finally, he found the words. "Because I don't want people to see cryptids as 'monsters'... and that goes for the creatures fighting now! Think about it. Most people who report seeing mystery creatures -- Sasquatch as well as the various lake creatures -- aren't joking or seeking fame. *They just want someone to listen to their stories.*

"But these people are treated as crazies., And the creatures they see? They're dismissed as illusions; products of overactive imaginations. Hell, the creatures people see could care less about humanity and are just trying to survive, and yet we call them *monsters?* If even just one cryptid kills another person – I - I -- don't know what would happen then. To be honest, I hope it never happens."

Chad was taken aback by Erik's heavy answer and went silent as well. It was true: he would be treated as crazy! Hell, he treated people who told him similar stories the same way before and now, guess what? He is now on a boat after having had his truck crash into the lake while a creature he had inadvertently transported there was now fighting a legendary cryptid reported by numerous people for hundreds of years.

The irony is that now *he* is one of those 'crazy people'.

Chad paused for a minute to find the words that would fit the situation. Suddenly, he heard Erik grunt as he saw the water boil, then churn -- and finally, explode!

"Stop the boat!" Erik yelled.

The yacht just began to stop as the finale to the battle unraveled before their eyes.

***

A huge surge of water bulged out in front of the boat, causing Chad to stop the vessel. The Giant Eel burst out of the water. It had new gashes running down its body and guts flailing in the wind. A rabid look adorned its already cold face. The Ogopogo quickly followed suit. It breached the water like a demented *Free Willy* knock-off and crashed onto the Giant Eel. The Eel charged for another electric shock, but that trick wouldn't work twice.

The Ogopogo ripped into the Giant Eel's stomach and tore out a large chunk of viscera. Blood spattered about like a sick, twisted version of fireworks. The warm and sticky liquid spattered the faces of Erik and Chad like crimson-colored mud. The reptilian lake creature grasped the Giant Eel in its powerful jaws and hurled the invader onto the front of the motorboat. The Eel thrashed around as it made an agonizing sound resembling a cross between a bellowing alligator and squealing pig being put to the slaughter.

Erik and Chad fell back and tried to scramble out of the way of the enormous eel's way. Chad slumped to his knees and nearly vomited at the sight of the monster fish's torn guts spluttering out onto the boat. He then began to get up and raise his fists to hit the creature in anger, only to be stopped by Erik.

The Ogopogo cocked its head as it saw Erik's restraining action. It didn't understand human language, but it seemed to realize that Erik was telling the other individual of his species to stop. All of that was soon washed away, however, as the Giant Eel slithered onto the edge of the boat and launched itself back into the water.

The monster fish was not in good shape. In fact, it was best to say it was on the brink of death. Nevertheless, it blasted towards the Ogopogo with all its predatory instincts focused into one last assault.

The Ogopogo was only too eager to oblige its opponent. The monstrous marine reptile swam toward the Eel, and at once the two descended into a vicious one-on-one battle. A frenzy of bites, claw slashes, and tail whips blurred into one malicious beat-down between the two competing alpha inhabitants of Lake Okandagan. The lake water seemed to boil as the Eel wildly lashed out against its opponent, finally losing consciousness as it lunged for the final blow.

The Eel's vise-like maw bit down in the direction which its opponent was located -- but it failed to see the Ogopogo had maneuvered out of the way. In a swift motion, the Eel's head was locked into place and yanked upwards towards the Ogo-creature. In a swift, graceful motion, the Ogopogo spiraled upwards and broke the surface of the water.

What happened next made Erik and Chad's jaws drop.

As the Ogopogo breached out of the water, it bit down onto the upper jaw of the Eel. In one brutal yet beautiful motion, it ripped off the jaws' hinges in a glorious yet gruesome display of water and blood. A wave of crimson spewed from the Eel's mouth as if a blood-filled bomb had exploded.

The Giant Eel went limp as its life was siphoned away in an instant. The barely visible pupils faded into complete darkness and its lower jawbone hung loosely from its face. The elongated mutant fish was clearly as dead as a doornail, to borrow one of Erik's analogies of choice. The Ogopogo triumphantly bellowed and tossed the Eel's carcass into the water, where it began to sink to the cold depths of Okanagan Lake.

The Ogopogo, "The Sacred Creature of the Lake," had won. The mysterious water beast turned and looked back at Erik and Chad. The expression in the creature's eyes spoke of thankfulness and wisdom before it sunk back into the waters of Okanagan Lake once again.

And just as before the battle started, the lake grew calm and silent once again.

***

Chad and Erik got back to shore and as they did so, the RCMP came up to them. The officers thoroughly questioned them over what happened on the lake. The story they told, as per Erik's suggestion, is that they were not exercising enough caution when the boat was struck by something. Chad fell into the water, as the story went, and Erik had jumped in to help him. They were attacked by the "whatever-it-was" that killed the unfortunate RCMP diver, and luckily Erik managed to drive it off. The rationale for the story is that Erik told Chad he could report the incident to the former's cryptid research organization and not worry about anyone thinking he was one of the "crazies."

"So, what happened is that we spotted the creature heading towards --" Erik gestured to Squally Point just to the south. "Though I will say, officers, you should check the area just before you get to there. I have a feeling you'll find it… there!" Erik pointed to an area further north.

"The kid has a point," Chad concurred. "Besides, if you don't find anything just keep a watch out. And if no other incidents happen… well, let's just say the creature I was carrying died from exposure to the freshwater environment."

The officers said they would note all of that when they took their crews onto the lake for investigation. Finally, Erik and Chad offered their condolences to Bill Melnyk's family.

After all the various parties had left, Erik turned to Chad. "What happens now, sir? Will you still be in the trucking business?"

Chad shrugged. "That's for my boss to decide. But, if you want to know my personal thoughts, I still feel bad for what happened." Chad sighed while evincing look that was packed with regret.

"Don't keep blaming yourself. It's no good to keep going over the same thing more than twice. Plus, the Eel is dead and at the bottom of the lake."

Chad simply smiled for a moment before a quizzical look formed on his face. "Hey kiddo… mind if I ask you something?"

Erik nodded, uncertain of what Chad is going to ask.

"How did you know things would go down the way they did? And how do you know all of this "cryptid" stuff? Seems to me like you're part of some organization by the looks of your shirt."

Erik feigned a shocked expression, and then sheepishly smiled. "Oh boy, looks like you caught me! Well, I might as well fess up -- you see, I'm just an aspiring researcher who has read a lot. That's all."

That answer still didn't satisfy Chad when Erik's phone suddenly rang. He took immediate note of it and motioned for Chad to wait a second. The latter nodded, turned his back and waited. It didn't take long for Erik to start answering -- to which Chad turned around when he heard something going on.

"What? You can't be serious! After all of that…" Erik spouted in intervals, clearly talking in between someone else talking to him.

Chad observed Erik's face becoming more serious. At the end of the phone call, which took less than two minutes, Erik sighed. His eyebrows cocked upwards in an "it can't be helped, then" manner as he gave his statement.

"I'll get there as soon as possible! Okay thanks, Aquila! *Nos vemos!*"

Erik ended the call and turned to Chad.

"Look, I'm sorry, sir, but I have to go," said Erik as he moved towards his car. Something else has come up. But, thanks for coming along with me and sorry for dragging you into the mess. Good luck to you and your family."

When Erik got to his vehicle, he sat down onto the driver's side, closed the door, and started the engine.

It was at that moment Chad realized something. The Giant Eel was only the beginning…

***

As Erik hit the road, his head was spinning in a hundred different directions. The battle with the Giant Eel only confirmed what he had suspected all along: the Ogopogo Tribe of Okanagan Lake are not man-eaters at all. They are merely powerful creatures that are not opposed to self-defense, and certainly do not welcome any invasive creatures into their lakes. The fight with the Giant Eel was proof of this theory.

Erik Halverson now left Peachland for a gas-up. It was clear that his next destination was to get to Kalamalka Lake. This was a smaller body of water outside of Okanagan Lake where another report of something in the waters was making waves in the local press.

Except that this time, what was being reported was worse than the Giant Eel. Erik sighed. It was time to get back to work as a cryptid researcher.

"One of these days," Erik said to himself, "I need to find a cryptid that will not rip my arm off!"

THE END?

WHY DON'T CANNIBALS EAT CLOWNS?

VAMPIRE vs KILLER CLOWN

BY KEVIN HEIM

July 1997

Prague had been awful, another huge mistake. January was badly hurt by the Inquisitor, Bloody Bill barely escaped from Police Commissioner Zbik, and there was a better than odds chance January had been fooling around with Count Daninsky the whole time they were in Poland. If he hadn't wrangled a favor from Pan Twardowski out of the trip, Bill would consider it a colossal failure.

Right now, his only concern was for Jan. The pain she was suffering would continue until Bill found a way to undo the damage. It wasn't right that vampires should suffer physical or mental trauma; suffering was for the living. Bloody Bill and January hadn't led easy lives when they were mortal. Becoming undead had been more of a blessing than a curse, at least until they split away from their vampire family and left England to see Europe on their own.

Bill knew they hadn't been ready, and with insanity taking more and more of January's personality every day, they were likely never going to be ready. But Bill possessed a poet's heart, even if it no longer came with a poet's soul. He couldn't give up on his dream of finding happiness for January and himself, no matter how many humans he had to kill for that happiness.

With that kind of dream comes ambition, and ambition breeds hope. They say America is the land of opportunity, and when he traveled to the New World decades earlier with his brood, Bloody Bill found that America offered a lot of opportunities. The vampires tend to be a lot more progressive in terms of finding interesting solutions, and the humans tend to be far less likely to prepare themselves against true evil. Americans are so faithless he was even able to set foot in some churches the last time he was there!

Two weeks later they were arriving in Boston, and despite the bountiful food available onboard the *SS Tipton*, poor January was no better. Bill didn't like problems that couldn't be solved with copious quantities of blood. But he hadn't expected an easy solution, which is why he had an old acquaintance waiting for him at the docks.

"William!" James, dressed as a uniformed police officer, greeted the pair at the bottom of the gangplank as EMTs raced aboard the ship to treat the few surviving passengers. "Always a pleasure. Pity the circumstances aren't better. Officially I'm here investigating the strange deaths, but why don't you meet me at my parlor in an hour? And try not to attract too much attention on your way there; I'm trying to keep Boston under the radar... or sonar."

"*Your* parlor? So, Carl is out? Congratulations, daywalker. But there's no time for social calls. I need -- Jan needs help now."

"That's one of the advantages of running the Parlor; makes it easy to provide transportation for those of us with... sensitivities."

Within half an hour Bill and January were safely avoiding the encroaching dawn in plush coffins loaded into black Lincoln Towncar hearses. He could hear and feel the ride well enough. Bill trusted that James had arranged a location for them far from the scorching light of day. He pushed the lid open a crack, and was relieved to see the cold dead light of fluorescent bulbs pouring in. The room appeared to be a medical examination room, an annex to a morgue. Bill wasn't sure if this was his final destination, or just the most convenient place to unload coffins.

He picked up a blank toe tag. "Arkham, Massachusetts. Now why do I feel I should know this place?"

Just as he began lifting the lid off January's coffin, the sound of heels on cement stairs echoed into the room.

"Ah, bollix!" Bill exclaimed and quickly shut the coffin.

Jan was still fitfully thrashing about inside but making no effort to extract herself. With no time to find a hiding place, Bloody Bill laid down on the nearest autopsy table and pretended to be the corpse that he was, eyes closed till he could tell what he was dealing with.

"Oh, I've got a live one here!" a chipper voice called out with a giggle as a door was thrust open. "Keep it moving, Doc; we mustn't keep our publics waiting! Or is that our privates? Doctor, *do* behave yourself!"

A muffled cry is the only answer the laughing man received, followed by the "thud" of a body hitting the floor.

"Why didn't you tell me this room was occupied?" The voice made its way over to Bill. "Hey pal, how about showing a little respect for the living? Now, why don't you make like a bat and die a horrible, painful death?"

Bill opened his eyes and sat up slowly. With luck he'd be mistaken for a zombie and no one would make a grab for the cross hanging over the door.

"Didn't know they had a med school at clown college."

Bill took in the twisted, painted face of the man standing over him with a bit of a shock. The man smelled human, but looked more warped, more "gone," than any vampire Bill had ever met. He wore pale blue scrubs over top of what looked like orange prison togs, except for the long sleeves trailing behind. This suggested the man was a psychiatric patient who until recently had been bound, straitjacket-style. And with skin that white, hair that green, maybe the word "human" didn't truly apply to the poor creature anymore.

"Clown? You callin' *me* clown? Kiefer Sutherland called, and he wants his hair back! But he said you should keep the duster; it makes you look dangerous. Like a wizard or something. That's not right, maybe it was... say, you remind me of a joke I once killed. Good times. Or were they? One thing I never could stomach about living in Nazi Germany; all the damn vampires. But they do have excellent taste in skulls!"

Completely thrown by all the inane gibberish, Bill hadn't even reacted before the razor had found its way to his neck. Shoving the gloved hand away forcefully, he grabbed the blade for himself and held it to his adversary's face.

"What are you on about?" Bill yelled directly into the clown's visage. "Did we meet in Germany?"

"Did we? What an absurd question! I'm sure I would remember something like that. Unless it was all in your head."

"You mean *your* head."

"Oh, right. Sorry, I keep getting us mixed up."

Once again, the garishly grinning ghoul had already out-maneuvered Bill. This time he'd twirled around to land himself a seat on January's coffin. It rumbled a bit, and January's voice erupted forth. "Billy, where have all the *mome raths outgrabed* to? I can't find a one in here!"

The clown put hand to chin and smiled, "Oh, I like this one. I'm trading everything for what's in the box!"

Bill moved to stop him. "Don't you go disturbing Jan!"

But the gangly clown with the too-wide smile was far faster than any human Bloody Bill had met before. He already had the coffin open and was helping January to her feet. "I don't see how that'd be possible; this delicate little flower is as disturbed as they come already!"

The clown gave a half-bow and kissed January's laced glove. "*Au chante, mademoiselle*. My name is Jackson Gray. Or, maybe it's Jack Grayson. Which do you like better? Remember, there are no wrong answers."

Not wishing to upset Jan, Bill opted to seek information from the clown's captive colleague. The supposed doctor, a buxom twenty-something blonde dressed more like a candy striper from an exploitation movie than a medical professional, was bound and gagged with duct tape, her eyes imploring Bill to aid her. Since she had to have seen him rise off the table, she must have been desperate indeed to seek help from the undead.

Bloody Bill ripped the tape from her mouth and pulled her upright. "Who's the dandy?"

"That's... that's Mr. Jay," the girl broke into sobs before she could finish. "But he's out of control. He needs his medicine or there's no telling what might happen."

"Right, then." Bill removed the tape from her hands and feet. "Attend to laughing boy. I have to find out who's in charge of this asylum before any more of -- Aaah!"

The doctor raised the barrel of her squirt gun to her lips and blew on it for effect. "Like that? Looks like this medicine is just what the doctor ordered!"

"Good one, Doxie!" said Mr. Jay. "Now, aren't you glad we stopped to kill that priest earlier?"

Doxie Moll gave the clown a broad, toothy smile. "You think of everything, Jasper! So, what are we gonna do with the not-so stiffs?"

"Why don't you put him in a room with a view of the sunrise, while Miss January helps me load these coffins back into the car?"

Jan moved, as if in a daze, to lift her coffin, never thinking to question Jasper's orders. "Are we going on a picnic? I like picnics. Billy, why don't you ever take me on picnics anymore?"

Bill, his game face showing through the smoldering holy water burn across his right cheek, grabbed the doctor and lifted her off the floor by the neck. "Just kill the bloody clown so we can get out of here, love. If the doctors are this crazy, we'll be better off looking elsewhere."

Doxie Moll, seemingly oblivious to her own predicament, started bawling at Jasper's attentions towards Jan. "You told me I was your medicine! What do you need a vampire for when you have me?"

"Bloody! Shut! The Hell! Up!" Bill slammed the doctor into the wall repeatedly, cracking the tile in the process, but even so she never took her eyes off the clown. "You two are balmy! You deserve each other!"

He threw the doe-eyed doctor across the room at her pathological patient-turned-lover.

"It's nothing personal, Moxie," Jasper offers as consolation, still working on hauling the coffin into the bed of the hearse. "Keeping you alive is a burden I don't need; just another mouth to feed. Janny won't be hindered by little things like breathing, or--"

POW!

Billy licked the blood from his knuckles, having just punched Jasper square in the jaw. Not surprisingly, even his blood tasted diseased, and Bill spat it out. "Enough! Are you too far gone to realize what I can do to you?"

"Heh. He-heh. Ha! Ha ha ha ha ha… ha ha!" The clown pulled himself off the floor, not even bothering to wipe the blood from his mouth. "I… don't… *care*! What you can do to me? What *can* you do to me? Kill me? Good luck; better men than you already *have*! Turn me into one of those… *you-things?* I don't *need* your necromancy, I'm *already* a god! And I eat demon wanna-be scum like you for breakfast!"

Bill caught the glint of steel as Jasper drew another weapon. He caught the arm, and saw it was a scalpel that was already streaked with blood.

"I'll bet you make a right scary clown at the circus and all," Bill said, "but against a true creature of the night, you're nothing. And I'm not waiting for breakfast. I'm eating you right now, bad blood and all."

With that, Bloody Bill sank his fangs into the white-skinned neck of Wicked Jasper. The sensation was usually an ecstatic one for Bill, savoring the elixir vitae as it flowed into him, carrying the very living essence of his victim with it. This time, there was no pleasure in the act, however. The blood was doing nothing to assuage his thirst. It was like drinking used motor oil, or maybe sandy sea water. Whatever it was in human blood that normally satisfied the demonic portion of Bill's vampire existence seemed to be completely absent in Jasper.

This would not satisfy his hunger, but there was plenty of time for that later. Now it was simply necessary to defeat a foe. Bill tore at the jugular to increase the flow and get this over with as quickly as possible.

Except... that's not what happened. Bill found himself swooning. He thought he might have even tried to let go of his prey but was unable to do so; it was as if he was being charged with electricity and had no control over his own muscles. He was mentally sinking into Jasper, getting lost in a life already lived, a life that should have ended already.

Bill had heard of vampires experiencing their victims' memories and emotions as they drained them, but never thought it was real. It always sounded like the kind of things those weepy "poor me; I'm the real victim" vampires would say to make themselves sound more romantic, and less pure fucking evil.

Bloody Bill himself was pure fucking evil, and proud of it. Emotions were for those with souls. Sure, he cared about January, but she was the vampire that sired him, and that might have created a blood bond between them. He'd heard of those happening as well.

Slowly, or so it seemed to him, Bill appeared to be trading minds with Jasper. If there was any precedent for this experience, it was likely a soul-gaze, something that wizards could sometimes initiate. So far as he knew, it didn't even apply to vampires. Now it was drawing him in, and it was overwhelming him. It was like watching a videotape of Jasper's life, backwards, with no way to stop it or look away.

Jasper came to Arkham a lot but left just as often. These moments flew by; apparently Jasper did not have a vested interest in what went on at the asylum and merely bided his time when forced to stay here. He had strong flashes of events in Boston, in New York, in Chicago, in Belfry, in Detroit; wherever the circus took him.

No, he was still seeing it backwards. When Jasper came to town, he brought the circus with him later. Garish colors, acrobats in tights, flashing lights, fortune tellers, screams, exotic animals, screams, freak shows, screams, showgirls, screams, thrill rides, screams, roustabouts, screams, screams, *screams!*

Wicked Jasper was far older than Bill thought he could be, older even than himself. Fifty years ago, Jasper was in Berlin, Germany, but he was called Casper there. Maybe Bill had met him during the war after all? Before that, he had been all over: Baltimore, Pittsburgh, Los Angeles, even locations as diverse as London, Paris, and Tokyo. Each time the clown showed up somewhere, a discordant carnival of chaos would spawn around him, as though he *was* the carnival. His presence transformed everything around him into... *him*, becoming part of his totality.

And the deaths. Bill was proud of the body counts he'd scored, and in fact used to brag about his kills to the other vampires in his old family. But Jasper (or Jack, or Huck, or whatever the clown's name really was) had killed *hundreds* of men and women over the years, over the centuries. He didn't dwell on the children though, which was a surprise. Plenty of boys and girls died by his hands, but Jasper seemed to consider them immaterial to his... work. The children didn't count. The children belonged to daddy.

Bill was starting to understand or coming as close as this madhouse whirlwind falling backwards through someone else's life could simulate. Jasper didn't need the deaths; he needed the madness. He killed, because killing created chaos, and he fed on the chaos.

He fed on the chaos.

Wicked Jasper was, in truth, a vampire. Not an undead human body playing host to a demonic parasite, but a vampire nonetheless. Whether he was Jasper or Jackson or Jim or Jerome or John, whether he seemed to be sowing misery or reveling in *schadenfreude*, the clown's true agenda was always chaos. He was an alpha predator that far surpassed those who required flesh or blood to sustain themselves.

Even his companion was just window dressing that he's replaced time and time again. Whether she was called Doxie Moll, or Moxie Doll, or some other name, she was always someone trapped by Jasper's charisma. He'd use her as his sounding board until he forgot she existed, or he scared her off, or he died (or *she* died).

And Jasper died a lot. Bill witnessed, in reverse, deaths by drowning, gun shot, electrocution, blunt force trauma… there were scores of deaths disrupting his corrupted life cycle. Moreover, each rebirth seemed to bring a new personality, new neurosis, a new face even; it was hard to tell with it all happening backwards, and Bill didn't have the presence of mind to psychoanalyze his gaoler.

Bill realized he was coming to the end but was helpless to stop it. Over 300 years ago, Jasper, no longer white-faced, was with his mother, a witch named Abbie, wandering the mountains of New England. Bill couldn't tell which colony they were in and frankly didn't care. The boy, once again called Jack, often went with Abby to meetings presided over by a tall man in black, in a building that resembled a small European church (at least on the outside). Jack and the other children were told that they were special, because Gray was their father instead of their mother. The women praised Black and Gray, using old world rituals. Bill had heard that some gypsies used to utilize such practices, though he'd never believed any humans willingly participated in rites that profane.

Bloody Bill, right at 100 years on this Earth, was terrified. As Jasper grew younger in his eyes, the odds of seeing the face of Gray, whoever or whatever that was, grew more and more likely. Bill has fought demons and vampires and other inhuman monsters before, and rarely batted an eye at the horror they represented. He usually took it as a challenge to prove he was worse than them. He'd even had encounters with the legendary Dracula, or at least with a vampire powerful enough to talk the talk and walk the walk.

But Gray and Black smacked of dark gods, as alien in nature to him as his demonic symbiosis would be to a modern physician, and indeed had been to a few doctors he'd tricked into attempting to treat him over the years. It was usually fun luring the scientifically inclined into getting too close to him in their efforts to understand his *condition*.

Bill wasn't going to fall for the same trick though. He knew he was doomed if he followed Jasper all the way back to his birth. With all his will he reached up both hands to his mouth, and when he couldn't push the skinny, emaciated clown away, he instead dislocated his own jaw to break the connection between them. The pain was terrible, but necessary. He'd wonder later about why he had to go to such extreme measures, but for now he was just happy to be in his own head again.

"Sorry, Blondie, but nobody rides for free!"

The Clown, now almost completely drained of blood, resembled a shriveled corpse with parchment pulled tight against his face in lieu of skin. Even his green hair had gone pale. The only real color on him at this point was the bright crimson where Bill had busted his lip moments earlier. How was he even conscious?

"You can pay the ferryman on your way out and be sure to tell all your friends!"

After saying that, Wicked Jasper clasped Bill's shoulders with both hands, ramming metal spikes through the leather jacket and straight into the bones. A surge of electricity rushed through him, dropping the vampire to the floor in convulsing spasms. Bill was only vaguely conscious, but he was aware that the suffering he was experiencing now, bad as it was, was nothing compared to what he's just gone through.

The clown doesn't know, not consciously. His shattered psyche can't grasp his own existence. Maybe Bill could use this to his advantage. Maybe there was still a chance of saving January.

Bill fought to stand up and vomited thick black blood, all he'd taken from Jasper. He was spent, and though he'd fed on humans less than 24 hours ago, it felt like he hadn't had a drop of blood in months. And on top of all that, he had a broken jaw and two taser conductors piercing his skin. If this came to a physical fight, he wasn't going to win.

"Wait! We can help each other!" Bill retched again, on his hands and knees, but this time only for effect. He popped his jaw back into place with a jerk and ripped the prongs out of his shoulders. "You want out of here, and so do we. If the four of us leave together, we can take turns driving, no stops. Get far away from Arkham and start a new act somewhere like Saint Louis or New Orleans."

It took a tremendous effort, but Bill stood up straight. He knew he'd be able to heal as soon as he drank more blood, human blood, so the discomfort was worth it.

Wicked Jasper cocked his head and sighed. "You have nothing to offer me, little batboy. Do yourself a favor and drop the savior routine; it's a lousy shtick and makes for –"

"Savior? Do you know how many people I've killed for fun? I'm no hero!"

BANG!

January's head exploded in a shower of blood, bone, and brain. The spraying ichor fouled the tiled wall and the coffin she had, until then, still been carrying. A cloud of pink mist clung to the air around her mostly intact face.

In the wink of an eye, Billy was at her side, cradling her body and holding what was left of her head together. She was a vampire, and human blood would restore the physical trauma. However, the exit wound was massive, and Bill was certain she would have brain damage, assuming she survived this at all.

"You see? A real monster would have left the girl and gone for the kill!" Jasper laughed as he climbed into the passenger seat of one of the hearses. "Come on, Doxie! You're driving the first leg!"

January worked her mouth like a fish, staring into nothing. Bill screamed.

"You bastard! Let's see how you feel when someone kills *your*— "

BANG! BANG!

Doxie Moll slumped against the open driver's door, then fell out. The blood pooled under her torso and spread quickly, indicating the shots were center mass.

"Sorry, doll," Jasper said with mock regret, "but I think we should see other people." Then he chuckled and turned his head to look back at the vampires. "Now, what was that you were saying?"

The clown slid over behind the wheel and drove out of the garage into the daylight, trailing his disconcerting laughter behind him. Bill didn't care. He was desperately holding January together, while he dragged her away from the coffin and over to the bloody corpse of the female doctor. She at least had smelled human and may have enough left in her to heal January's injuries.

Bill dipped his fingers in the pooling liquid and dribbled it over her wounds. He then wiped the rest onto her lips, forcing some inside her mouth.

The vampire was barely audible as he said, "Come on baby, stay with me."

If this was working, it wasn't working fast enough. Bloody Bill tore his left sleeve off with his teeth and bit hard into his own arm. His demon blood flowed over January's head, running into her hair, her eyes, her mouth, staining her Victorian dress.

Finally, her eyes fluttered, and she looked up at him with a weak smile. "Billy, I don't think I like this picnic."

"No worries, love. We aren't staying in Arkham anymore. We're going to find a nest where you can heal right proper. But first…"

Bill let her go as soon as she was sitting up in her own again. Then he bandaged his arm using the torn sleeve and headed for the stairs leading to the rest of the asylum.

"But first," he repeated, "I need to hydrate."

END

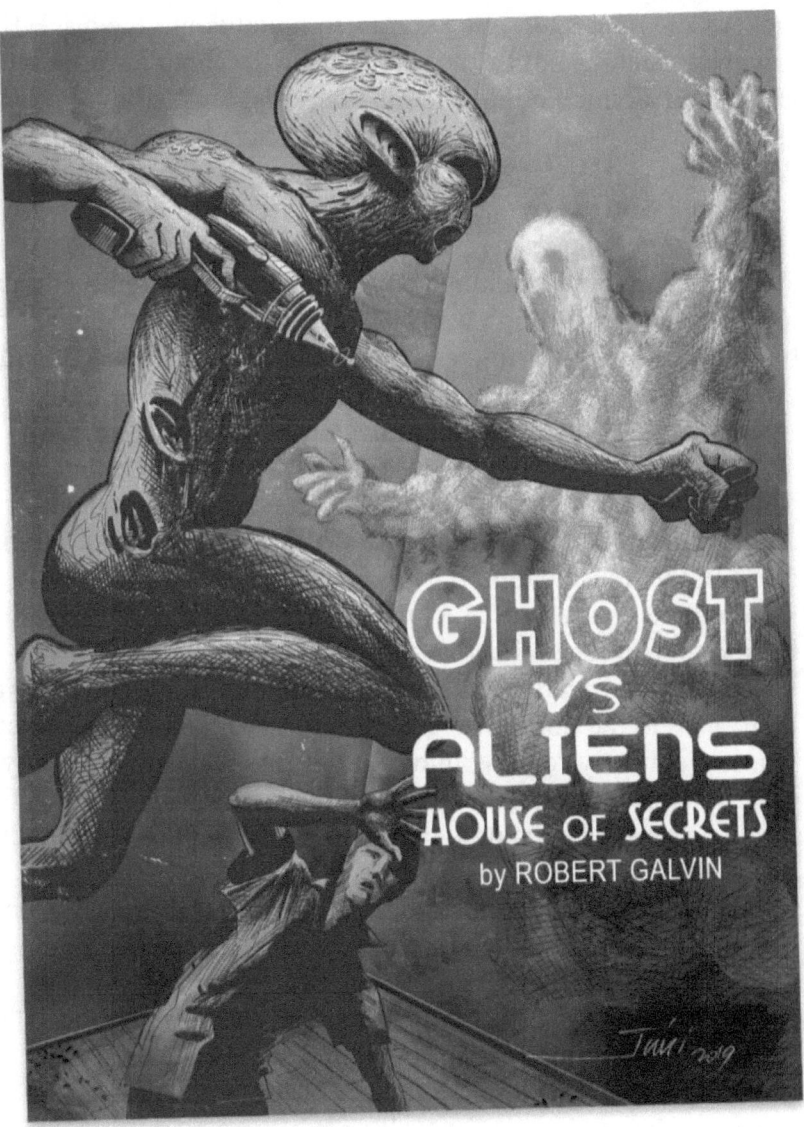

Middle-aged with a thin yet decent black beard, Dennis drove at a slow pace to his new little house, which he had purchased and moved to only a couple weeks prior. It was a bit isolated, but conveniently near a nice small town. His car began to make a racket s the rusted old thing stumbled noisily onto the brick-filled driveway. Dennis put the car in park and sat there for a moment. He sucked a bunch of air into his lungs and let it all out with a big sigh. Then he opened his car door and took a heavy step onto the driveway.

Dennis wore a grey jacket with a white shirt on the inside. However, the white shirt had been stained from an accidental spill at a coffee shop earlier in the day. His blue jeans were worn and torn from years of rough use. He wasn't too out of shape but had a bit of a beer belly starting -- which deep down he hoped to rid himself of; though in his current state, that was rather unlikely.

Dennis gave the house a quick glance, not necessarily for admiration, but more so because this is where his life had led him. The house wasn't exactly top tier quality. Faded paint and damaged wallpaper covered most of the walls. He wasn't living alone in the house either.

Many generations of arachnids had lived and died there, leaving behind their webs and corpses throughout, especially in the basement. However, German roaches mainly ruled the house as their own, to the point where they didn't fear Dennis too much and would frequently roam within his presence. Traps were set by an exterminator a week ago, but he told Dennis it would take a few weeks, or maybe even up to a month, to rid the house of the little pests.

So, for now, they continued their open romps about the floor and walls. Dennis loathed the existence of the insects, finding them the most annoying critters on Earth, beaten out only by the mosquito. Still, the house wasn't too bad. It had three levels: an upstairs, a main floor, a basement, and a working bathroom. At the same time, it wasn't the best quality house and there was a reason it was so cheap. Dennis gradually made his way through the small path to the equally small porch and then to the door.

Walking in, one could see that the residence was heavily worn out on the inside just as much as the outside, if not more. The house was very run down and beaten up. Only strands of sunlight, illuminating the amount of dust floating in the air, accessed the interior. The rest of the house was engulfed in darkness. Many of the few windows had thick curtains blocking out the sunlight.

The floor squeaked from the first step indoors. "Shit," Dennis sighed.

There was an attempt on the weary homeowner's part to clean up the place a bit, but he hadn't been in the mood to do so of late. As he walked in a bit further, he heard a loud crunch. Stuck to his shoe was now a crushed roach, but still alive and moving. How he hated those damn things! He stomped his foot down a few times to ensure the still-twitching insect's demise, then continued forth.

The house was sort of compact, as the kitchen was only a few steps away. There laid a table where Dennis would take a seat. For a moment he sat there, beginning to descend into his memories. He reached into his pocket and pulled out a small object.

For minutes he stared intensely at the item, lost in deep thought. A story was playing through his head, one derived via a memory from his own existence. Briefly, he thought of the good times, the touching moments that had helped him to become the man he is. However, as this story continued it took a wrong turn.

Like a switch had been flicked, his facial features changed. His face began to fill with the color of red, as did his now bloodshot, watery eyes. Dennis closed his lids, reflecting deeply on the past. It was hitting harder than the fastest truck or train, and it kept hammering him over and over. It was now all he could process; all he could think about.

Dennis clenched his hand holding the object into a tight fist and brought it up to his face. He began to shake, his eyes now spilling the tears they had accumulated.

***

Some time had passed since his breakdown, and he had since grown tired. The sun had vanished, and nighttime was about. Crickets filled the chilly night air with their noise. A long day had taken place, and Dennis had decided to bring it to a close.

The new mattress and sheets for the bed were soft and comfortable. He made certain his sleeping arrangements would be to his liking, as he could tolerate nothing less. Dennis hopped onto the bed, laying there for a while. There was a window to the side, through which a pine tree obstructed a good portion of the view. A few branches had lost their leaves for whatever reason. He studied the tree carefully as he laid there.

While doing so, the subtle movements of the pine tree's branches before him came about. It paused for a minute, then started again. He couldn't make it out, but guessed it was likely to be some sort of bird. Then, out of nowhere, it flew into view and onto the thick barren branches. It was an owl, now resting upon Dennis's house. Its blood-red eyes could stain themselves upon the mind, surging a chill through one's body.

The mysterious bird just stared at Dennis for an eerie minute before descending back into the branches. It was then he realized the scale of the thing. This bird was gargantuan; it had to be around six or seven feet at the very least! Dennis laid still for a while. He felt very uneasy but was amazed at how big the bird was. It unnerved him as much as it intrigued him. Despite this, Dennis was unable to stay awake to further investigate the anomalous avian and slipped into a deep sleep.

***

The sun shone onto Dennis's face in the morning as he woke. He was unemployed, so he didn't really have anywhere to be today, though he did have a list of job offerings on the table in the kitchen he planned to eventually skim through. Downtown, there was a hardware store Dennis had visited. There he had picked up a ton of cleaning supplies to clean up his place.

Dennis counted the cash he had brought with him and figured he had enough for a box of cigarettes, so he asked the vendor for one. The old man at the counter complied and placed it with the cleaning supplies. Dennis was informed of the amount owed, and he handed the elderly clerk all the cash he had on him. The old man counted it, then made a disappointed look.

Dennis was 25 cents short.

Though it pissed him off, Dennis knew he needed to ask for a quarter. There was a customer behind him that looked pleasant enough, so Dennis asked the guy if he could spare a quarter. Thankfully the man kindly gifted one to him. This gave Dennis some hope that maybe the residents in this area were good people who would treat him nicely.

All dreams were shattered when the old man behind the counter had an issue with this. "C'mon, what're you doing? Don't do that, don't give him that quarter."

Dennis was taken aback by this man. "The fuck is your problem? You're giving me shit for asking for a little quarter?"

"The fuck is *your* problem?" the old man responded. "You should've just had the quarter yourself!"

The generous customer behind Dennis then jumped in. "Calm down, calm down. Just let him use my quarter. It's nothing to make a big deal out of."

The old man seemed to agree and accepted the quarter. Dennis had a lot he wanted to say but didn't want to worsen matters. All he did was give the old man a look before walking out the door and heading to the parking lot.

"Don't mind Gary," a voice from behind told Dennis. "He's a bit of an old fart."

Dennis turned to see the man who lent him a quarter, giving him a look of surprise. He studied the kind stranger more closely now. The man was likely around the same age as Dennis, maybe even a bit older with some grey hairs on his beard.

"Name's Albert," the man continued. "You're the one who just moved in a little down the road, right?"

"Yeah," was Dennis's simple reply.

Albert recognized that Dennis wasn't really in the chatting mood, but he still wanted to pursue a conversation. "It's a nice house you got."

"Nah, I wouldn't say that," Dennis replied. "Thanks though."

"Yeah," Albert laughed a bit, "I guess you're right."

There was a brief pause in the conversation, before Albert continued. "Anything out of place happen to you there? I mean, out of the ordinary?"

Dennis was taken by surprise with this question. "What do you mean?"

"Well, that house has had quite the history, you know."

Dennis shook his head. He had no clue what the guy was talking about.

"Quite a few moved out," Albert continued, "claimed strange things happened there. You know, ghosts!"

Dennis laughed, as he couldn't believe the man was going there. "Ghosts? And you believe that shit?"

"I've seen it when I went ghost hunting with one of the prior owners. Some crazy stuff goes on up there. There was a suicide, a sacrifice, strange lights. A couple even claimed to have seen some creature resembling the Mothman!"

This conversation was now considered over by Dennis, as his new acquaintance seemed insane to him.

He began laughing. "Holy shit, you do believe in that. Well, I don't buy into those fairy tales!"

Before Albert could really reply, Dennis got into his raggedy car and pondered for a minute as he drove away. He thought of the owl. Before the thought could continue, he shook his head with a mildly amused look. As he told Albert, he wasn't going to buy into some fairy tales or stupid bedtime stories.

***

Dennis cleaned up around the house a bit, but after an hour or so he wasn't in the mood anymore. He went out to the front porch and plopped down on the chair, where he spent hours upon hours with a cigarette in hand. The sun began to retreat, the breeze in the air chilled, and the crickets stole the night.

Over and over Dennis reflected on his life. Slowly, he began to drift away. Before he could pass out, he heard a loud bang which immediately gained his full attention, causing him to stand up. He believed the sound could've been the front door slamming. If so, Dennis wondered if this could mean someone had just entered his house.

He opened the door as quietly as he could -- though it ended up squeaking anyway -- and walked in. Despite having three levels, it was a rather small house with not too many rooms. He cautiously walked through the entire residence and looked everywhere he could think of. No one was found; he was alone. Dennis was drained by then, especially after that weird occurrence. He had a small frozen dinner with a beer before heading up the stairs to bed.

It was three in the morning according to Dennis's clock hanging at the end of the room by the door. The room was barely illuminated by a night light on the left side of it. The temperature outside was slightly chilly, but nothing too bad. However, something was off, and it took Dennis a moment to discover what.

He suddenly found that his body was stiff, unable to budge from its current position. Dennis began breathing faster while beginning to panic. A cold sensation surged through his form as it dawned on him that he wasn't alone. It was then he noticed a dark black figure standing motionless at the end of his bed. To his right stood another figure.

The first figure laid a hand upon Dennis's exposed chest, which was strange as he had always gone to bed with his shirt buttoned up. But there was something odd about its hand, as it was holding something. It was just too dark to make it out.

As soon as this occurred, Dennis woke up in a sweat. He looked all over the room, shaking as he did so. The figures had vanished. He wiped sweat from his face with his right hand, completely in shock from what had just occurred.

***

Dennis had done some research that morning after the encounter, quick to find a logical explanation. He had found out about sleep paralysis, something that happens rarely when one goes to bed and partly wakes but is unable to move and hallucinates. Dennis found this answer satisfactory.

He sat back in his chair, staring at his computer. Within his mind he pondered the words of Albert. The owl, the door, and the figures in his room. He was lost with his thoughts for so long, his computer dimmed, preparing to sleep.

Dennis continued fixing up the place. In his mind, the more the house was cleaned, the more this would annoy and affect the pesky roaches. He swept the ground floor, ridding it of any dust bunnies. Following up, he mopped it with a bleach mixture.

Afterward, windows were wiped, and the cabinets were made as spotless as they could ever be. One cabinet he opened up took Dennis by surprise, but it really shouldn't have.

Corpses of fallen roach brethren were scattered everywhere.
The living roaches ran, slipping out through small cracks in the
wood. This was the thing that really made him hate them. They
knew they weren't supposed to be there, they would always scurry
off as quickly as possible once discovered.

Dennis cleaned out the bodies, which fell apart very easily, then
wiped the area thoroughly. Before he could shut the cabinet, he
heard something fall behind him. Laying on the ground was the
broom he had used earlier.

Dennis was startled but came to quickly shrug it off and went to
set it back up against the wall. As he positioned it back, a voice
charged throughout his body. Dennis couldn't make it out; even
more, he barely even heard it. He mainly felt the sound permeate
his flesh.

Hairs all over his body raised, the heat from his body escaped
him, and his rough skin became riddled with goosebumps. The
sensation he received in that moment made it feel as though his
soul shook within his body.

After an echoing scream, Dennis hit the floor. Shaken to the
core, he took a second to comprehend what had occurred. His
breathing intensified as he couldn't locate a source of the sound
anywhere in his vision.

He actually would prefer there be an actual person in the house
messing with him over whatever this was. The rational world has
reasonable solutions. If someone was there he could take care of
them, personally or with the police. But no one was in the room,
this was for sure.

Once he had calmed down enough, Dennis rose from the floor.
While looking unlikely, if there was an intruder, they could've
spooked him and run to another room. It had to be just some
random local trying to rile him up since he was new to the place.

Dennis searched room after room, yet deep down he feared the
truth: there was no one there.

Drenched in sweat, Dennis walked down to the last room of the
house to be checked, the basement. If there was someone here, this
had to be where they were. He had saved it for last since it so
happened to be the one he wanted to look through the least.
Carefully, he placed his hand on the doorknob. The noise of the
door cracking open filled the void of sound in the house.

He walked down a few steps, quickly looking around the filthy forgotten room. No one was found.

Dennis pondered the idea for a second that maybe he was just going insane, maybe there was no actual person or even a voice. It was all in his head and he had overreacted. Maybe he heard something else in the house which freaked him out. He took in a big gulp of air and released a great sigh.

As he was turning around, he saw a thing run past the door.

It moved too rapidly to be seen in a proper enough manner to make it out, but from what he witnessed Dennis could describe it as a little man sprinting away. He chased after it, but, as before, there was no one around the corner. The whole event happened so fast, he wondered if it was just his eyes messing with him.

***

Going to sleep was nearly impossible. The thoughts of the mysterious noise and the entities Dennis had seen kept his eyes open. With every second that passed came the greater expectation of something strange occurring.

Eventually, the urge to sleep had grown greater than to constantly stay up searching for the entities. Darkness overcame him as he passed off into a deep slumber.

However, Dennis didn't stay asleep. The same experience as the night before was destined to repeat. The figures were in their respective places as they were during the last visit. Dennis, while surging with fear, began to wonder if the teachings of the church were true, and the humanoid forms present were spirits or demons messing with him for unknown purposes.

One of them stabbed Dennis with a strange-looking device, immediately resulting in a spike of intense pain. A faint smile could be seen on the figure's face. It pulled the device out and punctured him again.

The figure at the end of the bed made a startling noise and lifted its scrawny arms out at the other. The grip on the device tightened as the closer figure frowned in response. It yelled at the other figure as it looked down, but Dennis couldn't make out what it was saying. They kept at each other until a loud creaking noise echoed from outside the room. A brief moment of silence followed. The two looked in each other's direction, seemingly contemplating their next step. The humanoid at the end of the bed turned to the door, while the other stared in the direction of the other. Everything then faded to black for Dennis.

***

The doorbell rang.

Dennis abruptly awoke. He sat still, thinking briefly back on what happened to him.

The doorbell was rung again, catching Dennis's immediate attention this time. He wasn't expecting anyone, nor did he really know many people in the first place. After throwing something on, he approached the door. He was intrigued by who could be standing on the other side. Through the peephole Dennis peered upon a familiar face. It was Albert, though he looked a bit down from earlier. Dennis carefully unlocked the door, then grabbed the handle and pulled.

Immediately, the first words out of Albert's mouth were, "I'm really sorry about earlier. I'm just a bit crazy."

Dennis was about to slam the door but second-guessed the action before committing to it. Albert did seem rather genuine with the apology; one could sense the distraught tone of his voice. The guilt of dumping all that supposed nonsense upon Dennis must've eaten away at Albert. Hence, Dennis kept the door open and offered Albert to come in. His guest thanked him, already feeling more relieved.

As he walked in, the floor squeaked as it always did on the first step. Albert didn't seem to be fazed at how filthy the house was. More so, he was surprised how much had been cleaned by Dennis. Albert thought he saw some movement in the kitchen, likely an adventurous roach.

Dennis comforted Albert, saying he forgave him. He offered a beer, which Albert respectfully declined, and then asked for more information on the house. Dennis cracked open a cold one and began gulping it down. A little spilled onto the floor but he didn't care too much.

Albert explained how the history of the house was rather vague. However, most understood that a couple of decades prior, a man named John had happily moved into the place with his wife. Back then it looked a ton better. The floor didn't squeak, the place was filled with sunlight, and it wasn't infested with roaches., which had now been taken over by weeds. It was truly a beautiful place.

No one knows exactly how it started; if it was due to a Ouija board, Satanic rituals, or maybe it was because the house was built on an Indian burial ground, but John's health began to decline due to horrific nightmares. Every night it started with the sighting of an entity. Then he would deal with visits from sinister figures. His wife grew more and more concerned with her husband, and John began to share stories of frequent insane encounters.

Not long after, the man splattered his brains onto a wall in the house. This would repeat itself a few years later. The place was believed to be haunted by the spirit of the dead man, so, naturally, a ghost hunter named Dan had bought the house. He managed to get on the good side of everyone in the town, even Gary. In fact, Gary was quite into the topic of ghosts back then.

Gary and Albert would chat a lot about the paranormal, sharing stories and whatnot. Once they found out a ghost hunter had bought the house, they had to join him. Albert became uneasy about this part, not wanting to share too many details; but whatever happened in their first night of ghost hunting was so bad it scared Gary away for good. A few nights later Dan would be another victim and the house would be up for sale again.

Dan had claimed to have seen a giant bird before his demise. Some believed the weird avian entity to be responsible for the death, but no one knew for sure. So, the house was abandoned and forgotten... sort of. It was put back on the market later, but in the hope it would be torn down and not moved into.

After Albert had mentioned the bird, Dennis pondered for a minute about the huge owl he had seen. Before the thought could continue, he shook his head with a mildly amused look. He wasn't going to buy into some fairy tales or bedtime stories. He couldn't even believe he was actually considering Albert's words.

Albert noticed Dennis thinking about something, so he asked, "Have you seen it?"

Dennis snapped out of his musings, looked at Albert, then shook his head side to side.

"You know, Mothman is always followed by tragedy," Albert continued.

Dennis let out a quick laugh, then smirked. "You really believe that bullshit?"

Albert was a bit offended by Dennis's behavior. "I think anything's possible. I think you listened to me for more than just curiosity."

As their conversation had paused, a noise came from upstairs. It sounded as if someone heavy was walking about. Dennis and Albert sat still, looking up to the direction of the footsteps. Dennis recognized it to be coming from his room. From there, the sounds moved to the direction of the stairs.

Albert was becoming excited, suddenly feeling years younger. He lit up and had to investigate. Dennis couldn't believe how quickly Albert stood and made his way to the stairs. Albert's heart rate had increased by the adrenaline rush the situation had gifted him. He ran up the stairway fearlessly, ready to confront this thing.

"Are you crazy?" Dennis queried. "Do you see anything?"

Albert was disappointed to have found no source to the noise yet felt that maybe it was for the best. Whatever was walking up there had disappeared.

Albert turned to Dennis. "Let's do an investigation."

***

Gary broke up with his wife in a nasty divorce after whatever had occurred all those years ago. It had turned him into a rather unkind and sad man, akin to Dennis a bit but on a greater scale. He wasn't just getting peeved about quarters that day at the store.

There was a knock at Gary's front door. He took a minute to look through the peephole before opening it.

"What do you want?" Gary hollered through the door.

On the other side Dennis held up a quarter, "I just want to talk."

Gary opened the door and stared at Dennis for a bit, dumbfounded. He saw Albert standing next to him. Dennis offered the quarter to Gary. He declined, but let Dennis and Albert in. Albert got to the point, explaining how Dennis lived at that house and was willing to explore it.

"You know I can't go back there," Gary said. "There's just no way."

Gary remained silent for a while, staring at the floor and thinking back on things.

Dennis reached into his pocket and pulled out an object. He didn't want to show it to anyone, he was just fidgeting around with it while thinking of things. As Albert and Gary argued a bit, Dennis moved this object within his grasp, examining it with only the sense of touch. Suddenly, it was gone. It had slipped and fallen to the floor.

Gary looked to the object as it fell, and Albert's eyes followed. Dennis's face became red from his slight embarrassment as they saw what the object happened to be. It was a small dinosaur toy, specifically of the long-necked saurian popularly known as Apatosaurus. Dennis quickly kneeled and picked it up.

"The hell is that?" Gary asked.

"It's my daughter's," Dennis replied while intensely staring at the toy to avoid making eye contact with Gary.

***

A year ago, Dennis had it all: a well-paying job and a beautiful family. They lived happily in a pleasant and safe suburban area. One day, they decided to go to the Science Museum in the nearby city to look at some of the dinosaur fossils and ancient American artifacts.

They spent a few hours there. His daughter, Nicky, really loved the place. She went on and on about facts on the dinosaurs, which impressed both Dennis and his wife. In the gift shop Nicky wanted all the expensive items, from big dino plushies to real trilobite fossils being sold. Dennis had to respectfully decline buying any of them. However, one toy caught her eye. It was a small Apatosaurus figurine. It was a rather cheap toy, but she loved it. Dennis happily got it for her before they departed.

Before sundown, they went to walk on the beach. Nicky played with the figure, making it run on the ground and destroy sandcastles. Dennis's wife stayed close. It was one of the happiest days of their lives. Then, as night descended, they drove home.

They were all tired, except Nicky who was still playing with the toy. Dennis continued driving, now nearing their house. He stopped at an intersection and looked both ways. No one seemed to be around, so he continued forth. As he did, a big car suddenly came speeding out of nowhere and slammed into the back of Dennis's vehicle. One could guess what had happened as a result.

Dennis and his wife didn't get along after that and their life together turned into a wreck. She got bitter and nasty towards him, despite it not being his fault but rather that of the drunk driver. After a brutal divorce, she walked out of his life for good.

***

After some minor pushing, Dennis explained this to Albert and Gary. Silence filled the air afterwards. Gary looked to a picture he had put face down. He picked it up to view the image it held.

He then turned to Albert, "He moved into that place?"

***

Time had passed, Dennis had calmed down, and the investigation was to begin. Dennis opened the door, and Gary got to experience the squeaky floorboard for the first time. Dennis's eye twitched. He hated that floorboard. As he continued forth a roach was walking on the floor. It paused and stared at him for a second, Dennis stared back. He tried slamming his shoe upon the annoying thing, but it scurried off too quickly.

Albert knew the hotspots of the house, but the main one was obviously Dennis's bedroom. Gary placed a camera up there, facing the bed at its end. Albert pulled out a spirit box, a device used to pick up ghostly voices, according to some people.

Nighttime was approaching; the day had passed by quite quickly. Everyone was ready. Albert turned on the spirit box, which then proceeded to make a very loud static noise that echoed throughout the house.

He asked some questions into the air. "Are you here with us? If so, who are you?"

No response, so Gary butted in. "You still here, you bitch?"

Still, no response. Dennis wasn't too sure about this ghost stuff but let them continue until they gave up. Right when the spirit box was turned off, a loud noise came from upstairs. It sounded like something heavy had fallen.

Albert put the spirit box down onto the kitchen table, causing a roach to scurry away. They paused, looked at each other, then followed Albert as he ran up the stairs. There, by the bed, they noticed the camera had fallen to the floor. Further inspection by Albert revealed the camera had been drained of its power.

"Don't worry, I knew this would happen," Albert declared. "An entity must've taken the power. I have a spare battery."

He took out the drained battery and slipped in the new. The device turned on and functioned as it just had, before dying again. Whatever it was, it drained the new battery in plain view of everyone. A loud screeching noise emitted from the lower level, grabbing their attention. The spirit box had turned on. The noise silenced then came back briefly, as if something was trying to communicate.

By now Dennis was freaking out, as he hadn't experienced anything like this prior. When Albert rushed to the stairs he paused. The sound of the spirit box became slightly fainter.

Albert carefully made his way down the stairs and looked around from the main floor. "Wait, it's not here."

He walked to the kitchen table to discover the spirit box had disappeared. The noise seemed to be emitting through the floor.

"The basement," Albert proclaimed. "It's coming from the basement."

Dennis looked to Gary and noticed immediately that his body had begun to vibrate.

"I'm not going down there," Gary made it clear. "I can't do this!"

True to his word, Gary bailed. He had checked out, going as far as to walk out the door. Albert tried reasoning with him, as Dennis focused more on the spirit box. Its noise continued to fade occasionally, as if it was taunting them.

While Albert and Gary argued, Dennis decided to toughen up and stand up to this thing. He tried flicking the switch for the basement lights, to no avail. Then he grabbed his flashlight and switched it on before moving down the steep stairwell. Webs were still everywhere down there, hanging above Dennis's head as he descended. Some even featured the corpses of ancient spiders.

The spirit box continued its obnoxious noise, still fading every now and then, yet a voice could never be made out. It simply laid there on some dusty boxes. Dennis stared at the object for a while and considered his options. He wanted this to be over. Instead of asking any questions, he grabbed the box and shut it off.

Dennis was relieved to finally rid the house of the noise. Then, he listened. There was total silence throughout the house. Albert and Gary had gone quiet. Dennis turned to the stairs and carefully ascended. As he approached the top, he peered around, seeing nothing but his dark house. The few lights that barely kept the place lit flickered and dimmed.

A chill came from behind Dennis as he stood by the table in the kitchen. The room went cold, as if the house itself had become a refrigerator. He turned to find himself face to face with a solid black mass. The sight of it burned Dennis's retinas with the intensity of its blackness.

"Fuck this," he said as he looked at the thing.

Immediately he rushed to the door. The second he opened it he stumbled back. There, *it* stood. With its blood red eyes staring back, it too sort of resembled a black mass. It kicked Dennis back into the house, sending him clear through the ice-cold cloud of supernatural darkness.

He could see its ebon misty substance being absorbed into his skin. His veins stung, as if electricity was flowing through the length of his body. A bright white light shined through the entire house, blinding Dennis as he helplessly passed out.

***

While Dennis walked to the basement, the argument between Albert and Gary had continued to the outside.

Albert shook his head while staring directly at Gary. "You gotta confront this thing, get some closure."

"What about you?" Gary replied. "What do you --"

Before he could respond, three sharp talons burst through poor Albert's chest. A spray of red struck Gary's face. The amount of shock and disbelief that took him over was enough to freeze his body in place. He could not believe what had just happened.

Albert fell to the floor, and with that the beast was exposed. At first glance, it did resemble Mothman a bit, but further inspection revealed it to be rather different. The creature's eyes met with Gary's as it waited for his next move.

A rage pulsed through Gary; he was done dealing with this thing. He remembered he had the perfect solution in the back of his car. Slowly, he moved towards the trunk while the bird-like entity followed curiously, as if it was studying the final moments of his prey.

Unexpectedly to the entity, Gary pulled out a rifle. He fired his weapon directly at the beast, hitting it with loads of ammunition. The creature stumbled back several feet as Gary went through a full round of ammo.

As Gary's rifle clicked empty, the beast looked at its chest, then back to Gary. Below its red eyes a toothy smile emerged. It had taken the bullets, all of them. Suddenly, it glanced back down to see green blood trickling from the minor injuries it had sustained.

Gary laughed. "That's for ruining my life, you fuck!"

This was the thing that had scared Gary for all of these years. The dark, cloudy mass-like being looked back up to him, and its eyes were glowing more than ever before. It shuffled towards him as he reloaded.

Gary tried to keep his distance, but the creature was faster than expected. The giant bird-thing jumped and seemingly glided towards the man as he fired again. The monstrous owl unhinged its jaws and engulfed Gary's head in them. He screamed in muffled terror as the beast crunched down. Afterwards, it turned to the door and noticed that the spirit box had gone silent.

***

Dennis awakened drenched in sweat back in his bed. He was breathing quickly and felt drained. A persistent itch could also be felt in his throat, so he wanted to get a glass of water. Fear started setting in, as he couldn't get his body to move.

Immediately he recalled his prior situation and began to question what sinister scheme was going down. A striking white light filled the room, providing it with a rather heavenly glow. The brightness of the light had not fully blinded Dennis, however, as he could still make out the three shapes entering his room at the end of his bed.

Closer they came, revealing themselves under the powerful illumination. The nightly sleep paralysis visits of the shadow people were not true. Dennis did not have sleep paralysis and he wasn't seeing shadow men being projected from the deepest regions of his mind. The dark silhouettes he remembered seeing had now changed in his memories, as if his brain tried erasing the terrifying beings' details to keep him sane.

He remembered the soft ashen-gray skin, the large heads, and, most of all, he remembered the soulless black bug-like eyes that were now once again staring into his soul. Aliens had been entering Dennis's house to study him, and now they intended to do so again.

Towering above the others at the end of the trashy room was a similarly built yet different being. It was as if one took a Gray alien and stretched it out to make it taller and even more slender. The aura of this being seemed familiar, but he couldn't understand why.

Once Dennis looked dead into its eyes, it struck him like a train. The giant bird he spotted outside his cracked window wasn't actually a bird. He was able to gain a better look at the avian entity now that it was lit up. This thing indeed wasn't a Mothman, and Dennis would have described it more like an Uber-Gray alien.

It was bigger and more fearsome than the other two Grays accompanying it, whose activities it clearly directed. The Uber-Gray turned to the smaller Gray on the right and nodded. The latter alien looked to the ceiling, and Dennis's eyes followed. Hanging above where the captive human lay in the bed was a silver rectangular object with small circular lights around the rim. Suddenly Dennis realized to his horror that the entire bedroom had been converted into some type of hi-tech but barren medical lab. Only the few devices required to conduct whatever the procedure was had been moved there from what he presumed was their spacecraft, all of which were easily mobile and able to be held in the aliens' long-fingered hands.

A humming noise began, which started low and rumbled the bed with increasing intensity as the sound grew louder. Pain surged through Dennis's veins, his skin tightened, and his body stiffened. His screams echoed throughout the room. This was it, he thought; this was the end.

Until, suddenly, a dark entity seeped out of his body. Black vein-like strands were sucked into the machine situated above him. It was as if something that had surreptitiously taken possession of his body in the house had been forcibly extracted from him.

The Gray put its hand upon Dennis's head. Out of nowhere, a sentence ran through his mind, one he didn't think of himself. It felt as if it was streamed through his brain, and the process gave him a bit of a headache.

This was unexpected. Through what must have been mental telepathy, it communicated to Dennis that everything would be alright. However, this didn't help, and the Uber-Gray moved closer to the captured human.

"Why?" Dennis tried asking.

The Uber-Gray took a second to ponder this, then leaned in close.

Research.

This it told Dennis telepathically. Maybe these beings were studying and experimenting with what remained in the house. It was difficult to understand, but it seemed whatever the Uber-Gray was after, it had acquired it.

Another standard Gray entered the room and helped the other guide the floating rectangular box. Meanwhile, the Uber-Gray stayed very close to Dennis. He was horrified of what the answer would be if he asked what was going to happen next.

To Dennis, it seemed as if the aliens had done this before, and that this was just another day on the job. However, as the Grays transported the metallic box, it came to a halt and began to vibrate again. The Uber-Gray turned toward the object, tilting its head. The box began to shoot out more and more sparks until it finally fell to the floor with a loud thud.

The device seemed to have malfunctioned. The bright white light dimmed just a bit as steam spewed from the box. The Grays looked at one another, almost as shocked as Dennis was. A black ooze poured onto the floor. It possessed an almost electrical quality to it. This was the same mass that Dennis had absorbed, yet it looked a bit different now as it had been given a more physical form.

The roiling mass shape-shifted constantly, as it appeared this was how it moved. Random jolts of energy would periodically cause it to twitch out tendril-like extensions. The Grays didn't want to touch it, as if it was toxic. The Uber-Gray snarled; the day had grown rougher for the tall, genetically-enhanced alien being due to this extreme inconvenience.

The Uber-Gray signaled for its smaller compatriots to join it in brandishing laser pistols and opening fire on the ghost. These beams of sizzling red energy passed harmlessly through its intangible ectoplasmic substance and singed the white walls behind it. Angered by the futility of this attack, the Uber-Gray extended vicious-looking talons from beneath the upper dermis of its elongated fingers and slashed at the cavorting ghost just as it passed through a wall to confront the alien face-to-face. Again, nothing occurred.

The ghost's intangibility also prevented him from retaliating in kind, so the dead man's spirit instead focused its emotional energies and projected pure terror and thoughts of suicidal depression into the psyches of the three aliens. They reeled for a moment, but their own highly developed psychic skills enabled them to quickly fend off this attack.

During this situation, Dennis had come to realize he could move again. He wasn't sure how; maybe the dimming of the light had something to do with it, but it didn't matter. The door was wide open, but first he'd have to get past the Grays and the ghost.

While the combatants were guilty with their conflagration Dennis darted for the door. The Uber-Gray was surprised at the balls its human captive exhibited by making a run for it. One of the Gray aliens immediately dashed after him, while the other stayed to help with the black mass.

Back upstairs the ghost had enough and decided to change tactics. By sensing the great amount of ectoplasmic matter that could be summoned from this environment, the discarnate spirit willfully congealed its substance into something roughly equivalent to material solidity. The now denser mass of the ghost settled to the floor as it began taking on the aspect of physical weight. It then quickly descended the flight of stairs towards the ruckus going on below.

Hence, a salient fact was made clear to the conscious spirit trapped between this life and the next: The being's astral consciousness had retained a sufficient amount of its ectoplasmic covering that it could alter its level of density at will. And there was a set of both pros and cons displayed by both degrees of solidity.

At its typical low level of density, the ghost enjoyed the following pros. It was entirely intangible so that it passed through physical barriers with ease, and both physical and conventional energy attacks – including lasers – passed through its billowy form without any discernible effect. It could also effortlessly float or hover through the air.

This mode was perfect for pursuing an enemy quickly and evading physical attacks. However, it came with one very serious con: much as it could not have physical harm inflicted upon him at low density, the ghost was likewise unable to inflict any type of physical harm against an opponent; its attacks had to be entirely on the psychic level, and these aliens seemed to have advanced enough mental abilities to resist such assaults.

Back downstairs, before Dennis could make it out of the house, the pursuing Gray tackled him. It then pulled what was clearly a weapon on Dennis and told him to stop resisting.

Meanwhile, upstairs, the ghost had decided to take advantage of the situation. Hence, it extended its now much denser ectoplasmic mass outward towards the standard Gray facing it, striking the diminutive alien in the face. The small entity stumbled down as if hit by a strong physical blow. The Uber-Gray retaliated by extending vicious claws from the ashen-colored dermis above its fingertips and slashing at the mass. The ghost shrieked, surprised that it felt pain.

Thus came the realization of the pros and cons that the greater density brought to the vengeful spirit. When its ectoplasmic substance was congealed enough to mimic solidity, the ghost could inflict terrible physical attacks on its targets. This included morphing its substance into various deadly shapes to accomplish this.

However, the ghost soon became aware of the very obvious con: Its quasi-solid form could *receive* injuries as well as inflict them, and it even "bled" ectoplasmic fluid in place of blood when cut. Significant damage in this form could very well cause a "second death" to the ghost by dissipating its etheric shell and causing the astral form sheathed within to involuntary pass over from the Earth plane into one of the afterlife realms. Finally, the now denser spirit also could not pass through physical objects or maneuver through the air in this mode, thus inhibiting its usual level of fluid mobility.

The Uber-Gray took its claws and punctured them deep into the ghost, holding its now semi-corporeal mass in place. The Uber-Gray then extended its jaws and crunched down onto the ghost. Shrieks of pain emitted from the ectoplasmic being as it morphed more rapidly due to the bite. The ghost tried releasing itself from his extraterrestrial opponent's grip but found severe difficulty. A liquid substance, maybe ectoplasm, drooled from the wound.

Just then, an idea had popped into the ghost's metaphysical head. Instead of getting away from the Uber-Gray, maybe it had to do the opposite. Hence, the billowy entity forced itself down the Uber-Gray's gullet. The extraterrestrial being gagged intensely, completely taken aback by what had just occurred.

Its head then began to vibrate. Green blood trickled down from its bulbous eyes. Its body had grown extremely stiff. The Uber-Gray fought to regain control over its form, but to no avail. Its skin twitched and shook more and more. The Uber-Gray's head expanded outwards and popped like a balloon, painting the sterile white room around it green. The rest of the Uber-Gray's body fell to the floor as the dark mass of the ghost exited the corpse.

The other Gray stood there in a state of complete shock as its leader had been slaughtered. The ebony mass comprising the ghost's ectoplasmic form morphed into a bunch of spikes of differing lengths that protruded out from a core. They moved rapidly as the ghost screamed in anger. It settled down, then turned its attention toward the smaller alien.

A laser struck its form, causing the ghost to shriek again. The Gray was armed and fired continuously at its ectoplasmic adversary. It responded by moving and morphing quickly, which soon enabled it to dodge most of the lasers. Its mass then enveloped the Gray's bulbous head, held it in place, and compressed it inward. This crushed the otherworldly being's fragile head to a pulp. Greenish blood poured from its pulverized pate to the floor. Once the ghost let go of it, the body dropped to the floor with a sickly thud.

There was only a single Gray remaining now. It was the same one that put its hand against Dennis's chest to read his vitals, among other things. There wasn't much choice left for the alien. It could sense that its leader had violently perished, as did its other friend. All it had left was Dennis.

It may have seemed bizarre, but despite everything that had happened here, Dennis felt bad for the alien. Looking into its eyes one could sense it was in deep pain and mourning. In just a few minutes it lost friends it had likely worked with for decades.

Morning was approaching as night faded away. The sun was just barely popping up. The alien lowered its weapon. Dennis was free. Before he could run, the alien "spoke" to him. A deal would be made: The Gray would leave the planet and leave Dennis unmolested if he helped to defeat the spirit. Dennis wanted to just abandon this place and leave it to the roaches. He wanted to run away so badly, yet he didn't. Instead, he agreed to the alien's deal.

***

The ghost made its way down the stairs, searching for its final kill. It planned to use Dennis as a host, if it could, to escape this place and to truly live again. As it descended the stairway, it caught sight of Dennis sitting at the kitchen table, chugging down a beer.

The ghost paused. It scanned the area, cautiously searching for the Gray. It briefly wondered if it had fled the manse in cowardice, perhaps even the planet itself. The spirit desperately tried to take a human form but couldn't manage the feat. It didn't take much time for it to realize that Dennis's presence at the table was a distraction, and that this was a trap.

Out of a corner, the Gray alien appeared and fired a salvo of laser beams at the ghost. Ectoplasm splattered across the floor. The alien then quickly converted its weapon into a cold metallic bludgeon and smashed the ghost's ectoplasmic form again and again, beating the fleshless entity down. The rage within the spirit grew as the Gray battered it.

The spirit threw the Gray to the other side of the kitchen. It then rushed at the alien while attempting to again morph spikes out of its ectoplasmic dark mass. A few were successfully formed and punctured the alien following a single blow of the ghost's limb. Screams filled the air as greenish blood squirted from the injured extraterrestrial.

Dennis thought fast and grabbed a knife. He ran up to the entity and dug the blade deep into its shifting center. The spirit screeched with pain. A giant tooth-filled mouth formed from its mass and latched onto Dennis, quickly tossing him away.

Dennis's knife had dropped near the Gray. The ghost continued stabbing the alien repeatedly and ruthlessly. Life had begun fading from the being from the stars as its vision started to blur. With what remained of its sight, it could see a glint of reflected light shining from a nearby portion of the linoleum-covered floor.

The knife was close by. With all its might the Gray reached for the blade. It succeeded in grabbing hold of the blade and stabbing the ghost with its razor-sharp business end. Ectoplasm seeped out over the floor as the ghost bled.

There was an area of the mass that seemed like a human head directly facing the Gray's visage. The alien brandished its blade and shoved it through what subtly appeared to be the jaw of the ghost. The spirit screamed in pain before quickly dissipating.

When Dennis had struck the wall, he hit hard. As the Gray alien dominated the ravenous ghost, Dennis began to pass out as the prior-encountered bright light filled the house again.

The final, victorious alien had been transported back to the awaiting spacecraft. which quickly left planetary orbit to return to the Gray homeworld in the Zeti Reticuli star system. The small amount of data that the sole survivor of the mission had managed to gather about the ability of ectoplasmic entities to "possess" sentient material life would just have to suffice for now.

***

Dennis woke in his bed, the sun shining in his face. He quickly sat up and looked around. There was nothing in his room.

He steadily walked down the stairs, searching for anything unusual. As he reached the last step, he heard a crunch. Dennis looked down to see he had stepped on a dead roach. The poison set up for them was finally working.

Passing over the squeaky floorboard, Dennis ventured outside to his porch and sat down in the rickety old chair he kept there. Birds were chirping crazily, squirrels were running about, and the weather was pleasantly warm. He laid his head back and let out a tremendous sigh. At last, he was alone, truly alone.

Or was he? Despite his best efforts, Dennis could not eliminate the feeling that he still wasn't alone. That *something* was watching him; or, possibly, more than just one kind of "something."

This strange house had already attracted disparate types of entities, and luckily this time circumstances resulted in a conflict between them that ultimately saved Dennis from being the ultimate victim of either. But what attracted beings from another world to this residence above all others in the city? What attracted a spirit trapped between the worlds – and one with so much etheric energy at its disposal, at that? And the roaches… those goddamned *roaches*. What attracts so many of them? Is it a normal infestation, or… something beyond that?

With these questions pervading his mind, and the continued feeling of being watched by something he couldn't (yet) see, Dennis found himself cringing at the thought of spending another night in that house of mystery.

END

WENDIGO VS. SKELETOID: GASHADOKURO BATTLES THE KEE-WAKW

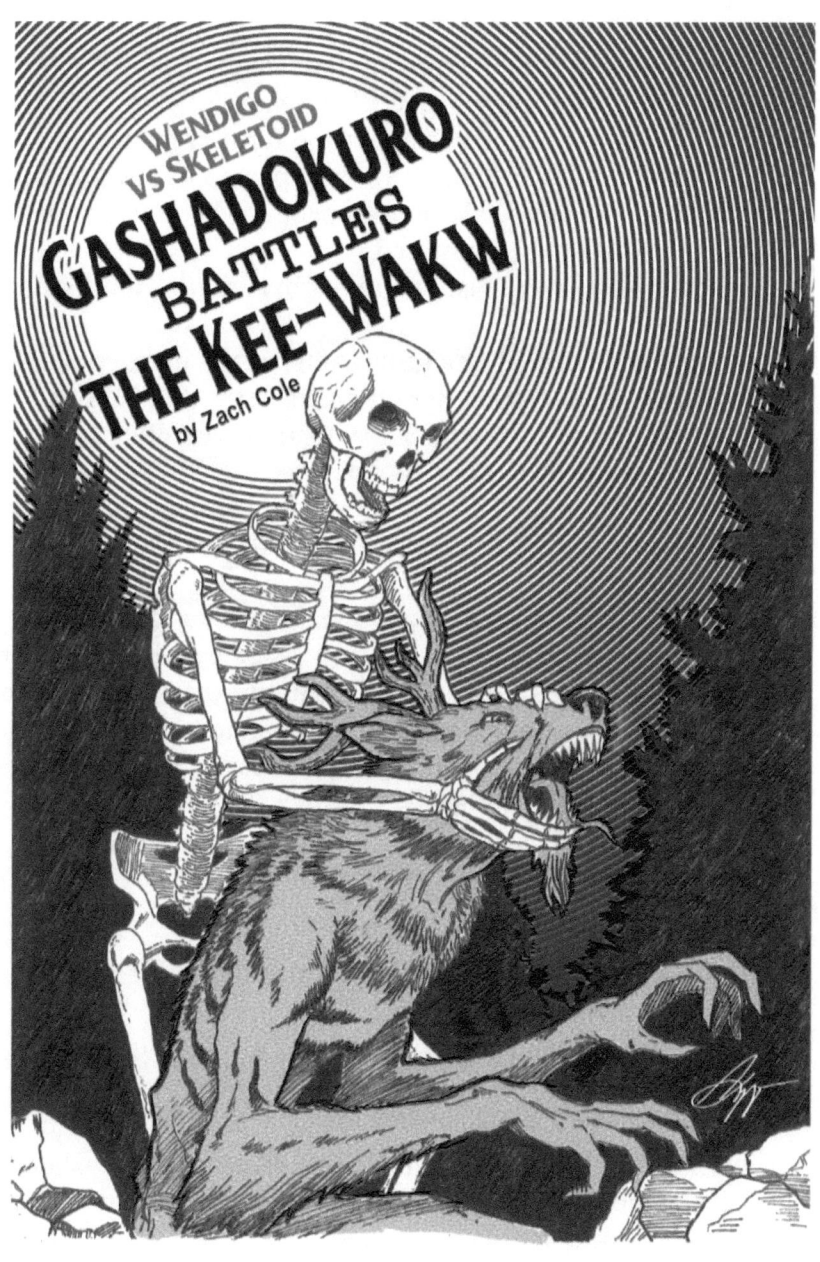

1

I've been following it from my homeland of Japan. The Gashadokuro., also known as the "starving skeleton." In Japanese mythology, they're spirits that take the form of giant skeletons and are fifteen times taller than an average person. They are said to be created from the amassed bones of people who died of starvation, or in battle without being buried.

I thought they were just that, though. A myth. But it seems I was wrong.

The creature rose after a group of terrorists invaded downtown Tokyo and began to open fire on innocent people. No one knows why... and no one ever will. The terrorists were killed after a firefight with the local police force.

Once the battle died down, the creature rose forth, supercharged with the souls of all those that were killed... and looking for revenge.

Strangely, it didn't attack anyone. Instead, it lumbered away from its blood-soaked birthplace and disappeared into the ocean.

I, Yoshio Tsubaki, was one of the police officers on the scene. I witnessed the rise of the creature. I killed the terrorists in a brutal firefight, and after getting a look at their faces, I knew where the Gashadokuro was going.

2

Appalachian Mountains, Maine...

"Those idiots! I told them to wait for my order!" Derek Jeffries growled, slamming a fist down on the wooden table he sat in front of.

"What exactly was the goal?" Raphael Hernandez asked.

"To let those damn Japs know we've not forgotten what they did during World War II!"

"Oh... right."

Jeffries backhanded Hernandez's shoulder. "That's the point of all of this!"

"I know, I know..."

The death of their comrades in Tokyo put a dent in their organization. Only six of their number remained. They were an anti-Japanese group that believed it was only a matter of time before the "Japs" started another war with the United States.

And of course, most of them were backwoods hillbillies. Most of them believed in many of the conspiracy theories floating around the Internet. And one of those theories was that Japan was gearing up for another war. The hate-filled group took it upon themselves to try and stop the Land of the Rising Sun before it could succeed.

Their base of operations, such as it was, constituted a cabin built deep within the woods in the Appalachian Mountains. Unfortunately, they knew little of the horror that was coming for them.

The horror of the Gashadokuro!

3

My plane landed in New York. After renting a car, I drove, not really knowing where to go. I just knew the Gashadokuro was going to turn up soon. The only question was where. Where would it turn up?

The Gashadokuro was filled with vengeful spirits. It would seek out those that wronged it and destroy them. That it had arisen in the first place meant that whoever was behind the attack in Tokyo was still out there.

My aimless driving ultimately brought me to the middle of nowhere in a place called Maine. That's when I spotted it lumbering in the distance, its eyeless sockets locked on the mountains behind me.

4

Jeffries growled in frustration as he stood from his seat.

"I'm going for a walk," he announced before making his way toward the cabin's front door.

Jeffries stepped off the wooden front porch of the cabin and into the surrounding forest. He didn't have a set destination; he just needed out of the cabin to clear his head of his frustrations. After twenty minutes of walking and feeling less frustrated with himself, he decided to head back.

Shit, he thought as he looked around at the endless trees surrounding him. *I'm lost. Maybe this wasn't such a good idea.*

Jeffries pulled his cellphone out and frowned as he realized that the device had no bars.

He began walking again, soon seeing a structure in the distance. Thinking it was the cottage he sought, his legs pumped faster. His spirit was crushed, however, when he entered the clearing and saw the structure wasn't the cabin. Rather, it appeared to be a mere slab of rock.

The hell is a slab of rock doing in the middle of the forest?

Upon further inspection, he found there were rocks of all sizes scattered about everywhere. They were obviously deliberately placed there and arranged intricately.

"What is this?" Jeffries wondered aloud while kneeling down and placing a hand on a boulder. "Some sort of Indian burial ground?"

As soon as his hand made contact with the rock, the ground rumbled. It was a gentle rumble at first, though it quickly turned into a rattling earthquake. The ground at the middle of the burial site heaved upward, sending Jeffries falling on his ass.

The man looked up with horror as the form of a giant creature rose from the ground. Dirt fell from its furry hide as it turned to Jeffries with blazing red eyes. Those eyes seared into his corneas as the creature's jaws opened, revealing rows of razor-sharp fangs and the black abyss that was its gullet.

Before the hapless man knew it, he was inside the abyss…

5

I knew I was lost. After reaching the mountains, I exited my car and decided to wander around. I didn't know why, but I had a feeling I was connected to the Gashadokuro. After a while of wandering, I came across a cabin. Upon setting eyes on it, I knew that was exactly where the Gashadokuro was headed for.

I walked up to the cabin and knocked on the door. A man resembling the stereotypical redneck answered the door. His brows creased in disgust at the sight of me.

Definitely the right place, I thought.

"What the hell do you want, you dirty Jap?" the man growled.

"It is coming," I said involuntarily.

The man's disgust grew even more pronounced. He pulled out a handgun and pointed it at my head.

"Get out of here. Now!" the man demanded. "Or, I'll blow your dirty Jap head off!"

I didn't budge.

As the man's finger began to tighten on his gun's trigger, a roar echoed through the air. It confused both me and the man holding me at gunpoint. The Gashadokuro doesn't have the vocal cords to produce noise. No, whatever made that ghastly sound wasn't the Gashadokuro, but sounded just as big.

The other man's eyes widened in terror a moment after his confusion.

"It can't be," the man muttered.

"What is it?" I asked.

The man looked me in the eyes, pure terror radiating from his countenance.

"Kee-wakw," was his only reply.

Trees rustled, gaining our attention. A horrific, fur-covered head with bunny-like ears and a mouth full of fangs appeared over the treetops. The monstrous entity let loose another rumbling roar.

The man slammed the door in my face, retreating to the make-believe safety of his wooden cabin. I watched as the Kee-wakw reached out with its boney fingers and peeled back the roof. The people inside screamed in horror as the huge beast reached in and plucked them up by the handful and stuffed them into its salivating mouth.

I could feel the anger of the Gashadokuro's vengeance being stolen away from it.

The enormous skeletal being soon appeared over the mountain opposite the Kee-wakw. The two creatures glared at each other, the sides of the Kee-wakw's lips lifting up in a snarl to reveal its blood-covered fangs.

I knew I needed to get out of the way of these two supernatural giants. I thus ran into the forest, back toward my rental car as the monsters charged at each other.

6

The Gashadokuro hungered for vengeance. It had followed the smell of the murderers all the way from Japan, only to have its vengeance ripped away from it by the lanky creature standing before it. The beast was covered in thin, tight skin and fur. A boney tail flicked side to side behind it.

The Kee-wakw made the first move, charging at the Gashadokuro. The Gashadokuro spun, dodging the Kee-wakw, and raking the sharp ends of its fingers across its back as it continued past. The Kee-wakw roared, bleeding from the gashes in its back. That was where the Gashadokuro and the Kee-wakw were different. The Gashadokuro didn't feel pain. In fact, it didn't feel anything. Nothing but vengeance.

The Kee-wakw retaliated with a backhand to the Gashadokuro's head, literally sending it spinning. The Gashadokuro reached up, grabbing its opponent's head in its boney hands to stop the uncontrolled revolution. The Kee-wakw looked amused with its enemy.

The Gashadokuro opened its jaws and lunged forward, latching onto the Kee-wakw's shoulder. The Kee-wakw threw its head back and let loose a pain-filled screech. It clawed at the Gashadokuro, crushing the components of its boney form until nothing remained save for the head still attached to its shoulder. It then grasped the Gashadokuro's head with its thin hirsute fingers and pulled with all the creature's considerable might. The Gashadokuro's head came loose and the Kee-wakw tossed it into the forest.

The Kee-wakw looked down at the pile of bones that was its enemy before turning its back to them and taking a step toward civilization miles in the distance. It could smell the many corrupt denizens within its borders and wanted nothing more than to feast upon their flesh.

But it never got the chance to take another step.

The clattering of bones caught its ears. The Kee-wakw turned around, its blazing red eyes widened in surprise as it found the

Gashadokuro reforming itself. The re-constituted body of the Gashadokuro reached into the forest, located its head, and popped it back where it belonged atop its body.

The Kee-wakw's surprise was only momentary. It again raked its claws at its enemy, scraping away the bones that comprised its body. But after every swipe, the bones that were ripped from the Gashadokuro's skeletal form were just absorbed right back into it.

As the Kee-wakw was scratching away at its enemy, the Gashadokuro reached up and wrapped its hands around the Kee-wakw's fuzzy head. The Kee-wakw continued tearing at the Gashadokuro's body until the pressure on its head became unbearable. By then it was too late, however. The furry beast let out a shrill shriek a moment before its head exploded in a spray of blood, skull fragments, and brain matter.

The Gashadokuro was victorious!

7

I watched as the Gashadokuro crushed the Kee-wakw's head in its skeletal hands. Despite it having no muscles, the creature was surprisingly strong. No... make that *supernaturally* strong. The skeleton-like monster was supernatural in nature, after all.

I could feel the Gashadokuro's satisfaction. Its revenge, while not the one it had originally set out for, was finally complete. It stood there for a moment before crumbling into the hundreds of bones that comprised its giant form.

The Gashadokuro's job was done, and so was mine. It was time for me to return to Japan.

END

ZOMBIE VS. ALPHA SERIAL KILLER: A DISTRACTION OF MONSTERS

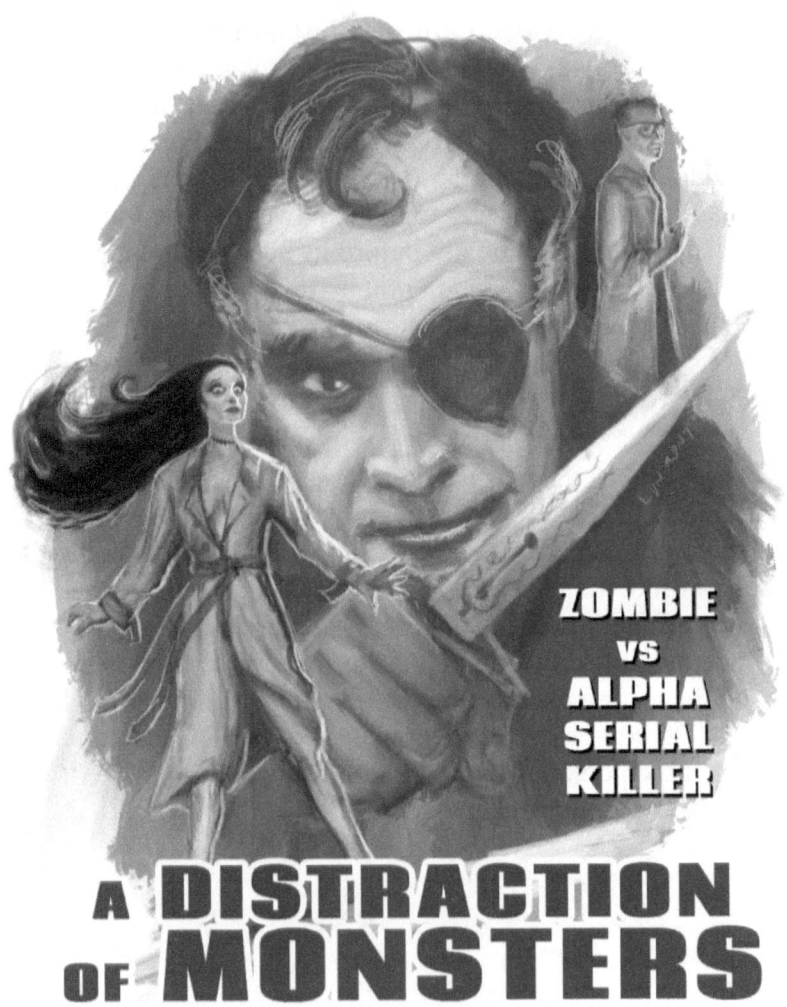

by Pete Rawlik

January 1918

Noel Vasseur, once of Paris but of late residing in the port of Cherbourg, drew the knife from its sheath and watched the way the blade caught the moonlight. There was something sublime about his knife; it was not an ancient weapon, nor was it new, though Vasseur thought about it as antique, for it dated from the eighteenth century. Its hallmark was Spanish, and the untrained might think it from Toledo or even Catalonia, but they would be wrong

Vasseur had spent an entire summer in Spain tracking down the origin of his weapon, which he traced to the Ramirez forge in Zaragoza. It was a beautiful weapon, lightweight, expertly balanced, and stronger than any other steel he had ever known. It sat in his hand like an extension of his own arm, like the killing claw of some deadly beast -- drawn only to kill.

And with this blade Vasseur had killed so very many.

He liked to think that it was all a matter of circumstance, that all the deaths had been because of the Great War that had ravaged Europe for years now. He liked to think that, but he knew it wasn't true, it was just a lie he told himself -- as if he could tell someone else -- so that he could sleep better at night. During the day and the evenings, he knew better -- Noel Vasseur, the last in a long line of butchers, was a killer of women.

It hadn't always been so. Not so long ago the only thing he had ever killed had been livestock -- cows, swine and lambs. But then the war had come, and he had been called to serve in defense of France against the invading Germans. It was then that he had found his dark passion in the battle of Mulhouse when a terrified young lady refused to stop screaming as the German offensive overran his position. Rather than let her draw the enemy's attention he had covered her mouth with his hand, and then slit her throat.

She hadn't died immediately, but rather had struggled and clawed into his left eye before she succumbed to the wound. It took him three days to work his way back to Allied territory and by that time his eye had become infected. The doctors, little better than butchers themselves, had no choice but to remove the festering orb. After that he had been sent back to Paris and later released from service.

But within him that dark desire grew. And over the years he had learned how to kill. First in Paris, then later in Lyon, Toulouse, and Nantes. Always he had stayed in the large cities where prey was easy and a woman who vanished might not be missed for a few days. But inevitably, as the number of disappearances grew, the police would become suspicious and Vasseur would move on. It had been a pattern that assured that he would not get caught.

Then he had come to Cherbourg, and the transitory nature of a port town created for him the perfect hunting ground with police long accustomed to missing women. Rare were the bodies of his victims that were discovered, but when it did happen the locals invariably blamed it on some seaman whose ship had just departed. No one in authority could conceive that a local man -- a Frenchman -- could be responsible for such things. It gave Vasseur the opportunity to act in an almost cavalier manner. He was an upstanding citizen; he supplied meat to the mayor himself. No one suspected that he was a killer. No one at all.

Not even the woman he followed.

She did not know who he was, and he did not know who she was. It was a fine arrangement, one that he had no desire to change. The only reason he had any interest in her at all was because she was his type. Tall, well-proportioned, with brown hair worn flowing over the shoulders. She wore a simple country dress, grey cotton, cinched at the waist with a matching belt.

A few weeks earlier and she would not have been able to wear such a dress. December had been particularly harsh, but by January it had warmed up a bit. It was still cold out, but not bitterly so. During the day some of the ice on the streets had softened into slush. It had refrozen with the night. The once smooth blue pools now transformed into crags of grey, contaminated with soot and dirt. He hated these cold nights, but on the other hand they presented opportunities that he couldn't afford to dismiss just because of a little chill.

He watched his prey turn down a side street, not quite an alley but not a thoroughfare either. He followed discretely, careful not to let his boots make a sound on the worn pavestones. It was dimmer here, and with each stride the light of the main street behind them faded. He quickened his pace but lightened his step to close on her. The blade shifted in his hand. He changed his breathing. Slow.

Shallow. Breaths. Almost silent in the night. He matched her pace, but with a longer stride he gained ground rapidly. In moments he was within striking distance.

He raised his arm up to the level of his eyes.

He broke stride.

The blade caught the moonlight and glinted into her face.

She turned and gasped, but only for a second.

He caught her in his arms, the blade sliding across her throat with ease as he dragged her into the shadows and spun her around.

That should have ended it, the warm blood running down her chest, her eyes filling with despair as he watched the life drain out of her. But these eyes didn't do that; suddenly, they filled with defiance. She charged at him, blood flowing behind her, filling the air with a fine crimson mist. He dodged her easily and let his training take over. The butt of the dagger came down on the back of her head and knocked her to the ground. He turned and planted himself firmly, one boot on the road and the other in the small of her back.

She was pinned there, struggling, gasping -- gurgling really -- for help. He couldn't let her flounder about like that. He took the knife and with a deft thrust borne from years in a butcher shop inserted the blade into the hole where the spine met the skull. There was a faint crack and an accompanying pop. A low cry escaped from her mouth. And then she went still.

Vasseur stepped back, frustrated. It had not been a good kill. With his foot he rolled her over and looked at the flush of blood that was escaping her throat. There should have been more. The blade had not cut as deep as it should have, but this was through no fault of his. There was a scar on her throat. She had been injured there before, and thus his attack, his perfect attack, had been fouled; not foiled, just *fouled*. Not that it mattered, as she was dead. And his bloodlust was satisfied. All he had left to do was to claim his trophy and dispose of the body.

He lifted her left arm and tugged off her glove. A small cylinder of wood fell out and rolled away. It wasn't much to look at, just five centimeters or so long, and slightly larger in diameter than a pencil. A curious thing to be kept in a glove, he thought. And then he saw it. The small finger on her left hand was missing, severed at the second knuckle as if by an expert. As if he himself had already taken a prize. As if he himself had previously killed her.

But that was impossible.

The dead were dead.

And nothing could change that.

Could it?

February 1918

It had taken Vasseur a month to find the empty grave.

He had travelled through the countryside under the ruse of being a butcher looking for new sources for his shop in Cherbourg, which wasn't exactly true, but neither was it a lie. And the locals had become accustomed to strangers passing through their villages looking for a steady source of supplies. The war had been responsible for that.

And so Vasseur had made his way through the countryside visiting farmers and dairymen, and more discretely, the churches and their associated graveyards. It was a slow, perhaps even tedious process but it had ended much sooner than Vasseur had expected. It had ended in the village of XXX, and with the grave of Chloe Herveaux who Vasseur had killed late in October of the previous year.

Herveaux had been found frozen in the river and buried in the churchyard where her family had worshipped. It was from Simone and Beatrice, Chloe's younger sisters, that Vasseur had learned of the disturbed grave. The young women had been praying at the church, lamenting with the old priest over the issue. Vasseur had engaged them in conversation and learned that the grave had been robbed not long after the service. Beatrice was particularly upset and had taken a vow to name her first daughter after her lost sister.

In contrast, Simone seemed more angry than remorseful, and spoke at length concerning whom she thought responsible for the matter. It seems that a pair of American doctors had taken up residence not far from the village, in an abandoned mill. They claimed that they had been discharged from service, or perhaps they were just on leave, but either way they had settled into the old mill and used the aging water wheel to power a crude electrical generator and strings of queer lights that could be seen for miles around. They bought a suspiciously high number of pigs and claimed to be surgeons pioneering new methods in organ transplant and reconstructive surgery, a skill that would likely be in high demand after the war.

To Vasseur such information gathered from a young woman seemed unusual, but Simone scoffed at him. She was no simple country girl, as she planned on being a nurse when she was old enough to study and had a cache of books on anatomy and medicine that she routinely studied. She had even been to the mill to clean for the two American doctors, and seen them keeping organs alive in jars of saltwater. These same organs were stimulated into movement by discharges from coiled copper electrodes which the white-haired senior physician called Pretorian coils and seemed to take great pride in.

Vasseur apologized for his rudeness and promised to pray for their sister. At this Simone had snorted and then dragged her sister away. Beatrice smiled at him and waved goodbye. He waved back and thought that perhaps in a few years he might have to return to this village and see what kind of beauties these two had grown into. Perhaps they would be worthy of his special attentions. Perhaps.

That evening he made his way out to the old mill. It was indeed an odd sight to see, the crumbling stone and wood building all lit up by electric light. One did not expect to see such things so far from the city, and yet here it was casting queer shadows over the frozen landscape. He rapped on the door and after a moment was greeted by the sound of a fumbling lock and the creaking of ancient hinges. The figure on the other side was younger than he had expected. The girl had spoken of white hair, and this was true, but the tow-headed visage that answered the door was at best in his thirties, and not the elder physician Vasseur had imagined.

"May I help you Sir?" asked the American in English.

Vasseur's English was passable. "You will forgive me, *Monsieur*. I have come to discuss a matter with you, a medical matter, a rather grave matter."

The man shook his head. "We are not seeing patients. There is a doctor in the next village over, he can help you." Then he went to close the door.

Vasseur inserted his boot and spoke rapidly, "I must insist. It concerns Mademoiselle Chloe Herveaux."

The man stopped. "What about her?"

Vasseur smiled. "Perhaps you can explain to me why I saw her in the streets of Cherbourg just last month?"

"I know nothing of such things," the man stammered, his glasses suddenly fogged up.

"I think you do," responded Vasseur, "and I think that the Gendarme would be very interested to know what goes on out here, and why the dead no longer stay dead."

The man took a deep breath, "Perhaps you should come inside." The door slid open.

Vasseur crossed the threshold and after a few more steps turned and took off his hat and coat. "I was told there were two of you."

The man -- the doctor -- close the door and took Vasseur's hat and coat. My partner is away on business -- a buying trip. We have difficulty gaining access to the materials we need here." He tossed the hat and coat on to a small chair. "Now what is it I can do for you, Mister...?"

"Vasseur, Noel Vasseur."

"My name is West, Doctor Herbert West. What exactly do you want?"

"That is an excellent question, Doctor. I am a man of wealth and rather obscure tastes, ones that I believe intersect with your own. I suspect that we might come to an arrangement that might benefit both of us."

Dr. Herbert West proffered a chair to his guest. "What exactly are you suggesting, Mr. Vasseur?"

The conversation was slow at first, circumspect; but in its own roundabout way it was useful. Secrets were revealed, and bargains struck. Hours turned into days, and then into weeks. It took time, but with Vasseur providing the raw materials and West sharing his knowledge the one soon mastered the skills of the other.

And in that manner Noel Vasseur, butcher and murderer, learned how to reanimate the dead.

August 2018

The thing that was once Chloe Herveaux tore out of the fluid-filled bladder that had once more reanimated her. She coughed up the sludge that filled her lungs and screamed as her memories flooded back to her suddenly conscious mind.

There was a mirror on one wall, and in this she caught a reflection of herself. She bore only a semblance of humanity. Her throat was a mass of crisscrossing scars and similar wounds were scattered over her arms, legs, and torso. The black oil healed her wounds, brought her back to life, gave her strength and the strength of will to do things she hadn't thought possible, but there was a price. A terrible price. She moaned in agony as her senses brought the world back into focus and she could feel it around her. Moreover, she knew that if she wanted to live, she had to get out.

There was a dress and some shoes. Nothing fancy, but she put them on to hide her ruined body. She had to get out. She had to run. She had to find someone who could help her, who would put an end to the torment Vasseur was inflicting on her, and all the others.

The others.

They hung there, each in their own canvas bladder, black oil dripping from the seams. How many were there? Four -- no, five -- counting her own. All in various stages of being bathed in the reanimation fluid that West and Vasseur had concocted. West hadn't come to this place by chance, he had been drawn here by an account he had found in a private library.

There was a long lost and forgotten cave, and in the cave a Roman temple to Attis, the dying god, and in the temple a pool fed by some chthonic spring. In the pool was a black slime, an alga of some kind. And on the shores of the pool, feeding off the alga were lizards long thought extinct that frolicked in the darkness. There was something in the alga, something miraculous; or, perhaps fiendish.

How did she know this?

Vasseur had told her. He had killed her more than a dozen times and, in his triumphs, had whispered the secrets of his dark gifts to her, of how he was able to torture her and all the others over and over again. He was proud of it, reveled in it. And mocked her each time he slaughtered her. Panic welled up inside her. She had to get out. Her hand reached for the door, but then stopped.

She had done this before.

Many times.

Vasseur was out there. He was always out there.

Waiting. Waiting to kill her.

She needed to do something different.

She looked around the crude little laboratory. There had to be something that she could use against Vasseur, something she could use as a weapon. And some other way for her to escape.

There were various tools -- screwdrivers, hammers, chisels, and the like. There were medical implements as well – needles and silk, syringes, scalpels, a bone saw. There was the well for the house, and the small pump that fed water to the glass reactor full of black algae and the small tubes that harvested the black oil into a sealed decanter. Copper tubes ran from the decanter to each of the artificial wombs that incubated her fellow prisoners. The substance had to be metered in carefully, otherwise the process would go awry and the subjects would return malformed, not only in body but in mind as well. Her eye went to the syringe, and then to the decanter of viscous black grease.

She had a plan. She just hoped that she had time to execute it.

***

Vasseur smelled the smoke before he saw it. It came drifting in on the wind and he recognized it almost immediately as what it was, a wood fire -- but not just wood. There was an acrid, greasy stench to things that told him paint and other chemicals were involved. It came drifting in from the east, brought in by the sea breeze. It could have been from the town, but somehow Vasseur knew that it wasn't. Somehow, he knew that the mill was ablaze, and he only had minutes to stop the flames from consuming everything he had worked for, the delicious secret that he hid and nurtured there.

Vasseur wasn't far from the mill, and within minutes he could see the flames flickering in the windows and smoke pouring out from under the roof. As he passed through the garden wall, he felt the heat. Even from outside he could feel the heat, could see the plants that had colonized the ancient stones withering from it. It didn't matter, he broke through the door and plunged blindly into the inferno that raged beyond. His knife was gripped in his right hand, his left arm raised up to the level of his eyes in a futile attempt to block the heat from his face.

He was surprised to find that the laboratory was relatively intact. The flames had engulfed the other parts of the mill, but here the only things burning were a few curtains and the door that connected to the rest of the building. The lab itself was mostly undamaged. He noted that the glass reactor full of alga was gone, the artificial wombs that hung from the ceiling were all intact -- all save one.

Chloe, it seems, had been reborn on time, but where was she? What had she done? Vasseur scanned the room and noted that the flames were spreading. He needed to save what he could before it was too late.

He climbed up on a table and pulled one of the canvas bags close to him. His other hand brought the knife up to the thick ropes that suspended the apparatus from the ceiling. With furious speed he began sawing at the ropes, desperate to cut them and drop the sack to the floor. So intent was he that he failed to notice the syringe sticking out of the bag, not until the contents inside began to kick. But by then it was too late.

Two slender arms, too thin to be as strong as they were, burst through the canvas seams and clawed at Vasseur. He pushed away and tried to balance on the table but then turned in panic as he heard another bag split apart and dump its contents onto the floor. The viscous oil gushed away and the lithe female body that rose up from the floor screamed in rage.

Vasseur crouched into a defensive position, but all around him the same act was being repeated. One by one his victims were being reanimated prematurely and coming out of their faux amniotic sacks far more dangerous than normal. He counted four out of five; Chloe was nowhere to be seen. She had done this -- built a trap and then drawn him in. He smiled at the thought, proud of what he had helped her become. Clever girl.

When the screaming stopped the attack began.

They rushed him from all sides, but he scrambled up the dangling rope and into the rafters. He thought it would have given him a moment or two to think but he was wrong. The three women -- once his victims, now his attackers -- sprung from the floor and with preternatural strength joined him in the infrastructure of the roof. They moved with frighteningly inhuman speed, and not like a human at all, their arms and legs at odd, almost insectile angles. They moved like spiders or ants, swift and sure-footed and oblivious to any potential harm.

Which put them all within striking range. Vasseur struck out with the blade, stabbing instead of slashing, looking to effectively damage rather than artfully kill. The tip drove home between the neck and shoulder of one of the creatures. It screamed in agony and rage as it fell to the floor. Its head hit the ledge of the well and snapped back in an impossible position. It didn't move. Vasseur would have preferred to check whether it had survived, but the other three were closing in.

He leapt to the floor and spun around to face whatever followed. Two dropped to the floor on either side of him, while the third flung itself directly at him. He dodged it easily, stepping to one side and then plunging the blade into its back. Another scream filled the room as the monster fell to the floor and flopped there in agony, its spine severed. It wasn't dead, but it was severely wounded, disabled even. He ran at the thing and kicked it in the skull, silencing it forever.

Vasseur then turned to face the remaining two attackers. The one to his right was weary, circling for a better position from which to strike. The other was on his left in his blind spot. He turned his head to see where it was but instead was rewarded with something hard cutting into the hole where his eye had once been. Now it was his turn to scream, but that's not all he did. His reflexes kicked in and his right arm brought the dagger crashing down into his attacker's head. There was a satisfying crunch as the point penetrated the skull and black oil erupted all over his hands. He kicked the flailing reanimate away and turned to face the last of his attackers.

She struck first, scratching at both his arms with her own claw-like fingers. Those nails drew blood from the back of his hands, and against all desire he dropped his only weapon. She lashed out at him with a well-placed kick to the mid-section, sending him reeling into the wall, narrowly avoiding the burning curtain. He tried to shake off the hit but had little time as the she-devil charged him.

Unarmed, Vasseur's one good eye darted for something he could use to his advantage. He grabbed the curtain and pulled the fiery cloth from the wall and whipped it between him and the rushing attacker. A burning shroud enveloped her and then exploded as it hit the wall. For a moment a living being of fire walked in that room, but it could not resist the flames. It fell to the ground and lay still as it burned.

The laboratory was lost. The flames were everywhere. Vasseur should have felt some sort of remorse at the loss, but he didn't. The battle had been invigorating. It had been costly, but he felt more alive than he had in years. He picked up his precious dagger and with joy in his step walked out the door, the mill succumbing to the flames as he did.

He didn't stop walking until he was on the hill that overlooked the property. Vasseur turned back and watched as the entirety of the homestead collapsed inward. He frowned a bit. His favorite coat and all his papers had been destroyed. None of it was of tremendous value, although there was a ticket to hear the pianist Orlac's upcoming concert in Cherbourg. A small loss compared to everything else that had happened. Not that it was the thing that concerned him most. Chloe had escaped. She had to be dealt with. He moved off into the night, trying to pick up her trail.

***

It wasn't until two days later that amidst the smoldering coals of the burned-out mill that something stirred. A half-burnt board shifted, as did some melted metal that once could have been copper tubing. More debris was pushed away, and slowly from beneath the ancient well was revealed, and from this, two slender hands caked in ash pulled up a body drenched and water-logged but with a semblance of life.

As Chloe came out of the well, she smiled at her cleverness. She glanced down at her refuge, the glass reactor that she had used bobbing slowly up and down, its former contents washed out by the well water. But she didn't care about that. She had lived, she had beaten Vasseur at his own game.

She never heard Vasseur creeping up behind her, never saw the dagger that plunged into the back of her skull. Chloe had been a clever girl, but not clever enough.

Vasseur had searched, but could not find any trace of her, and so began to think about things more logically. There were very few reasons to take the glass container, and none of them involved fleeing through the landscape with it. And even if he couldn't find her, he should have at least found the reactor. If Chloe hadn't escaped into the countryside, then there were very few other places she could have gone. Only one, really.

It had just been a matter of time, of being patient and waiting.

Now that Chloe had been dealt with, Vasseur would once more travel to see Doctor West and persuade him to again provide the necessities to make the dead live again. This time finding the doctor would be much easier. This time he knew where he had gone. West had told him.

There was an abandoned medieval village where an order of heretical knights had once worshipped a dying god. A place on the Spanish and Portuguese border called Berzano.

END

by Alex Dumitru

"For the woods are lovely, dark and deep.

And I've got promises to keep.

And miles to go before I sleep.

And miles to go before I sleep..."

-Robert Frost

1

The Himalayas, 1978

He had chosen a beautiful day for his death.

Stars had given way to cool gray skies, then to a brilliant blue dominated by the bright white sun. The mountains shined and sang to him in the howling, windswept voice of the Himalayas. They sang his song, and he listened. He hoped in his heart to hear this song until the very end, but of course that was not the way of this. Not his people's way. Not the way Sound of the Spear was destined to die.

Sound of the Spear felt something nuzzling at his side, distracting him from his reverie. It was Koga, his hound. But he had left Koga with--

Spear turned, his massive shoulders hunching for a moment under dense, matted white fur. But there was no call for it. They had come, as he had supposed they would. In his people's tongue, which wasn't truly a language of words but of thoughts and meanings carried by the spirit, there was one which held the meaning of both 'tribe' and 'family.' Both had come now and stood before him on the ridge of ice and stone he had been meditating upon. He laughed in his heart, but only let the barest hint of smile show on his broad, flat face.

His eldest daughter, Heart Singing Songs of Ice led them. Behind her trailed her young ones: Shining Eyes That Dream, hopeful and slightly cowed in the presence of his great-sire, nestled against his mother's knee. Last to Be Seen stood tall and calm next to her mother, so like her; so like his long-ago lost mate even more. And in Heart's arms was the youngest, whose name had not yet been spoken by the wind, sleeping quietly despite the strong gales. But what were winds to his people? Not something to hide from or to fear. That was the way of the humans below, not of his tribe. The wind was the voice of the Primal on this world, and they merely listened and watched for its signs and wisdom.

Wide Place to Begin, the father of Heart's offspring, loomed behind them all. His bulk seemed to reach for the vault of the winds. He held his enormous paw up and hailed Spear. Wide Place was no warrior in their tribe, despite his size. He was a gentle soul and so greeted him with reverence and not in the warriors' way of shaking spears and rattling bones. Sound of the Spear was the only warrior in this part of the mountains. Heart had promised him they would cross into the Primordia soon to search for more of their kind if the time came to fight, that she wouldn't endanger their tribe. Wide Place had sworn to protect them if there was no other way.

Spear knew that he would give a vicious fight if need be, gentle giant or not, but Wide Place knew nothing of their peoples' way of combat. And he hoped he never had to learn. Spear was glad his daughter had not mated to a warrior. Her sisters had left the mountains years before to other far away climbs, and his son had fallen to the enemy before even then. It had been a good way to die, but sorrow echoed in his heart ever after. No such fate for others of his tribe, he hoped and prayed to the winds.

Spear approached them, his massive feet crunching in the snow. Out here, this far beyond the usual reach of the humans, there was no need for stealth, no call to hold the voice inside. He looked at his daughter, her eyes a gleaming yellow, and pressed his forehead to hers. The clarity of thought and emotion was made greater this way, and his soul reached out to speak with hers.

My ears are already back in the Primal. I did not hear you come.

A laugh from Heart, then she thought back: *We would not have found you in time if not for Koga. He knew where you walked.*

Spear nodded, pulling away from his daughter. Now he knew who to blame. Koga looked up at him, the only one left of the many hounds he'd raised over the years. Once he had been a mighty beast, much like Spear had once been. That day, however, was long past. But he had told Koga that it was not yet time for him to go, that the tribe needed him a while longer. Koga understood in his own simple way, but still the great shaggy beast looked to his master, asking for another run, another hunt. One last time. But not this time.

To seek me in my time, that is all I ask, Spear said. *Now my time is over. Seek me no more.*

Heart nodded. The rest followed her motion, his meaning clear. Spear stepped to the side, knelt to Shining Eyes, and pressed his brow to the youngling's crown.

There will be many times of joy ahead in your years, may you walk this world and others in the centuries to come untethered by this moment of sadness. They pass like the night, long in the happening, short in recalling. Shine bright, like your eyes, for your mother.

An overwhelming pride flowed down into the pool of sadness, and with that the young one was tempered, no longer mourning, but now less a child. Spear nodded.

He stood and moved to Wide Place. Spear had to reach up, as even his size was dwarfed by the giant before him. Rough-skinned hands, thick-nailed and ancient, pressed to Wide Place's skull.

Be sure to remember the promises you made to my daughter. You wouldn't want the Sound of the Spear to haunt you. His mind spoke thusly with icy authority but his heart carried the warmth to keep such a snow glowing. Wide Place nodded, his eyes pools of amber that chuckled in the dawn light.

Spear moved away from Wide Place and came to Last to Be Seen. He gave her an actual smile.

Last to Be Seen, but not last to be loved.

But, it was always you who could find me first, even at my youngest, she thought back to him.

Spear nodded at the happy memories they shared in that moment, all their games of hide and seek high above the world, her skill, his occasional fear that he may have actually lost her, his skill always leading him to her in the end.

Be sure to always know who to hide from, and who to let see you, daughter's daughter.

She nodded. *You have taught me how, greatsire.*

Spear moved back to Heart, ready for his final goodbye.

Do you know what I have listened to this morning and night, daughter?

She tilted her head. *Surely the winds. They have sung for you all this past night.*

Yes. And do you know what they told me?

She stared at him, confused. One was not normally supposed to divulge what the winds spoke to another of his people; often it was too personal, too dense even for their understanding to truly impart to another.

Father?

They told me the name of this one... Spear said to her, laying his hand upon the sleeping child.

He roused, opening wide eyes that Spear had barely had time to get to know. His heart ached at the last task, but it was a sweet ache.

They told me... he is Rising Day at the End of Sorrow. You will remember me by this, and he will carry my memory forward in all our worlds.

Heart held up the young one high above her head, the infant squealing in surprise. He held his little paws up and they were silhouetted against the piercing morning light. Rising Day looked down at Spear and laughed.

You must leave me. And I must leave you, Spear told them. *My time has come.*

Heart nestled her younger son into her arms again. Tears were rarely shed amongst the Yeti, as their world was too cold for many of them. But there were more than enough amongst Spear's tribe that day.

Walk serene and primal, father, they told him as one.

Sound of the Spear pounded his chest with one powerful fist and howled up to the wind. His voice could be heard echoing and re-echoing across a thousand stone chasms.

Spear held his arms up as his cry receded, shutting his eyes to better enjoy feeling the cold wind in his fur one last time. When he opened his eyes, the tribe had gone. Even Koga. The farewell was painful, but necessary. Now the time had come for his next necessity.

Spear knelt in the snow and rock, much as he had all the past night. He drew the runes of Passing, each with a careful precision learned over the centuries, first from his own great-sire, Eats With a Wild Heart, then from his father, Tames Only the Fearless. They held no more mystery to him than the lines in his ancient face, or his thick jagged teeth, but unlike these details of flesh they had never ceased to fill him with reverence. These were the symbols that took him home, the ageless world all his people came from, where they were most close to the Primal.

Primordian, said Spears in his mind as he finished the last rune.

Home, said his heart as the mystic power seeped into the weave of the worlds.

Welcome, said the folds of space and time with drew back for him in the moment of Passage.

It was time.

Sound of the Spear rose on aged, aching legs, and for the final time passed from the world we called Earth to the world he called home.

2

The Primordial Realm

The portal opened on the other side in less grand a fashion than it had opened on Earth. Spear simply was not there, then suddenly he was. The Primal spread out before him in dense, rolling waves of untouched wild. He was amongst the birthplace of all his kind, but of his people specifically. Great frozen vastness spilled over endless tundra. The spires of ice that stood taller than any artificial structure on the world he'd come from pulsed and sang their chilled purple song. Far in the distance, he saw some of his people, a great line of them walking towards the horizon. Some were aware of Spear's presence but sensed his purpose in his isolation and made no move to trouble him. The Dying Place was a journey each of his people made alone.

Gazing up into the untamed sky of the Primal, Sound of the Spear got his bearings, then opened his mind. He let his inner eye search in the way he'd been instructed by the winds when they had spoken his destiny to him, and he followed where they led him. Almost without looking, while barely being aware of it, his great feet began to move, and he strode off into the icy wild.

Spear didn't know where he was being led as a physical place. He had never trod there in his many hundreds of years. But that doesn't mean he had never been here before. All his kind could visit this place in dreams. But until a few nights ago, it was a place Spear had not gone for many, many years. Not since the death of his son.

He did not wish to make the pain of his loss greater by reminding himself that there was no other way to be with him. He preferred solitude to the torture of ghosts.

Spear knew the Dying Place would find him, just as much as he found it. His trance of movement seemed to pass as his feet found ground; they had only ever trod there before in dreams. He saw the glow of indigo ice crystals blocked by a grove of ancient trees. The ground beneath him became treacherous, and he looked down to see what had nearly tripped him.

A skull. Broad, with thick sloping brow, and great lantern jaw lay a few feet away long with the rest of the skeleton that had once supported it. Spear knelt and gently, in a reverent hush, reunited them. He had arrived.

Peace washed through his soul. The journey was over.

The crystals stood in a spiral grove that was enclosed by the white, leafless trees. They sprouted from the ground at impossibly ornate angles, looking less like trees and more like the antlers of a buried herd of elk or deer, bleached white by millennia of exposure and the strange, ethereal influence of the crystals. The spiral shape of these objects put Spear in mind of a great sleeping snake, and he walked between them, now mindful to keep his feet away from the other bones and remains around him. There were many places like this in his world, all for the different denizens of the Primal. Some were at the bottom of deep valleys or hidden away underneath miles of ocean; others were in the darkest part of the woods where only the swiftest paw could carry you. Others still were located in the bogs and mires of impenetrable swamps, a place where one met their end by simply being swallowed up by whatever lived there, animal or vegetable. All were different, all were the same.

The creatures that called this dimension home did not die in other worlds. When their time came, they returned to their world and prepared to meet the Primal Spirit. If death came to them unexpectedly, they were collected. Spear had only ever known one of the Collectors, but his encounter had left him chilled for many seasons after, especially on nights when the wind was still, and he thought he heard the flapping of leathery wings.

Spear was looking for his place amongst these honored dead when he heard the noise. Not flapping wings, or even the rattle of bones, but... panting. Something yet lived in this place of the dead. Had he come at the time of another? Normally this was a time spent alone; hence, he wasn't sure what to do if he intruded upon the death song of another. But this was no death song. No dirge of an ancient soul, celebrating its return to the Primal. These were desperate, small noises. Something panting, something wounded. It was far enough off, he decided, to not be an issue.

Was some other creature dying near the place of death? Well, that is what it was there for. No need to concern himself with it. The aged hominoid resumed his search for his own place. Sound of the Spear had always assumed his place would be obvious to him, something natural that he knew by instinct, like how to eat or how to mate. No one had taught him; these were things his spirit simply arrived knowing. He presumed this was the last piece of information woven into himself that he simply knew, but now... he found himself feeling lost.

Spear hunched his shoulders. The anger welling inside him was out of place here. It did not belong. This was a place of peace, acceptance, of passing over one final time. Anger had no place here. And its unbelonging only made him feel it more keenly. He became angry that he was angry. This was not a good way to die.

The albino-haired being whirled. Where? Where was that panting? What dared to disturb him, to ruin this moment? His people rarely felt anger, but when they did it was profound. It was part of the warrior spirit he had used to protect others when he was young. Now that he was old it felt needling and acidic in his chest, a corroding sludge in a rusty container. His white fur, yellowing in places, bristled, and his crooked teeth clenched. Mighty fists curled and he stalked towards the noise that reminded him of miniscule dying sounds.

The opal light and the soaring trees became mist to him, something to be looked past and through, not at. His long legs carried him past them, back out of the grove and away from the crystal spiral and its attendants of bone and dust. Spear's once-keen eyes strained at the dark, his ears trying to home in on the sound and narrow it to its origin. Moving into the empty, bleak winter woods that lay beyond the grove, he slowed, breath pouring out slowly in vaporous drifts. It was close.

Perhaps this was part of it, Spear thought, his mind clearing as his pace slowed. He had never been told what the order of things was in death. Who was there to tell him? He let go of expectation and focused on just his new reality.

There. Behind that tree. Even in this dim light, he saw the small scaly hand protruding. It lay limp on the ground, fingers curled up, and the tiny claws on the tips made it look like a dead spider that had rolled onto its back. Spear felt he had seen some of these creatures before. But if he was right it was far from their usual home. The hand moved only slightly, with the panting breaths he had followed to this much smaller, less grand place of dying.

He rounded the tree. The creature was small, looked to be male. His bald head was leathery-skinned, green, and oblong. His eyes had once been a luminous yellow but were steadily dimming. A pointed nose hung over a curling mouth full of narrow, jagged teeth. His other hand was held to a hideous wound in his side. Bluish ichor seeped from him into the snow-covered ground, marking his trail from deeper in the wood. But here his trail stopped. His life essence pooled here and soon he would know no more. The great yeti knelt beside the twisted creature.

I am called Sound of the Spear, he told it, casting his mind out. *What kind of creature are you? Why are you here in this place?*

The creature looked up at him, without fear or malice. It swallowed once, then gasped. He was going to speak with words, it seemed.

"I am… calls many things. Mostly by… humans. They calls me Spriggan, Nixie, Dark Elf, Goblin… little names for what they calls little people. I calls myself Nalvoq. No one shall calls me that again. There is no one left to speaks it to me…"

Spear titled his head. It had been long years since he had heard physical speech this closely, but even so it sounded strange.

Why is there no one? Are you the last of your clan?

After a moment of taking in the thought, parsing the meaning, Nalvoq spoke again.

"No one left, cuz they's all been killed, or driven off to far down places, deep away from the killin'. But Nalvoq, silly little kobald, he stays. He says, 'No, he no wants to go'…"

Who? Who killed them? Spear furrowed his heavy brow. *Was it the humans?*

An ugly, choked, rattling sound burbled from the goblin. After a second Spear realized it was... laughter.

"Humans never catch old Nalvoq, theys don't remembers how. Don't knows he exist no more...me and my little brothers and little sisters, we stays in the forests and in the hills, play in the rivers and keep the Old Ways. Keep the balance right. Till *he* comes..."

Here it was, Spear thought to himself.

Who?

Nalvoq laughed again. "Who? Who! Hoo! Hoo! That's him alright. Thought him for some forest guardian at first. Then we sees him closer. Those wings, those horrid eyes. Those great red eyes... he weren't no owl."

The flesh on Spear's bones tensed. A shiver passed through his heart. A cold, killing wind.

An Interloper, his mind said.

Enemy, his heart said.

"Go away from this place," Nalvoq says. "Lift your charms, pull away your protections. Or die. Some runs away. Lots die. Now... now old Nalvoq, he dies. Alone. Unavenged. Comes back to the Old Realm to do it. Where we's all comes from..."

Spear stood. This was why he saw no place amongst the Spiral. It was not yet time. One last thing to do.

"Nal...voq..." Spear spoke.

The goblin started, his yellow eyes snapping up from their dreamy trance. The word was guttural, raspy, spoken by a voice that was better suited to howls and grunts. He now had the little creature's attention.

You are wrong. You have heard your name again. You will not die alone. You will not die unavenged.

Nalvoq appeared confused. His wrinkly brow creased further, trying to understand.

"Are...? You're one of the Guardian tribes... aren't you?" Nalvoq said.

Spear nodded. *My people stand in the far-off places, we watch for the Interlopers. And when they come, we kill.*

Nalvoq chuckled, a less offensive sound this time.

"Well now…" he said, as the yeti picked up a thick length of branch and a stone. "That's the best news I's heard in all my days."

As Spear sat down and set to work fashioning his namesake, he asked the goblin from where in the Second World he'd come.

Nalvoq told him.

Sound of the Spear laughed.

Only humans, he thought, *would try to make a wall out of corn.*

The grizzled yeti sat and worked on his spear. They talked. And Nalvoq did not die alone.

3
Cornwall, England 1978

It was night when Spear passed into the world again. And he was thousands of miles from where he had last crossed. This was just one of the gifts of his people, of living in the Primordial Realm. Humans suspected their existence, some outright believed, but none could prove it. They didn't have the gift to walk in multiple worlds.

The object that was his namesake felt heavy and familiar in his hand. It had been a long time since he had actually held a weapon, but despite the newness and the un-blooded quality, his hands still knew how to make the tool for killing. The stone blade was wide and jagged, wickedly sharp, and bound with hair he'd cut from the ends of his mane and bark. All the warriors of his people made their own weapons, ones that would pass back into the natural world once their purpose was served.

Spear felt strange. This morning he had been so ready to die. Now, he stood in this place he'd never set foot in, oppressively hot in comparison to his old haunts, with a fresh blade in his hand. And he was not here to die, but to kill. The wind had not spoken of this. But he felt ready.

The hirsute warrior was near where Nalvoq had told him to go. He had said that the Interloper made a habit of haunting the area around an ancient human shrine-building. A holy place to the humans was just the sort of locale that drew their unhallowed kind, he knew. Nalvoq told him that it had been a handful of seasons since the creature had come. Humans had seen it, some mad old wizard seemed to follow it, they whispered.

It wasn't real, most of them said in their cups. But Nalvoq knew it was, for he had felt the talons of the thing sink into him, had watched it butcher his friends. He had looked into its huge red eyes as it sealed his fate. *No more,* Sound of the Spear swore. He started walking.

His fur stood out in a wash of moonlight. He could smell no humans nearby, but his senses told him that their village lay away in the night, close enough to be worrisome should this hunt take long. Up ahead, he could see the house of worship rising up from the ground. His breath caught. He had seen holy places to the humans before, glimpsed them from afar in the mountains of his home. They were sprawling places of a quiet beauty and dignity, filled with humans in yellow and orange robes, the rising voices of their intonations reminding him of his own howls to invoke the Winds.

This place… was not like that. It was jagged to his eye, strangely menacing. Graves spread out around it, ancient stones to mark the burial of humans long dead, almost forgotten. The way the stones jutted up reminded him of diseased teeth in a wide open, sickly maw. The word the goblin had used for this place felt more accurate as he looked at it. "Church."

To Spear the word had the quality of crunching bone, and this building did not change his mind. He saw a gate at the front of the yard, inscribed with words he did not understand, and which looked grim to his eye. The piled stone of the church was ancient, Spear could see. He had rarely seen something that had built by the humans that was older than he was, but this structure was easily one of those exceptions. The weathered stones, the angular spires, all showed the signs of having been built in his grandsire's time. An ancient site, steeped in death, and radiating corruption. Remote from the humans who had made it, and who claimed to speak with their gods here.

This was the perfect place for one of the Enemy.

In the woods beyond, unseen by Spear in his fascination with the aged pile before him, something stirred. Something watched. And in its black heart, it smiled.

Spear drew closer to the church, the place the humans called Mawnan Smith, though neither he nor Nalvoq had known those words. He ran a hand along one of the tombstones, his other holding tight to the shaft of his weapon. His eyes scanned the tops of the vaulted roof. He watched for the perching thing he hunted but saw no immediate sign of it. The presence of this place felt stained with it, however. It couldn't be far.

The old yeti's thoughts drifted to his son, once again dwelling upon the dead in a place of death. His fall had been on a hunt like this one. They had been called upon to aid another tribe with an Interloper in a far-away land whose name Spear had forgotten. That one had been powerful, insidious, had taken long hours to track, and had been nearly impossible to bring down. Spear had not landed the killing blow; that had fallen to Finds the Safe Cave, the head of that party. Spear had instead held his son as his life had passed from him and waited for the Collector to come and claim him to be taken to the Dying Place.

The yeti folk did not have vengeful hearts by nature. But Spear knew that this was what he wanted and the ability to feel this is what made him a warrior amongst his tribe.

Such dark, sad thoughts, a slithering, hissing voice crawled across his mind. *They're utterly delicious, old one.*

Spear whirled about, his weapon up, grasping it now in both hands. *Too old,* he thought to himself. *Distracted.*

The slithering voice in his mind agreed. *Yessss... you shouldn't have come alone, Guardian. How long has it been since you last killed? For me, it has been mere hours... one of us is blooded. The other is... faded.*

Spear roared a challenge to the Interloper. To speak to him like this it had to be close. The next sibilant hiss in his mind chided him.

We don't fight like that, noble beast... you know that. Your son never saw his death coming. Why should you? The pathetic little creatures that lived in these woods are no concern of yours. And now that they are out of the way, my plans for the village are not your concern either. I can smell your death on you, old thing. Go now; die quietly. Or, I will make your death long...

Spear turned around, feeling the eyes on him before he saw them. The Interloper stood on a gravestone, seeming to have no weight despite the bulky torso he saw. Each Interloper was a little different from the others; some barely had heads, while others were lithe and long, with tapering skulls and razor-like wings. All had wings, and they all had the same bulbous, lantern-like red eyes -- and, of course, they all shared in their malevolent nature.

This one, as Nalvoq had said, was like an owl. Long black talons extended from two-toed feet that dug into the mossy stone it perched on. Feathers rippled on its hide and from the wings that lay folded at its sides. Like an owl, Spear had not heard the creature in flight. Instead it had glided up with less than a whisper. And the swooping angles of its face were completed by a beak that sat between two unblinking eyes that shone like burning coals.

The Owlman's head cocked to one side before it "spoke" again. *.So… it is more than just age that makes your fur white. You're of the mountain tribes. Rare to see a warrior of their ilk these days. Fewer of you than there used to be…*

Spear pointed his namesake at the Interloper. The yeti eyed Owlman over the headstones, and neither blinked.

I am Sound of the Spear, of the tribe of the Windswept. Enough talk.

The Owlman spread out its wings in a display of intimidation, its crimson eyes flaring. An aura of menace spread from it as the wings expanded, an oncoming rush of fear that the Interlopers used as a weapon in its own right. This wave of terror-inducing psychic force pounded against Spear's mind like a wave of the tide against a rocky shoal. The white-haired warrior held his ground, gripping his spear tighter.

A long death it is, then, the Owlman thought. Then it sprang at him.

Spear lunged forward, thrusting at his enemy. But as fast as it sprang at him it was suddenly gone from his view, moving in midair so quickly he barely felt the talons move across his shoulder. A torrent of red blood welled out from the painlessly split open hide, the delay lasting only until the dull ache exploded into a fiery screech of pain that went down the length of his arm. This weakened his grip, but the weapon stayed in his hands.

Spear spun as the Owlman cavorted about him. His world became a dark kaleidoscope of flapping feathers and glinting razors. It dawned on Spear that the Owlman had hidden claws in the folds of its wings just as they flashed and slashed, tearing into his chest. The yeti grunted and shoved outward with his wooden weapon in both paws.

The taloned feet of the Owlman locked around the spear and Spear felt a colossal tug on it as the creature flapped hard, trying to disarm him by ripping the staff away from his grip. But the yeti held fast, his great muscles bulging and flexing beneath his blood-dappled pelt. He roared as he swung his whole body around, causing the Owlman – who was clinging to the shaft of his spear – to follow first back, then upwards again. Once more, the flapping sound it made was almost eerie in its utter absence. The Owlman's burning red eyes were for a moment all Spear could see as it rose higher into the English night sky, then vanished entirely for a moment as it banked and swooped back in for another dive at him. The winged entity's luminescent eyes blazed brighter than ever as they swiftly closed the gap between the primal creatures, and they clashed again.

Despite the winged creature being smaller than Spear by a few feet and several hundred pounds, the force with which the Owlman struck the yeti. The white-haired hominid gasped inward as the talons dipped into his flesh again. The overwhelming force of the blow caused Spear to fall backwards. It began to dawn on Spear that this creature was unlike other Interlopers he had seen. It liked combat. It delighted in killing in a way that set it apart from its kin.

Most Interlopers were harbingers of disaster, of misery in the human world. Some subtly influenced it, others came to psychically feed on the desolation and despair. But this one came to cause it. First to remove the safeguards of the quietly woven centuries of spells by the little ones, then it would cause fear and terror from this hub of strange decay.

You begin to understand, don't you, beast? it told him. *It has begun already, a few sightings to breed the terror. A while to forget before I remind them. Then they'll begin to disappear. Little ones at first…*

A black claw dug into Spear's hands, a long-toed foot wrapping around his wrist.

Humans always do get so upset at the loss of their cubs… I've done it before, but this time will be my masterpiece. This village will remember forever what I'm going to do to it.

Spear reeled as the assault both physical and psychic bowled him over onto the ground. He was down, and he thought it was not going to be long now. If he didn't make some sort of progress soon, he might as well stay down and die here. The Owlman had gotten too close, moved too quickly. His spear was useless at this range, nothing more than a pointed walking stick.

It had been foolish, naive of him to think that this was how he was going to end his life. It had been too long since he'd been in battle. He'd forgotten it wasn't a glorious thing, or a noble thing. It was about killing, none of those soft sentiments. And because of those empty sentiments and a promise to a goblin, he was going to die here, far from his home, from his proper place in the Primal.

He would just be more meat for the Collectors to haul away before the humans could find this fool and expose them all. Death had come to Spear, but it sang a different song than he had expected…

4

The Himalayas

In the night, Eyes That Shine with Dreams tossed and turned. He had started nestled against his mother and the newly named Rising Dawn, but he had gradually moved away on the floor of their cave. Between his parents, he groaned, and his fuzzy face contorted. As his noises grew louder, the others of the tribe about him began to stir. Last to Be Seen woke from her doze to look over at her little brother. She knew immediately that something was wrong. The baby began to fret as Shining Eyes grew ever more distressed.

His name had been spoken to him in dreams, and that had proven to be more than just happenstance. Those dreams had guided them to a safe cave after they had to abandon their last home. A group of climbers had gotten too close during the time Rising Dawn's birth drew near and they'd had to move on for fear of the humans finding them at this delicate moment. He'd seen this place on their first night out in the wilds and guided them to it the next day. Now he dreamed, but it was clear he dreamed of something awful, something that frightened him.

Last to Be Seen began to rise and draw near her brother, but was fearful to wake him. Such gifts were often not things to be tampered with, and she feared what might happen if she interrupted such a trance -- and also what would come of it once he woke. But suddenly he awakened all at once, with her hand still hovering in apprehension.

The Spear must break! his terrified mind screamed as he sat upright in one juddering motion. The rest of the tribe startled awake at this psychic explosion from their second-youngest member. With that, Shining Eyes collapsed into the arms of his father and began to wail and weep. The chorus was soon joined by his infant brother, and both parents were occupied in calming their young. But Last to Be Seen stood quietly, looking out the mouth of their cave, into the night. He listened for the wind as Shining Eyes said over and over:

The Spear must break! Please... the Spear must break! it must...
The spear must break...
The spear --

5

Cornwall, England, Mawnan Smith

Must break!

The thought-wave exploded through the minds of both the Owlman and Sound of the Spear, and his attacker reeled back momentarily, blood streaming from its claws as it screeched in mental pain. The yeti beneath it was bleeding out slowly but surely; the Owlman had kept its promise that Spear's death would be a slow one, as each cut was deep but not yet fatal. Black and grey wings folded up to the sides of its bulbously avian head, trying in vain to ward off this inner attack from outside.

It was just the opening that Spear needed. Despite the horrid pain of a hundred cuts the Owlman had laid into his flesh, the message was clear: This was the end, and this was the way it had to be. He was no fool; hee was the instrument of the Winds, sent by the Spirits of the Primal itself to stop this Interloper from carrying out its evil scheme.

He was the Spear. And sometimes, the Spear must break.

The yeti flexed his mighty hands with the last of their strength and the wooden shaft in his hands splintered and cracked apart like a twig. The loathsome creature was able to see its victim clearly for just a moment, the haze in its mind being wiped away by the clear strong *crack!* below it. Then the yeti turned his spear head and the jagged end of the broken shaft toward the sides of the Owlman and drove them home.

The monster screeched again, this time in pain and fury. Black blood pumped out from the wounds, raining down onto the yeti's snow-colored coat. The Interloper writhed as it struggled to get away, flapping its deadly wings frantically. But the yeti held fast and twisted the splinters of his spear towards him, making it impossible for the Owlman to lift off without dragging Sound of the Spear up with it. This resulted in the winged entity inadvertently holding on by its mortal wounds and eviscerating itself.

Noooooooooooooo...! - the Owlman shrieked in his mind. *You can't you can't stop this let me go-oooo...! Noooooo...!*

They weren't what Spear had expected his death song to sound like, but they would do. He strained and drove the points deeper into the Owlman and more blackish grue and ichor streamed out, more like the thick juices inside an insect than blood now.

The beating wings began to slow. The screeching gave way to a wheeze that rattled deep in the Owlman's chest. The yeti grinned, an almost human gesture. The Owlman laid its claws against the yeti one last time, but now they had no more vicious speed, no more power to cut. They hung limply from their flaccid feathered limbs, as the strength ran out from his attacker, and it had now become his kill. And his killer.

Sound of the Spear heaved and threw the Interloper off himself. He rose unsteadily, legs shaking. He'd forgotten that victory usually felt like this, that defeat would almost be preferable if just to escape the dull hollow ache of the hard-won kill.

The grizzled yeti sagged under his own heavy weight. Suddenly he was too heavy for himself. He summoned up the last of his strength and began to call up the Passage, inscribing the runes one final time in the soft earth with one jagged nail.

6

The Primordial Realm

The fold of space began to draw back and the door opened. He passed through gratefully, happy to leave the Interloper to be rounded up by a Collector. The Primal woods before him were close to where he had found the goblin. The Spiral wouldn't be far. Just a few-

Noooooooooo!

The scream exploded through his mind as he felt claws dig into his back, the hit taking him to one knee as he stumbled forward. The Interloper squealed and raked him with insane vigor. Spear felt the ends of his broken weapon catching in his fur, still lodged in the beast's sides. He reached up over his shoulders with arms that felt carved from stone and drenched in his own lifeblood, clasping his heavy hands onto the Interloper. With a bellowing roar he hurled the Owlman over his shoulders and out in front of him. Not letting go he swung it by one winged arm. The yeti put all his strength into the throw and again didn't let go, his force instead cracking the Interloper like a whip. Bones snapped inside the wing, and the Owlman snarled back at him.

It lashed at the yeti with its feet, ripping into his guts yet again, trying to disembowel him on the spot. The cuts roared through his body and the yeti let out a bellow of pain. Spear swung his free hand out and grasped the pointed head of his weapon, ripping it free from the Owlman and falling upon it as it had done to him in that graveyard a world away. The winged beast's tearing beak ripped at his flesh as the yeti pulled away and sat up, with only his will alone holding his innards inside. He raised his primitive weapon and its stained stone head glinted in the moonlight of another universe as he brought it down on his feathered foe again and again. Streams of black blood followed each impact, a stench of thick sticking corruption filling the air of this Primal world to which both belonged, but in which only one was to survive.

With one last wrenching strike, the yeti howled up into the sprawling night, untouched by humans and heedless of whether they heard him now. None would. No human would know what he had done for them this night. And as he watched the light finally dim and go out of the Interloper's eyes, he decided that was good.

Spear stumbled away, one arm now held to his stomach, the other loosening and then letting go of the broken spearhead. It dropped without noise to the ground. Or, at least none that he heard;. the world had gone very quiet to Sound of the Spear. He looked around at its utter stillness, so close to this place where his people chose to die. The peace was good, but it made him miss the howling, singing voices of the winds in his mountains, and he wished he could listen to it one last time.

But instead, he heard another song. It came from beyond these snowy woods, from the white trees that stood like the antlers of a stag, and the great humming spiral crystals that they surrounded. It came in a clear strong voice he knew so well, but for a moment could not recall.

Then it came to him. It was his son. He was calling him to come home, to hunt, to laugh. Spear walked towards the place of Dying and followed the song, the last song. The only song left.

His Death Song.

END

BONUS FLASH FICTION!!

GOOFUS BIRD VS. HOOP SNAKE: HOW HIGH AM I?

"Whoa, man," Bill Chan whooped after taking another hit. "This is some good shit! I don't think I *ever* had a ride *this high* before."

The teenage stoner giggled incessantly as his body seemed to joyfully spasm. Bill, being the burnout that he was, made sure to protect his bong, keeping it tucked between his legs. He did everything he could to make sure it didn't fall or break while also trying to enjoy the buzz he was on.

"Roland, you really outdid yourself with this green, bro," Bill babbled on, despite being the only one there in that part of the forest. "I may ride this stuff to the Moon... yeah, that's it. I'll smoke all this shit, go to the Moon, and become their high-ass king."

Bill started laughing hardily as he brushed his long blonde locks out of his face and looked at the mountains far ahead of him. From where he sat, there was a clearing in the tree line big enough where he could see many of the rocky forms towering over most of creation. Instantly, Bill started zoning out on the purple hue shown from the mountains at his angle.

"Whoa," Bill let out as he continued to space. "That's so, like... beautiful and shit. Nature's purple haze."

Bill stared blankly for a second or two before he busted out laughing. He then looked down at his black Hendrix tee shirt slightly hidden underneath his denim vest, which matched his torn-off shorts. However, as Bill was sitting there laughing, everything else became suddenly still, save for what sounded like rustling nearby. Once the stoner's ears picked up the noises, he quieted himself and listened intently. His eyes slightly widened when it sounded like the rustling was getting closer.

"Oh, shit!" Bill said in a panicked voice. His body started jittering and trembling as he looked around and tried desperately to think of what to do. "What if that's like a ranger or something? Oh, man, oh, man, oh, man, I-- *Fuck!*"

Bill reached out a hand in an unsuccessful attempt to try and catch his bong. It fell and smashed into several pieces against a rock sticking out of the ground.

"Oh, shit!" Bill Chan shouted as he stood up. He gazed down mournfully at the shattered pieces of his treasured bong before his panic quickly took over again. "What am I gonna do now? How am I supposed to--"?

Bill was interrupted by what sounded like a loud holler filling the air. It was almost like the kind of noise someone might make when getting their toe stubbed or a finger caught in a doorjamb. Yet somehow it also sounded very inhuman, which actually made it chilling in a way. What was worse for Bill in this case was that it sounded like it was very close and getting even closer.

What the fuck?

Another holler, almost exactly like the first, nearly made Bill jump out of his shorts. It was so much more frightening than the previous screech because it sounded like it had come from right behind the young stoner. Bill screamed as he turned to see what terror awaited him and... his face was struck with the butt of a giant bird flying backwards.

The force was so strong it knocked the man off his feet, making him crash back-first onto the ground. "*Ow! Son of a bitch!*" he screamed aloud.

The dude's eyes widened when he realized what had happened. Bill struggled to sit up and then looked for the creature that had knocked him down. It didn't take him long to see the rather unusual sight of what looked like a twelve-foot-tall tan pelican-like bird with a big red mohawk and incredibly long, skinny legs. It was still flying backwards too, while still making its horrible hollering sound.

"What the hell else was in that grass?" Bill asked himself. "It had to be laced with some other shit for me to be seeing this."

Suddenly, just as Bill had managed to push himself back up to his feet, his legs were swept out from underneath him by an unseen force that struck from behind. Bill crashed onto his back again and screamed out in agony.

"All I wanted to do was get high!" Bill complained before he sat up to see what else had hit him, groaning all the while. What he saw next made his eyes widen. "Okay, now I know I'm stoned."

The second creature was just as bizarre as the first, being a sixteen-foot-long copper-colored snake with the tip of its tail looped back into its mouth. Stranger still was that the freaky reptile was rolling like a wheel and it seemed to be intentionally going after the odd, backwards flying bird. Bill could only watch in disbelief as these two beasts of weirdness seemed to be locked in a rather awkward race for dominance.

What the hell am I gonna tell people back at home if I ever try to explain this trip?

Bill's eyes widened in horror when it looked like the two monstrous oddities turned back his way. Remembering what happened last time, the stoner dude quickly got to his feet, slipping once or twice before running as fast as his feet could carry him. He screamed at the top of his lungs, all the while moving at top speed. Occasionally he could look back to see that both the backwards-flying bird and the wheel-like rolling snake were easily gaining. Although they seemed less interested in catching *him* and more concentrated on their race.

"Why the fuck is this happening to me?" Bill cried.

He had to skid to a stop and jump to the side with a scream when he realized he was about to go careening over the side of a several hundred-foot-tall cliff. After a couple of heavy breaths, he looked to see the hoop snake had not stopped and had gone rolling over the side. He then looked up to see the Goofus bird hollering in victory as it flew not so majestically (and posterior-first), into the open sky.

END

ABOUT THE AUTHORS

Pete Rawlik is a long-time collector of Lovecraftian fiction. His first professional sale was in 1997 but didn't begin to write seriously until 2010. Since then he has authored more than fifty short stories and the Cthulhu Mythos novels *Reanimators*; *The Weird Company*; *Reanimatrix*; and *The Peaslee Papers*. He is a frequent contributor to the *Lovecraft ezine* and the New York Review of Science Fiction. In 2014 his short story "Revenge of the Reanimator" was nominated for a New Pulp Award. In 2015 he co-edited *The Legacy of the Reanimator* for Chaosium. Somewhere along the line he became known as the Reanimator guy, but he fervently denies being obsessed with the character. His collection, *Strange Company and Others*, was released in 2019. He lives in southern Florida where he works on Everglades environmental issues.

Kevin Heim was born in 1969 and began writing fiction shortly after he learned how to read -- so for almost ten years now. In 2012 he contributed two short stories to *Psychopomp*, a defunct ezine, which introduced his version of the Frankenstein Monster and his original character Ivan Ronald Schablotski, both of which have a small but mediocre fan base. Since then he has submitted stories for a number of Wild Hunt Press anthologies, including *Dorian Gray: Darker Shades* (2018), *Attack of the Kaiju Vol. 2: The Next Wave* (2019), *Boogey Knights* Vol. 1, and *Mansion of the Macabre* Vol. 1 (the latter two upcoming in 2020 at this writing). His most notable achievements are having visited the Elvis American Diner in Jerusalem, Israel, and getting thrown out of St. Peter's Basilica in Vatican City, Rome. Kevin lives in Salem, Massachusetts, where he likes to dress up in costumes and pretend that fictional characters are real people.

Matthew (Matt) Dennion lives in New Jersey with his wife and two daughters. Matt works primarily as a teacher of students with autism and an SLE (Structured Learning Experience) Coordinator. He has loved giant monster and superhero stories his entire life. He began writing short stories for Black Coat Press and *G-Fan* magazine in 2007. In 2015 he began writing kaiju novels for Severed Press. His current works for Severed Press include *Chimera: Scourge of the Gods*; *Operation ROC*; *Atomic Rex*; *Polar Yeti*; *Atomic Rex: Wrath of the Polar Yeti*; *Kaiju Corps*; *Atomic Rex: Conquest of Chimera*; *Operation Megalodon*; and *Valley of the Dinosaurs*. He has recently began writing comics book in collaboration with other creators. His comic works include *Draco Azul/ Atomic Rex: Shadow of the Raptor* with Andres Perez and *Irokus x Atomic Rex: Avatars of the Apocalypse* Vol. 1 with Frank Parr and Wayne Smith.

Matthew has a line of self-published novellas including *The Kaiju and the Crime Fighter and Other Tales* and *Raptor Tales: Heroes and Monsters*. He self-published the first edition of the anthology *Attack of the Kaiju Vol. 1: Age of Monsters* and he has short fiction in *Attack of the Kaiju Vol. 2: The Next Wave* from Wild Hunt Press. All of Matt's novels and comics are available on Amazon in print and digital formats and can be purchased on Amazon. Along with his friends Andres Perez and Chris Martinez, Matt has also created the charity publishing venture Kaiju vs. Cancer, through which creators use their monsters and heroes to team with St. Jude Children's Research Hospital to battle childhood cancer! The first of these anthologies to be published was *Courage on Infinite Earths: A Kaiju vs. Cancer Anthology*.

Born on May 15, 1991, in Washington state (where he still currently resides), **Cody Bratsch** has had a fascination with all sorts of creative ventures and forms of storytelling ever since he was a kid. Cody's has watched and read a massive selection from them all and has come to adore a great many of them. His debut as a published author was in the short story anthology *Attack of the*

Kaiju Vol. 1: Age of Monsters (self-published by Matt Dennion), and his work has also been featured in *Attack of the Kaiju Vol. 2: The Next Wave* from Wild Hunt Press.

Alex Dumitru is from Northwest, Indiana, where he lives with his family and a very small dog. He was first inspired to write kaiju literature after becoming a fan of the *Ultraman* franchise from Tsuburaya Productions, and this inspired the creation of his own published sentai character, Massive. His debut (and that of Massive) was in Matt Dennion's self-published edition of *Attack of the Kaiju Vol. 1: Age of Monsters*, he made a major contribution to Zach Cole's linear horror anthology *The Experiment* from Wild Hunt Press, and his newest work can be found here and in *Attack of the Kaiju Vol. 2: The Next Wave* from Wild Hunt Press.

Tyler Shepard been obsessed with monsters great and small since he was two years old. It has been a life-long dream for him to become a writer. His motto: "The more blood the better, I always say!" *Duel of the Monsters* Vol. 1 is Tyler's debut as a published author.

Zach Cole is the author of the novella *Tsuchigumo* (his debut work), *Kaiju Epoch*, and the Jeremy Walker Thriller series (beginning with *Blue Moon: A Jeremy Walker Thriller*) and is the mastermind behind the multi-author linear horror anthology *The Experiment* from Wild Hunt Press. He was born in Wooster, Ohio, beginning his love of monsters at the age of two after viewing *Mothra vs. Godzilla*. He became a writer around the age of ten, penning Godzilla stories and even comics containing his own monstrous creations. His love of books started with the *Goosebumps* series, reading anything that had to do with monsters, big or small. He lives in Wooster, Ohio.

Dustin Dreyling is an avid fan of science fiction and horror, with a soft spot for all things kaiju. Originally hailing from White Bear Lake, Minnesota, he also likes proofreading novels, playing video games both old and new, and taking care of his planted freshwater aquariums. His first published story was featured in Zach Cole's linear horror anthology *The Experiment* from Wild Hunt Press, and his work can also be found in Wild Hunt's kaiju anthology *Attack of the Kaiju Vol. 2: The Next Wave*. His first novel, batch one of a kaiju horror series *Primordial Soup,* will be released in early 2020 from Wild Hunt Press.

Breyden Halverson lives near the famed and mysterious Okanagan Lake in British Columbia, where reports of mysterious creatures lurking in its depths have abounded. He is currently at the University of British Columbia, a graduate from a local college, and an aspiring author of creature/monster fiction. Kaiju are his specialty, but cryptids and original monstrosities from his own imagination are also on the table. He is a self-made artist as well, and he is featured on the popular art-sharing site DeviantArt, which you can see for yourself at: https://www.deviantart.com/kelownazilla2017. Aside from those things, he is also a researcher of lake monster sightings and is an eyewitness himself; he plans to continue the search for such creatures. Breyden's other hobbies include drawing, camping, kayaking, reading, travelling, anthropology, and sociology, as well as learning the Spanish language. His aim in life is to become a specialist in Gothic fiction and to teach it as well. His other work has been featured in Matthew Dennion's self-published *Attack of the Kaiju Vol. 1: Age of Monsters* and Zach Cole's linear multi-author horror anthology *The Experiment* from Wild Hunt Press.

Matt Hickman is the product of too much '80s TV. 'Nuff said! (We do not worry about being sued for saying that, because there are no mice around!)

Robert Galvin is an author who has been witness to a couple of unidentified flying objects and been in the presence of possessed dolls with eyes that surge energy and chills through one's soul. He grew up with the paranormal, listening to the radio show *Coast to Coast AM* and watching shows such as *Monster Quest*. The first tale he forged and published was his short story, "Goregod" for Matt Dennion's thrilling anthology *Attack of the Kaiju Vol. 1 Age of Monsters*. Some of his work can also be seen in Zach Cole's linear horror anthology *The Experiment* from Wild Hunt Press. Contact: robertgalvin125@gmail.com

Christofer Nigro has been a lifelong fan of fantastic fiction in all mediums, from cinema to TV to prose to comic books to board games to video games etc. This includes horror, sci-fi, super-heroes, anime, tokusatsu, and pulp adventure. The public first saw his writing online with the original websites for Warrenverse: The Amazing World of the Warren Comics Characters and The Godzilla Saga; he also reconstructed the MONSTAAH website with the permission and blessing of its creator, Chuck Loridans (all three are slated for a refurbishment). He got his start as a published author with Black Coat Press in several of its annual *Tales of the Shadowmen* anthologies and has had short stories published by Sirens Call Publications, Pro Se Press, Pulp Empire, Grinning Skull Press, Horrified Press, and Local Hero Press.

He also contributed to Matt Dennion's self-published *Attack of the Kaiju Vol. 1: Age of Monsters* and the charity anthology *Courage on Infinite Earths: A Kaiju vs. Cancer Anthology* established by Matt and artist Christopher Martinez to aid St. Jude Children's Research Hospital to battle childhood cancer. His first two kaiju novels *Dargolla: A Kaiju Nightmare* and *Megadrak: Beast of the Apocalypse* were published by Severed Press. He established Wild Hunt Press in 2018 to continue publishing his work and those of other authors.

MEET THE ARTISTS

Illustrations and Graphic Design by **Lungga Creatives:**
Facebook @lunggacreatives

Lungga Creatives are:

Elden Ardiente (Cyclops vs Dragon, Ogopogo vs Giant Eel,
Zombie vs Alpha Serial Killer)
Contact: ldnrdnt.com and Instagram @ldn_rdnt

Jimi Bautista (Ghost vs Aliens, Werewolf vs. Vampire)
Contact: Instagram @jimibi

Jim Faustino (Intro/Hosts, Vampire vs Killer Clown,
Mothman vs The Jersey Devil)
Contact: Instagram @drawingerojim2 and DevianArt:
humahawinghangin

Myke Guisinga (Invisible Man vs Alpha Serial Killers,
Goofus Bird vs Hoop Snake)
Contact: mykeguisinga.carbonmade.com

Glenn Lugapo (Wendigo vs Skeletoid, Yeti vs Owlman)
Contact: Facebook @Glenn Lugapo

Cover Art by **Glenn Lugapo and Elden Ardiente**

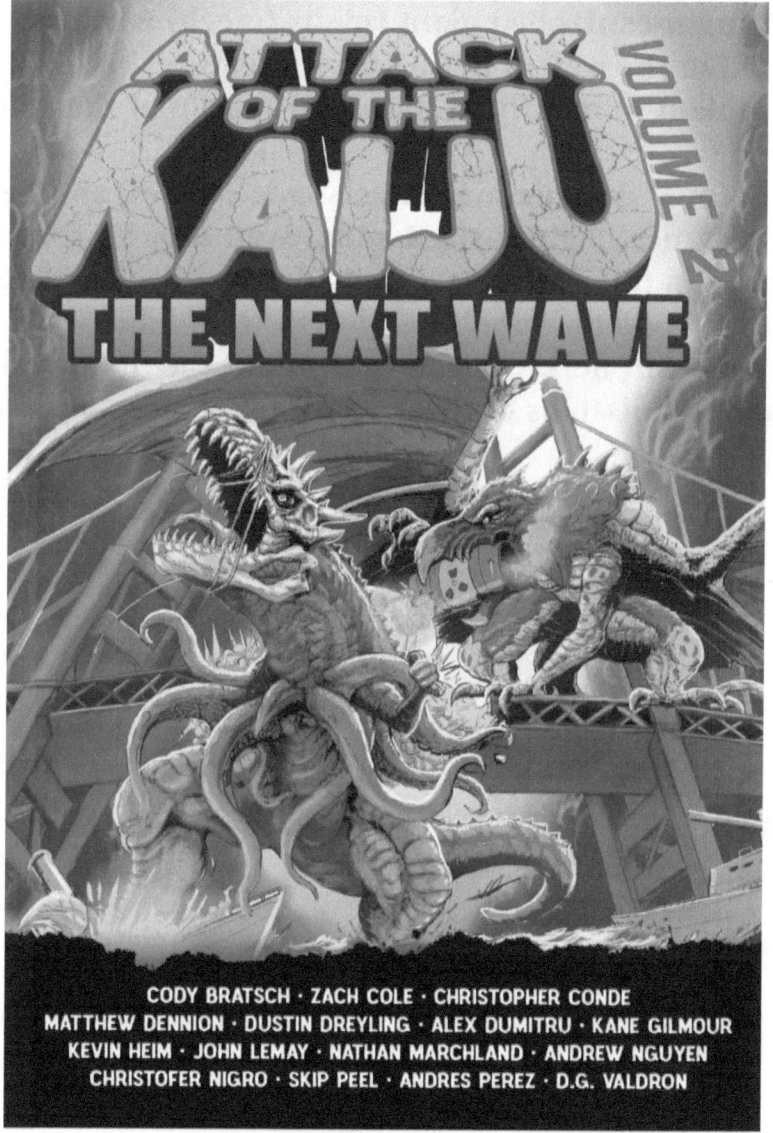

CODY BRATSCH · ZACH COLE · CHRISTOPHER CONDE
MATTHEW DENNION · DUSTIN DREYLING · ALEX DUMITRU · KANE GILMOUR
KEVIN HEIM · JOHN LEMAY · NATHAN MARCHLAND · ANDREW NGUYEN
CHRISTOFER NIGRO · SKIP PEEL · ANDRES PEREZ · D.G. VALDRON

New from Wild Hunt Press!

Attack of the Kaiju Volume 2: The Next Wave
features thirteen short stories by fourteen authors
that cover the city-destroying excursions of the most
powerful monsters in fantastic fiction – along with
some of the king-sized superheroes (sentai) and

human-controlled giant robots (mech) who dare to stand in the way of these titanic creatures' attempts to supplant humanity as the alpha species of the planet.

A lot of destruction, cataclysmic clashes, and heroic resistance to giant-sized odds await all who read the tales in this anthology. Consider yourself fortunate that you do not inhabit an Earth where daiakaiju are real -- but here you can read about the titanic trials and tribulations of those who cannot sleep as easily.

New from D.G. Valdron!!

GIANT MONSTERS SINGS SAD SONGS

D.G. Valdron

Also New from D.G. Valdron!!